May Snow

May Snow

Dottie Rexford

May Snow
by Dottie Rexford

Published by Windpath Books, P.O. Box 1042, Dunkirk, NY 14048
www.windpathbooks.com
ISBN: 0-9741185-0-8 (Hardcover)
ISBN: 0-9741185-1-6 (Softcover)

Cover and Interior Book Design by Pneuma Books, LLC
For more info, visit www. pneumabooks.com

Cover photograph courtesy of Tom Martin & Roy Newman
For more info, visit www.tommartinstudio.com

Printed in the United States on acid-free paper by Thomson-Shore, Dexter, Michigan. www.tshore.com

09 08 07 06 05 04   6 5 4 3 2 1

Publisher's Cataloging-In-Publication Data
(Prepared by The Donohue Group, Inc)

Rexford, Dottie.
    May snow / Dottie Rexford.
      p. cm.
    ISBN: 0-9741185-0-8
    ISBN: 0-9741185-1-6
1. Widows--Fiction. 2. Aged women--Fiction. 3. Man-woman relationships--Fiction 4. Friendship--Fiction. I. Title.

PS3568.E82 M39 2004
813' .54--dc21   2003107402

*For my mother, Arley Louine Abramowicz
and my daughter, Anne Catherine Purcell,
beautiful and strong, women of character*

1
June

Rose Celador walked as fast as she could down the uneven sidewalk. Her ankles hurt and it helped to slap each foot down hard against the pavement. Down. Up. Down again. Legs straight from the knee, ankles firm, she deliberately chose the sharp, swift pains that shot up her legs and into her groin rather than suffer the lingering ache that kept her awake well into the night when her stiff arthritic ankles, her old and tired ankles, had bent too many times.

Rose was anxious to get home. There was so much to do before Charity, Grace, and June got there. There was the porch to sweep and the rockers to damp wipe, and she needed to press the creases out of her cloth napkins. Charity would notice the creases. She didn't want to antagonize Charity. Not now. Not when Charity and Grace and June were all so angry with her. And she wanted to run in and see Anson. For support. Just for a minute. To touch him, beg with her eyes for words from him that would give her the substance and power to stand dauntless before her friends, to tell them of Anson's love for her, and to argue her integrity.

I didn't cheat, she thought. *We're right for each other. I didn't cheat.* Ah, but they were so angry.

She stepped down hard on a crumbled bit of cement, lost her rhythm, and stumbled. Pain flowed hot in her ankles as first one, and then the other, bent to balance and keep her upright. She drew in her breath at the depth of the pain, the completeness and the power of it. She made herself keep walking, concentrating on each step, counting them, and knowing that each one brought her just a little closer to easement. Ten was the magic number. And when she reached it, she let loose her breath in a grunt.

Damn legs. One of these days they would lead her straight down Ellsworth Street to that new nursing home. Well, not if she could help it. Didn't she just go dancing the night before last with Anson on the dock? They held her up just fine. If the hurt was extra for a few days, well, that was just a small price to pay. She was seventy-three years old and in love and not about to give it up. If that meant losing jealous, mean-spirited friends, so be it. Her shoulders slumped. She wanted both. Anson and her dear, old friends. *I can't hurt them,* she thought. *But I can't bear sharing him, either. Oh God, why can't it just be simple? I don't want to hurt anybody.*

The church chimed nine o'clock. She was almost home. It was a short walk from the bakery to her house — a block along the park, then across the street to the nursing home, and three blocks down Washington Avenue. Anson's house was directly behind her own. Their backyards met. She had bought gingersnaps at the bakery — a day old and cheap, tough and stale, but oh, so good against long-used and fast-fading taste buds — especially when those firm and spicy cookies were dipped in lemonade, soft and soggy and spongy. Anson loved gingersnaps. She would separate some out and take them over to him before the ladies came.

She saw the ambulance when she turned into her driveway. Her first thought was that it was a mistake. She had heard the siren when she was in the bakery. It was for the nursing home. She knew it was. It always was. The ambulance was always going there. It shouldn't be in Anson's yard. Someone had made a mistake. Then she saw the coroner's car.

Her second thought, as she dropped the bag of cookies, was, *Oh, my God, they've killed him.*

2
September

The Previous Year

Rose leaned back in her rocker, yarn and needles untouched in her lap, and inhaled the faint dry smell of dying leaves wafting across the porch. She pushed her foot rhythmically against the smooth wood floorboards, sliding her chair into its lazy, soothing motion. The day was pleasantly warm, blanketing her in soft, sleepy comfort.

"This is so nice," she murmured. "If only we could keep winter away. Far, far away."

"It'll come whether you want it or not," said Charity. "Might as well prepare for it." She lit a cigarette, inhaling deeply.

"Maybe not," said Grace. "Maybe winter won't come at all. Maybe the grass will stay green and the sidewalks clear and the days will be long and we can fish all year and throw away our boots and toss out our mittens. We'll never fall on ice, and we can feed the seagulls without freezing our fingers. Say your prayers, Charity. Wave your wand. Make it happen."

May Snow

Charity patted the white wings that curved up from her forehead and spread over the steel gray waves that sat solid and neat and motionless against her head. She looked at Rose and shook her head. "She thinks I have magic. She grows old and reaches back to childhood days of dreams and fantasy." Turning to Grace, she continued, "If I could, I would stop the howling cold of winter and keep our bones warm and dry. But I can't, so get ready."

Rose smiled. She loved them both, her friends. She had loved them forever, for decades and decades. They were familiar, comfortable, an extra heart, a place to go, an endless memory, a shared life.

"Remember the old locust trees in our front yard?" she asked, reaching deep into her pot of experience. "Remember you and Grace would come over at night with your mom and dad when there still was just a little light left, and they'd sit with my parents on the porch while we'd hunt for bug shells stuck on the bark?"

"I remember. The bark was sharp and it hurt," Charity said.

"And we'd run around the trees. And hide and tag each other. And roll in the grass."

"I remember," Grace said, squirming on the cushion she had thrown on the top step of the porch and adjusting her soft round bottom to find a better spot. "We'd come over after Dad was done in the vineyard. Dad let me hold the buggy reins on the way to your house. He called me his princess and the buggy was my coach."

"He spoiled you," Charity said.

Grace shrugged. "I was the littlest."

"Remember when Will and Anson and Joey and Thomas

pulled the bloomers off Miss Thorpe and ran them up the flagpole?" Rose picked up her knitting, automatically adding stitches to the heavy woolen blanket growing in her lap, her mind still reaching to a time long ago but still vivid.

"I was scared to death," Grace said.

Rose laughed. They had cowered together, the sisters and her and Gretchen Hirsch, the old German's daughter who ate grass because she liked it and besides, if ever there were no food in the world, she used to say, she would be ready, and they wouldn't. Shaking and not daring to speak with no place to hide in the one-room schoolhouse, the girls prayed the boys would finish their business and leave.

Alice Thorpe, a mean and insensitive teacher who neither liked nor understood children, had fought loud and hard, kicking, cursing, and crying, but the boys, wanting revenge for the indignities suffered from the sting of her ruler and the sharper edge of her tongue, were relentless. They held her arms and tugged at her bloomers, laughing as her shoes hit hard and bruising. At last, when the garment was off, they held it high and ran with it to the flagpole where they raised the white cotton and lace to billow in the air, helplessly flapping in the sky until the old German farmer, Gretchen's father, lifted his fists at the boys and chased them away. Then he brought the bloomers down and clumsily folded them — pale against his thick-veined hands — and he took them away with him.

The girls stood at the window and watched. He didn't come in to get Gretchen, and she didn't acknowledge him, either. Rose never did see them touch each other. It made her feel sorry for Gretchen, but she never told her that. She didn't think that Gretchen would have responded with warmth.

May Snow

Gretchen didn't often show feelings. But, even then, Rose knew that she should have said something or smiled at her or shared her sandwich or poked her and laughed with her when Grace told a joke. She should have made the others like Gretchen. She had thought about this, many times, in bed after prayers when she felt closest to God and His wrath.

"You want to remember childhood, Rose?" Charity said, pulling smoke deep into her lungs, blowing it out in a long stream. "I'll tell you what I remember. I remember coming to your house and finding you sitting out in the trees, hugging yourself and crying because you were so tired. And I remember your neck all sunburned and red and your hands all scratched and calloused. And your back hurting. Many times. Many, many times that's what I saw. That's what I remember, Rose."

"You never liked the farm," Rose said. Her hands were still; the needles drooped.

"You were out in those fields with your father all day long. All summer long," Charity said. "He worked you so hard."

"He didn't have anybody else," Rose said. "You had brothers."

"And still you loved the farm."

"I did. I do. I think about it all the time." And she did. Often. She remembered the hard work and the hurting. But the memories were good. Her father had loved her. He had cared for her well.

"You even married a farmer," Charity said.

"You couldn't wait to get away from farm life," Rose countered.

"A man with a top hat and a Tin Lizzie, That's all I wanted."

"And that's what you got," Rose said. "A man with a top hat

and a Tin Lizzie, handsome and charming, with a good job and money to spend." The first time Rose saw Maxwell he was driving that shiny black car, smiling a smile that melted the soul of every woman who had the tiniest iota of the maternal within her. He did like women. Then and all the days of his life. "You got what you wanted and I got what I wanted — a good man, a farmer. He took good care of me."

"Until he died and left you sitting on that great big farm with its mortgaged barn and hungry animals and corn-laden fields and equipment that sometimes worked and sometimes didn't." Charity's lips pulled thin over her teeth. "Margaret grown and gone and no hired man."

There was a fly walking on Rose's arm. She watched it move over tiny lines and liver spots. A shiver went through her. She moved her arm without wanting to and the fly flew away. She followed it with her eyes. It didn't go far, landed on the railing, stayed a brief moment, lifted its wings, soared and circled, and landed on Charity. Charity reached out and slapped it, quick and with good aim. The fly dropped to the floor. Charity kept rocking.

While Rose watched this, her head flashed full of shapes and colors and smells and sounds racing and tumbling and crashing against the flood of feelings let loose by Charity's words. It had been such a good life, life on the farm, married life. Thomas was a hard worker and he had loved her. He made sure she had everything she needed to keep her happy. The same with Margaret. He knew what was best for their daughter. He kept Rose from the heavy farm work, kept that for himself and the occasional hired help. She grained the cows, curried the horses, raised the calves. She drove the wagons while the men pitched hay, and later, the tractor while Thomas and whoever was hired for the season hoisted and threw the bales that Margaret had shoved and pushed and rolled into rows to save the men steps. She cooked, cleaned, canned, chauffeured Margaret, ran for parts for broken equipment, mothered cows in labor, kept the accounts, darned socks, tended ailing parents, planted flowers near the milk house, washed the cows' bags and udders twice a day, killed and plucked chickens, prayed and believed, made casseroles and cookies for church suppers and school functions and funerals and The Grange, and she played with Margaret whenever she could. And, always, she stood by Thomas, helping whenever, however she could, listening, fetching, obeying, loving, making him special, making him happy. It was a good life and she missed it.

"I got what I wanted too," Grace said.

Startled, Rose looked down at Grace sitting on the top porch step with her back against the railing, swinging her right leg that crossed over her left while she scrutinized the slim lower half of it, that and her delicate ankle and foot. Reluctantly Rose pulled herself from her reverie and watched the foot dip and bend and dance in the air all by itself. Grace the dreamer. The foot was probably enticing a lover or locking the gaze of an entranced audience. Maybe this was the foot that dazzled the prince and fit the glass slipper. Whichever, Rose was sure it was not simply a foot moving without thought or direction. Grace's foot wasn't like her foot, a foot meant for balance and walking. Grace's foot was surely meant to please and entice — a foot made for dreams.

"I got what I wanted too," Grace repeated. "I got Stan.

Stanley Girdlestone. Best talker in the whole world." She tilt-ed her head, examining the swinging extremity. "He thought I had great legs."

"You did," Charity said. "A long time ago."

"Sometimes," Grace went on, "sometimes I feel like I could lift myself out of my body and leap and spin and fling myself all over this earth. And I try. I get up and try. But my body is so big. And stiff. And it hurts. So I close my eyes and I keep dancing inside and it feels so good... so good that sometimes I cry."

Rose lay her hand on Grace's shoulder. "If I could," she said, "I would go out in a pasture, heft a newborn calf in my arms, hold it with my back straight and tall, and jiggle it gen-tly, just a little, and judge its weight."

"Well, if I could," Charity said, "I'd wear only silk the rest of my life and high, slim heels every day. And lots and lots of jewelry. With real jewels."

"No," said Grace. "That's a wasted wish. You really could do that if you wanted. A wish should be a heart dream, a pas-sionate need unfulfilled or that takes you back to a remem-bered time that can never be again, like climbing a tree and singing with the birds or playing marbles. I'd love to sit on the ground with my legs crossed and play marbles."

"You probably could do that," Charity said. "If you could stand the pain."

"I'd swing a hoe," said Rose, "break apart the dirt with a powerful wallop. Welcome the sun and sweat again."

"I'd climb a mountain," said Charity.

"Touch a cloud," said Grace, eyes to the sky.

"Dig a hole to China," said Rose.

May Snow

"Pilot an aircraft carrier. Or ride an elephant. Or slide over the ocean on the back of a dolphin." Charity leaned down and rubbed the back of her strong, muscled legs.

"Mix a new color," said Rose.

"Taste the wind again," said Grace, face still uplifted.

"You can still do that," Charity said, straightening up and smoothing her hair.

"Maybe. But I don't."

"In a time long ago, I'd sit in a red velvet chair with people in rapture all around me sharing the magic of a castrato's soaring song," Charity said.

"Feel a man's hand on my melting spot," Rose said softly.

She sighed, saw Charity grip the arms of her rocker, and heard Grace draw in her breath. She was silent with them, knowing each was in her own empty, dark, needing place and thinking of husbands, all dead, gone evermore, leaving them spots unused and untouched and aching.

Rose struggled to remember the feel of strong hands searching her body, touching her everywhere. Inside she strained to capture the ecstasy of joining. She could not. Shyly she looked to the others. They were not looking at her. Their eyes were closed, as hers had been.

"I want to sing in a field," Rose said softly. "A hay field smelling strong and sweetly ripe.

3
September

As Route 5 winds its way along the banks of Lake Erie on its way to Buffalo, it makes an oblong loop away from the water, rendering the lake invisible to passing eyes. On the two-mile stretch before the road heads for the shore again and on the north side between the two-lane cement and the capricious Lake Erie sits Canadaway savoring its precious spot, hoarding its treasured beaches and docks from outsiders.

Once Canadaway was a thriving, flowering community, an exciting place to dwell, buzzing, alive with laughter, gossip, hard work, and growth. The nearby cattle farmers, Rose's people, were rich with need. They needed animal feed, seed, fertilizer, equipment, repair, and food for their own bodies and brains and souls. They needed gathering places, market places. The tomato and bean farmers, too, drew to Canadaway for respite and replenishment. And the greatest consumer of all, the core of Canadaway, the essence of Canadaway, were the grape farmers. Vineyards surrounded the town at its peak.

May Snow

Most are still there, including memorial rows set in the village green, and although they are no longer owned by so many and their holders live in bigger and distant towns, many of the old in Canadaway who were raised on those farms, like Charity and Grace's people, remember. They are the natives with old, firm roots. They are the ones who look at the endless rows of grapes surrounding their town and see the fresh, green buds in spring, the large lush leaves in summer, the rich earth golds and reds in autumn, and the bare, fallen vines in winter. They are the ones who smell the grapes ripening and know when the little purple marbles are bursting with sugar and scent and are ready to be picked. They are the ones who have held the clusters and squeezed and felt the sticky juice spread on their hands and through their fingers, leaving purple-red stains and the odor of wine in the creases of their palms. These are the people who have sucked the thick, white pulp from the berry, spit out the skins, and felt the cool, sweet fruit slide down their throats. They have pulled the unneeded vines that had been cut by the trimmer and left in the dirt to the row end, piled them in a heap, ignited them, watched them flame, smelled them burn, and then partied. Their ears have heard the click of shears, their cheeks have been caressed by velvet leaves and stung by snapping vines, and their lungs have filled with insect-killing sprays and ached.

Now the town limps. The market for tomatoes and beans is gone. The growing season in New York is too short and the taxes are too high. Old Dunning's canning factory squats closed and empty, boarded up tight and growing shabby. Tearless Dunning had moved to warmer fields, longer crops, and a fatter wallet, leaving the farmers without a vessel to swallow up their product. And from other distant places, swollen purses reached and purchased little farms, coupled this one with that, pushed out fences, mingled herds, bought in bulk, sold for less. They ground up the dairyman, grabbed his pride and twisted it, took his child's future and changed it, robbed him of the right to choose his task to fit his clock. They forced his move to a little house in Canadaway.

Canadaway grew smaller, fewer families every year, with so many old bodies walking its streets. The village and its old folk were shrinking, but they still had heart and still had fight. Always with guts they struggled, with hope, to hold fast to pride, recapture vision, and hold tight to life.

"I tell you, Mother," said Margaret, "Robert never calls anymore. And when he does, duty drips so thick from every word it practically chokes him. Like he's doing me this great huge favor." Absently Margaret picked a radish from her salad, dipped it in dressing, raised it to her mouth, put it down before she bit it, and shook her head. "He doesn't have to call me. I never asked him to." She lifted the radish again, looked at it, set it down, folded her hands in her lap, and leaned toward Rose. "I know it doesn't matter. I know he loves me. I know he's busy, and I know Jenny takes first place now. But I really wish he'd call just because he wants to. I don't want him to be homesick. I only want him to miss me just a little." She gripped her hands together. "How can my life be so dependent on his every need for so long and then suddenly, poof, he's grown and gone and it's like that time never was. Like I'm invisible. Used up and discarded. This is the child who worshipped me, wanted to marry me when he grew up. I can't grasp it. I know I have to and I know it's supposed to be this way. But I just don't like the feel of it."

Rose and Margaret huddled at the end of the horseshoe counter in Hunter's, crouched on stools twisted toward each other, straining to catch the words that passed so softly between them so that none of the other lunchers could hear them and know their secrets.

"Give it time, Sweetie." Rose gently spread her fingers over the hands folded tightly in Margaret's lap. Slowly she rubbed her thumb back and forth over her daughter's taut-skinned knuckles. "He's full of Jenny now. He needs to get used to her, comfortable with what they are now, and with all that new responsibility. There's room in his heart for both of you. He just doesn't know that yet. Give him time. When he learns it, he'll be there for you."

"No, he won't," Margaret said. "She'll always be first."

Rose sighed. Margaret was probably right. And that's the way it should be. Forsaking all others. Including mothers. That's what marriage was. Only that didn't help Margaret. She doted on that boy. Too much. Had made his need turn into her need as he grew up and away from her. Rose ached for her, wished she could pull her from a want that couldn't be fulfilled to a craving that could be fed.

"What about Forrest? How's he doing with all this? Now that Emily and Robert are both out of the house, maybe you and Forrest could do more things together." Margaret swung away from her mother. "Yeah, right, like run around the house naked or maybe lay by the pool and feed each other grapes."

Rose took a long swig of iced tea, setting the glass down carefully. "I was thinking more along the lines of travel or

18

finding a hobby together ... like golf or gardening ... or reading a book in the same room."

"Now you're mad."

"No. I only want to help you through this. It does pass, you know. You get used to a tidy, quiet house. You even get to like it." As she spoke, Rose reached over and lightly brushed her daughter's arm. What she wanted to do was hug her hard, rock her, pat her back, but judging from the quick, involuntary jerk of Margaret's arm away from Rose's touch, then the sudden flash of guilt and remorse that distorted her daughter's face, she knew it was best to push that desire right out of her thoughts. It didn't surprise her. From day one her only child had struggled to please those she loved and she'd anguished when she hurt them. Floating in Rose's maternal memories was baby Margaret, little sweetie-pie, eyes squeezed shut, fists raised and shaking, mouth stretched wide, screaming in the middle of the night, wanting a dry cloth on her tiny, wet bottom or needing warm milk to fill her tummy, knowing what would please her. Then, suddenly she was silent, succumbing to her father's sharp call for quiet. *He needed his sleep. And that,* Rose thought, *was probably the beginning of Margaret's awful and continuous struggle to keep herself real and whole and visible while, at the same time, she shared from her great well of kindness and caring, wanting to give pleasure, and make happiness and peace for all. If there were a burden lying on the side of the road, Margaret would stop and pick it up.*

"It'll be all right," Rose said. "You'll see. You and Forrest will find things to do together. Just give it time."

"You don't know, Mother. You really don't. Forrest isn't like Dad. He's never home. He's always working. I'd love to be doing *things* with him. I've done everything I can think of to entice him to stay home to do *things*, to keep his home peaceful and easy and pressure-free so he has the inclination and the energy to do *things*. But he's never there."

"Then maybe you need to be looking for something to fill your time without Forrest."

"I've got the garden club. Flowers in the summer. Book reports and lectures in the winter. I know a lot about dirt, Mother. Excuse me, soil. I know a lot about soil. Soil and compost and seed quality. And potted plants."

"Something *you* really like, Margaret. Not something Forrest chooses for you."

"Ha, you're a fine one to talk. Dad's been dead for years and you're still making decisions based on what he would have thought or done. Listen to yourself, and when you hear what you're saying and do it yourself, then you can give me advice. Now eat. I've got shopping to do and shirts to iron and dinner to make before Forrest gets home. If Forrest gets home. Just eat, Mother. I'll be nicer next lunch."

❄   ❄   ❄

The old ladies rode out of town on their bikes. Charity led the way down Route 5 on her two-wheeler, fields on one side, vineyards reaching to Lake Erie on the other.

"Smell those grapes," Grace said, twisting her head and sniffing.

"Pay attention to where you're going and don't lally gag," Charity shouted back.

"They'll be ready to start picking in a couple weeks," Rose

said. Her mouth juiced thinking of the sweet, fresh fruit sitting moist on her tongue.

"Let's go," Charity called.

Rose watched as Charity lifted her rear from her bicycle seat, pushed hard with her lean and heavily-veined legs, and pedaled fast. Charity's mouth opened as she sucked in air. The wind molded her shirt against her sagging breasts and trim midriff. It raised her shirt and spread it behind her. It battled the gels that tamed her hair and lifted the waves that flowed from the stiff, white wings that even the rushing air could not move. She stood on the pedals, legs straight, leaned into the wind, and coasted. Her face was red, her mouth open and smiling wide.

"She's trying to pull us along faster," Grace said, drawing alongside Rose. "It never works. I know exactly how fast I want to go and that's exactly how fast I'm going to go. But she keeps trying."

Rose and Grace were on three-wheelers. Rose had bought hers so she could sit and rest her legs when they screamed their pain; Grace, so she wouldn't tip and fall when her attention wavered and her eyes lost sight of the path before her. The wire storage baskets on each bike were packed with blankets and books and games and food. They were headed for a picnic.

They turned onto Clover Lane and followed the flat dirt road as it curved through fields and pastures. Massive oak and maple trees, trunks thick with age, bordered both sides. Their upper limbs locked overhead, framing a dark, cool tunnel slightly warmed and lit by sun rays flitting and glittering and dancing between the leaves, kissing them with fire. It was a day from God, a gift to lay aside the scars of the blistering summer heat and gather strength for the bleak, cold winter days ahead. It was a trick. It fooled the brain into thinking that the balm could last forever. A kind and healing magic.

Thinking they would add a touch of earthy color to Charity's living room, Grace stopped and slid into the ditch to steal cattails for drying. Charity had motioned Grace back to her bike, complaining the cattails would shed and spot her rugs, but Grace shrugged and smiled and went into the trench anyway. She broke off the cattails and filled her arms with the wild flowers. When she was done, ready to get back on her bike, she discovered she couldn't get out of the ditch. There was no place to plant her feet on the slippery slope, and her hands weren't free to grab grass and pull herself out.

"Charity," she called.

"Damn you, Grace." Charity climbed off her bike and lay it down carefully. She stomped to the ditch and offered a hand to Grace. Grace tilted her head, lifted her eyebrows, and waited. She shifted the load in her arms just a little.

"Put the damn cattails down and give me your hand."

Grace shook her head.

Rose sat on her bicycle and waited. She was too tired to get down and help.

"Then stand there and rot." Charity marched to her bike, lifted it, and poised her foot on the pedal, ready to push.

"Charity!"

Rose smiled. This was stuff she knew and could predict.

Charity climbed off her bike again, dropped it on the ground. Grass bent and broke as her feet crashed across the blades and took her fast to the edge of the ditch. "You've been nothing but trouble since the first day I laid eyes on you."

Grace lifted the cattails to her. "Don't crush them. Give them to Rose, then come help me out."

Charity clenched her teeth and took the weeds, stepped sharp to Rose, and held them out to her.

Rose bit her lip. It was not the time to smile. She pointed to the basket.

Silently Charity threw the cattails in, went back to the ditch, grabbed Grace's hands, and yanked her hard.

"You're hurting me," Grace said.

"I wish." Charity released her hold and braced her body. She hooked her arm gently under Grace's and helped her out.

Grace kissed her sister on the cheek. "See, you really do love me."

"You always did get whatever you wanted," Charity grumbled. "Get on your bike and let's go."

So on they rode to Grimmers Pond, a swollen, rounded stretch of creek that dipped wide and deep — a hole for swimming, fishing, picnicking, and quenching wild animal thirst.

Slowly, with effort, Rose pumped her bike across the bumpy field. Her legs ached fiercely. She parked in the shade of a great maple at the edge of the water and sat on her three-wheeler, head down, shoulders slumped, heart beating fast, and hands gripping the handlebars while she waited for the pain to subside.

Charity touched her shoulder. "You okay?"

Rose nodded. She heard Charity walk away. She felt the tension leaving her body. Lifting her arm, she wiped her face with the back of her hand, looked to the water, and breathed deeply

of the fragrant grass and sweet air. This was a place of comfort
and memory. Her father had brought them here for picnics. She
had played here with cousins and neighbors, with Grace and
Charity, with other farmers' children. She had hidden here
when she craved a private place, swam naked with Thomas in
the dark here before they were married. She hadn't let him
touch her, only look. Until they came back on their wedding
night and celebrated. Her body tightened at the thought, and
she trembled. She had brought Margaret here. She had seen the
trees grow larger, the fields cover with snow and crop. She had
seen deer feeding here, rabbits and wild turkey, geese migrat-
ing with mighty clamor, minnows sunning, flowers spreading.
Here she felt safe and pleasantly full.

"Don't put that blanket on the ground," Charity called out
to Grace. "Spread it here on the picnic table."

"I want to eat on the grass," Grace said.

"If you get on the ground, you'll never get up."

"Watch me." Grace bent and dropped to the grass, hitched
on her bottom to a fallen tree, got on her knees, clutched the
trunk, and hefted her body — first up on one leg, rear sticking up, then pulling up her other leg, she straightened,
turned, spread her arms, and bowed.

"Cute, Grace. Such poise. Now bring me the blanket."

Rose took a blanket and padded to the place where two
aged maple trees had grown close together, old friends joined
at the bottom, leaning away from each other to catch their
own separate sun and splitting just enough to form a good
spot to sit. She eased her back against the spicy, rough bark
and closed her eyes. She sat quietly, vaguely hearing the familiar bickering between Charity and Grace — words hurled

not to hurt, just to sting a little. She shifted their words into the background along with the birdsong and rustle of leaves gently touching each other while she thought about Thomas and pretended he was at the pond casting his line, catching their dinner. The sisters would leave her alone while they spread out the food, played a board game, or took a walk. Charity was the oldest and Grace, the youngest and silliest and most pampered, but Rose was the one who had tired the most from their ride. They knew that, and they'd give her time to recover.

"I think I like this place better than the beach," Rose said, sliding onto the picnic bench next to Charity after her rest.

Charity put down her cards. She was playing solitaire. Grace was wandering along the edge of the water, tossing stones, watching the ripples, dreaming.

"If we were at the beach, you would say you liked the beach better," Charity said.

Rose smiled. "Probably." She picked up an apple, rubbed it in her hands, and smelled it. "I do like fall. But it goes too fast."

"Then cold, cold winter."

"Cooped up in the house too much of the time."

Grace hurried up from the pond. "Good, you're awake." She sat. "Let's eat." She picked up an egg, took half in her mouth, wrinkled her nose. "Where's the salt?"

After they ate, they walked the creek bank reluctant to start home. This would be the last trip to the pond before winter. They wanted to savor its pleasures as long as they could.

Rose lifted her face to the sky. "Outside air feels so fresh and moist and clean and crisp and inside air feels so used."

May Snow

"This would be a perfect day if Maxwell were here ... and we were alone," Charity said.

"It is a nearly perfect day," agreed Grace. "All we need is a gent for us to feed and for him to pick us flowers."

Rose looked into the creek and remembered the silky feel of the soft, night water sliding over her while the crickets sang and Thomas' gentle fingers explored, coaxed, and teased her to splendor. She hugged her body and felt the throb.

"I miss a man," said Charity.

"We've been without for a long time," said Rose.

"Do you ever dream there's one walking beside you?" asked Grace. "Or do you see Gilbert and Anson fishing on the dock and pretend they're arguing about which one of them you like most instead of who's got the best fly? Or when Manny White delivers the mail, do you ever pretend he slipped a love note in among the bills? I winked at him once, and I think if I'd crooked my finger and wiggled it at him, he would have run upstairs with me."

"He's married," said Charity.

"They're all married," said Grace. "Or dead. At least all the old ones."

"Not Gilbert," said Charity.

"Or Anson," said Rose.

"Or Charley, Charley, full of barley," said Grace. "But who'd want him?"

"Gilbert smells," said Charity.

"Anson doesn't," said Rose. She pictured the men. Charley was a bit bloated and Gilbert did have some bad stomach problems, but Anson, strong of limb and spirit, would be a man to reckon with. "It would be nice to have a man to cook for."

September

"Baloney," said Charity. "It would be nice to have a man to take you out to dinner."

"We should have a contest," Grace said. "See who could use her charms best and get Anson to take her out on a date."

"Not fair," said Charity. "He'd either pick Rose's cooking or your bed. I don't think white sparkling laundry or shiny furniture, my specialties, would turn him on. Although his house could probably use a good cleaning."

"It would be nice," Rose repeated.

"He's rich too," Grace said. "All that land, all those cows. He could afford us all."

Rose looked at her. "You're right. He could." And a plan started to form in her mind.

❄   ❄   ❄

"I am bombarded by beauty," Anson said, opening his front door to Rose, Grace, and Charity.

"It's your lucky day, Anson Stone," said Grace.

The ladies had sat late at the picnic table and considered the rewards of sharing a man. They agreed that too many old ladies, to wit themselves, lived long and widowed, and there weren't enough aged men surviving for each of them to have one for her own. Each agreed she pined for the solidity of a man to affirm her womanliness, to declare her body worthy, to speak in the tongue of the other half of the world, to prop and be propped. If there weren't enough, why not share? Equally and fairly.

So they came to the house of Anson Stone with a plan and he led them into his parlor.

May Snow

"We have a proposition," Rose said softly. She scooped up Gossip, one of a pair of tabby cats. The other was Rumor, so named by Anson because they were female cats and he thought it was funny. She smoothed Gossip's fur while she struggled to choose the words to explain and capture his favor. Her cheeks were pink as she looked at him. "It's been a long time since Thomas died. And Maxwell and Stan. And for you, Bernice." She paused. "This is hard." She wished he would look away. Or that she could. "We miss them."

"We want to share you," Grace interrupted.

"Share me?"

"We want you to keep company with all of us," said Charity. "We want you to take us to dinner, talk to us, go to bingo, maybe church, notice our clothes or hair or shoes or fingernails or whatever your man eyes see. We want you to be a man friend for all of us."

"We want equal shares," said Grace.

Rose put Gossip down. She wanted it too. Whoever said it, however it was said, she wanted it too. Someone alive to help her, to point out the choices, and to help her pick.

Anson grinned, a slow, amused, knowing smile.

He thinks we're lacking, Rose thought. Uncertainty flashed and was gone. We need his balance, and he needs ours. It's a good thing we're proposing. This is a chance to fill a hole he must have too. She wondered at his thoughts as the smile left his face and his eyes moved past Charity and Grace and then settled on her for a long, quiet moment. She wanted to touch the center of his cheek where the skin sank tight. She felt her hand begin to lift and steadied it, let it drop, remembering she was old.

September

Anson looked away from her. "Why would I want to give up my freedom?" he asked. "It's been a long time since Bernice. I like to do what I want, when I want."

"Maybe you owe us," said Charity. "You men use us up and then you die without us ever getting our share of pleasure. You can atone for three men here and make it even."

"And what do I get?" Anson asked.

"A meal, home-cooked. Woman talk, maybe more. Variety. Appreciation," Charity answered.

"I like what I have."

"We'll make it better," said Grace.

"You don't have to," said Rose. She was aching and frightened, ashamed to be asking, embarrassed they might be refused. "We're okay and happy without you, without this. It's only a thought, a try for more. For you too."

Anson met her eyes again. He nodded. "Okay then. Once a month each of you gets a crack at me."

"Once a week," Charity said.

"Too much."

"Once a week," she repeated.

"Twice a month," Anson said.

"Once a week," said Charity. "Give it a shot."

"I pick the days."

"You pick the days," she agreed.

"Sundays are out," Anson said. Rose knew he was remembering Bernice. "And Fridays me and the boys have fish and talk all night. Saturdays I shop and clean ..."

"We can do that," Grace interrupted. "See? A plus for you."

"We want at least one weekend night to rotate," said Charity. "An out-on-the-town night."

May Snow

"Could be expensive," Anson said.

"You can afford it," Grace said.

"Who's doing the asking here? Not me. You're the one choosing to change my life."

"For the better," said Grace.

"I don't know."

"We'll pay our own way," said Rose. She had enough money. Not much to spare. But enough. She wouldn't take from him what she already had. It was crucial that he know that.

"Monday, Wednesday, and Saturdays," said Charity. "Monday for cleaning. Wednesday for cooking, and Saturday for going out. We'll rotate."

Rose watched Anson as he thought. She willed him to agree, praying Thomas would understand.

He nodded. "I want my evenings. You can come in and clean and cook and I'll be civil, but I want my evenings."

"Except Saturdays," agreed Charity.

He nodded again.

Rose let out her breath.

❄   ❄   ❄

Charity made calendars to mark with alloted visits with Anson. She divided the weeks, rotating their days. One copy for her and Grace's house. One copy for Rose. A copy for Anson. Rose watched as Charity carefully scheduled the first week's assignments to coincide with the tasks each performed best. Charity gave herself Monday. Spit and shine and all in its place, that was her strong suit. If it wasn't clean, if it wasn't perfectly placed, it wasn't finished and she wasn't done. Rose cooked tasty food, so Charity gave her Wednesday. And Grace, charmer Grace, got Saturday. Right. Appropriate. She'd break Anson down and make him laugh and then want to laugh some more. He'd have fun spilling out of his ears. They were all good, the best, at their appointed chores. The next week, when they rotated, would be riskier.

When Wednesday came, Rose was prepared. She had spent the whole day Tuesday scrubbing, scraping, dicing, slicing, stirring, boiling, baking, sautéing, and putting together seven little casseroles suitable for freezing. One for each day of the week.

She waited until the noon hour passed, lunch time gone, to pack the food and make herself ready for the trek across her backyard and his to his back door. She didn't want him to think she expected him to invite her to sit and watch him eat, or worse, to share what she had agreed to provide. This was too embarrassing. What would she say? Here. This is my part of the bargain. Now eat it so you can do your part and make me whole and complete by your presence.

She should never have agreed to this. Best to drop the basket on his step, ring the bell, and run. Like May Day.

Except he would know who left the gift. And he would think her foolish.

She sighed. This was like a trip to the doctor. You showered and scrubbed every inch of your body, and you washed your ears good because you knew he would stick that thing in your ear and you'd be absolutely mortified if it came out waxy. And you dressed in clothes easily shed, so you could get in and out of that paper dress fast without showing much skin. And you thought it through a hundred times so nothing would surprise you, and then you gritted your teeth and did it, and it wasn't as bad as you thought it would be, and it felt so good when it was over. She would get through this too. She had said she would do it, so she would.

But then she was done. No more visits. The idea had been fine. But the doing was too hard. It would have been different if Anson had been the one knocking on her door.

"Forgive me, Thomas." She picked up the basket, pressed her lips together, straightened her back, and marched to Anson's.

He opened the door, stood there in his everyday tee-shirt and jeans with a big, red handkerchief stuffed in his back pocket, poking out just a little, hanging ready to mark the end of a fresh seeded row or tie a calf's legs together or swing at the back of a too-long log to warn the driver behind him. It was an old farmer's tool and his signature. He reached with strong, gnarled hands and took the basket, swinging it easily from her. He looked at her, and the smile that came was slow and known and friendly. And she was all right.

"Mighty heavy basket for one supper." He took her arm and led her into the kitchen, placed the basket on the table, and began to unpack it.

Rose watched him pile one neatly wrapped bundle on top of another. The stack grew tall. And taller. Like a child building a block tower, he carefully placed each foil square exactly on top of the last, then ran his hands down the sides to even them. When he was done, he turned and bowed.

"Could be I overdid it a bit," Rose said, smiling.

"Just a mite," Anson agreed. "Shall we shove them in the freezer?"

September

"There's one for every day."

"I can see that."

Rose burst out laughing. "It could have been worse. I could have made *big* casseroles."

"Wouldn't have mattered. Plenty of room in the freezer. You're forgetting Charity was here Monday. Not only did she shine my whole house, including places I didn't know could shine, she crawled deep into my refrigerator and created all kinds of space — clean space, space without mold, orderly space." He opened the freezer door at the top of the refrigerator. "Behold, there is no fuzzy ice clinging to the sides, there are no little packets of goodies from long ago dinners sticking to the bottom shelf, there is no *food* either. All is empty and ready for your bounty."

"Looks like she did a pretty good job."

"Thorough."

"Very thorough," Rose said and grinned.

"I sat and watched her do it," Anson said, returning the grin. "I sat and watched her clean the whole house."

"Was it interesting?"

"No."

"Then why did you watch?"

"I offered to go for coffee and get out of her way."

"And?"

"She got mad. Said my part was to keep her company. I told her it wasn't much fun to sit in a doorway and watch her dig crumbs out of a corner."

"But she didn't relent," Rose stated, knowing Charity.

"She didn't relent. The agreement is, she cleans, I entertain. In a manly manner."

May Snow

"Did you?"

"Apparently. She stayed to finish the job."

After the casseroles were put away, they went outside to sit on the porch and talk. The air was balmy, redolent with the faint, dry scent of dying leaves that still dressed the oaks and maples with vibrant color, some gently separating from the trees as, one by one, they slowly drifted downward, spreading over the grass and lacing a crisp carpet of many colors that dried and crushed and blended with the soil to nourish the mother trees, making it richer as they circled home.

Anson motioned Rose to take the chair near a small, ornately carved table. Rose hesitated. There were no spectacles on the table, no Bible on the crocheted doily, and there was no tapestry knitting bag filled with soft yarns and needles sitting on the floor. But still the chair was Bernice's and Rose could feel her there. She looked at Anson and he was looking back at her, standing by his chair, waiting for her to move. She could not tell from the set of his face what he was thinking, and she wondered if Thomas was there too — if all four of them were held there in time until she moved into a space that had never been hers and shifted the weights of their relationships.

Quietly, slowly, she lowered herself into Bernice's rocker, slid into the slope of her curves, into the pieces of memory and soul that lingered. She felt a peaceful fit.

She stole a glance at Anson. He was sitting in his chair. He looked relaxed, comfortable. His fingers tapped a song on the arm of his chair. His head nodded to his music. She thought he looked happy.

4
October

"Look, Margaret. There's Forrest." Rose pointed through the window and across the street to where her daughter's husband was hurrying by the storefronts, guiding his woman companion by the elbow and moving her quickly through the lunch crowd. "Who's that with him?"

Margaret wiped her mouth carefully. She laid the napkin firmly in her lap. She didn't look out the cafe window. "I don't know," she said. She poked a cherry tomato with her fork, swearing under her breath as it squirted juice on her blouse. She glared at her mother. "I guess she's a business acquaintance. Or maybe she works in his office. I really don't know. Or care."

Rose dipped her napkin in water and handed it to Margaret. "Pat it. Don't rub." She tried to keep concern out of her voice. Margaret had initiated this lunch, had chosen this cafe in Northridge where she and Forrest lived, had picked this time. She had insisted on this table next to the front window with its clear view of the long row of shops and offices and restaurants across the way. Margaret had called that morning, and Rose had known immediately that all was not well with her daughter. She'd heard it in Margaret's tense tone and crisp words; she'd sensed it in her changed patterns of pause and inflection. She didn't know what the problem was and didn't know what Margaret was seeking from her. Then Rose had seen Forrest, and Margaret hadn't looked. *Because she had known,* Rose thought. *She had known she would see Forrest. And Rose was with her because she could not bear to see it alone.*

"You knew you would see Forrest, didn't you?" Rose leaned across the table and took her daughter's hand.

"I don't know what you mean." Margaret didn't move.

"How did you know Forrest would be having lunch with that woman?"

"Leave me alone, Mother. Please, just leave me alone."

"Look at me, Margaret."

"I can't. I can't look at you, Mother."

Rose rubbed her daughter's arm. She wished she could be sure what to do. "I'd take the pain if I could," she whispered.

"Sometimes people, friends, say things they don't mean or don't know… or only think they know. They think they're being kind." Margaret raised her eyes. She bit her lip. "I have to know the truth. And I saw. Forrest was taking a fellow worker to lunch. In plain view. Right down the main street of where I live. There was no hiding. It's all right. I'm all right. We're all right, Forrest and me."

"Margaret," Rose said softly, her heart breaking for her daughter. "Oh, Margaret, I don't know what to say to you."

"Mother, please. You don't understand. It's nothing. Please

don't say anything to anyone, and please, let's just drop this *now.* It's nothing, really."

"Oh, Margaret."

"Don't worry about me. I'm fine. We're fine. Forrest and I are fine." She drew in a deep breath. "I love you, Mother."

"I love you, Margaret."

"I guess I wasn't much nicer this lunch."

Rose squeezed Margaret's hand. She wanted to cry. "Sweetie, you were fine."

❋   ❋   ❋

On a crisp Sunday afternoon in early October, three sweatered old ladies met on Rose's porch to discuss their shared experience with Anson.

"I think we need to face the problems head on," said Charity. "We need to write down rules and stick to them."

Rose blew on her cocoa and sipped it carefully lest it burn her tongue. She wasn't sure if the thermometer God put in her mouth worked anymore. Sometimes she would stick her finger in her food or drink to test the temperature before she sent the nourishment to her stomach, but she feared Charity's critical eyes, so she swallowed and prayed her throat would not get scalded.

Charity's words puzzled Rose. She rubbed her fingers up and down her cup absently, enjoying the warmth, while she sought to recall any moments with Anson that were less than perfect. There were none. For her at least, and, she hoped, none for him. He seemed happy enough with the arrangement. She knew the three of them amused him, probably even more than his cats did. The ladies seemed to add spark to the sameness of his days.

"I don't understand," Rose said. "What problems?"

Charity looked at her and frowned.

"I don't like to clean," Grace said. She licked melted marshmallow from her spoon. "I don't like to cook much, either. Those are two big problems for me. Anybody want to trade their days? I sure like Saturday nights."

"She's right," Charity said. "We do too much for him."

"Is that it?" Rose asked. "You think he expects too much from us?"

"Nobody said he expects us to do all the work we do," said Charity. "Though I don't hear much thanks." She pushed her cup away. It clinked against a mason jar holding Queen Anne's lace and bachelor buttons, the last of the season, in water dyed a deep and vibrant green. Rose had picked the flowers along the edge of the Little League field across the street from her house. She'd arranged them in several jars then put them on little porch tables and on the porch floor. Every canning glass was filled with a different bright color, and when the white Queen Anne's lace sucked the liquid through its stem to every minute and fragile blossom, Rose would have a magnificent bouquet.

Charity lit a cigarette. "We agreed to cook and clean," she continued. "It's part of the bargain and we should do it. That's no problem. Besides, I don't think Grace kills herself when it's her turn to do any work." She lifted her hand, palm out toward Grace, to silence her sister's imminent complaint. "No, that's not it at all. It's not the work and it's not Anson. I truly enjoy and look forward to my days with him.

October

You know Maxwell wasn't easy to live with. You saw it. But sometimes I can't help but miss the strength of his hand on me." She glared at Grace. "And I don't mean the sting of his hand, but the fire he lit when he touched me. There's power in a man's body. Solace. I can do fine without it. I manage fine by myself. But, still, I miss that feel of being a woman, that feeling that comes when a man looks at you and knows you're something that he can't be and that he can't own, when he hungers to have that part of you and knows he can't. It gives you a control bigger than anything else. I can't get that from another woman. I have a chance to get it from Anson, and I don't mean to let anybody keep me from getting that command back. I want to feel like a queen again. And, by God, I'm going to."

"Is that why you stayed with Maxwell all those years?" Rose asked. "Because *you* had control over *him*?" That was not how Rose remembered it.

"She stayed for money," Grace said. Her mouth twisted. "Look what she's got. Big house. Closet full of clothes. And everybody in town bowing down to her just because of the things she's got, all the while knowing what she had to do and what she had to ignore to crawl up that pedestal she thinks she sits on. There aren't too many secrets in this town. Some, but not too many."

"Shh," Rose said, laying her hand on Grace's arm to gentle her. "She's your sister. Go softly. She loves you dearly."

Charity looked straight ahead, rocking, smoking.

Grace squinted and drew away from Rose. "I don't let her control me. She lets me live with her, but she does it because it makes her look generous." She spoke in low, bitter tones.

"She really doesn't like the idea that Anson might get to like one of us better than her. And he might, you know. That's what scares her."

"Does it scare you?" Rose asked.

"I won't let it happen."

Rose looked from one sister to the other. Both were angry beyond their common, love-tempered, sharp-edged teasing. Bitterness pierced their words with wounds that dripped of old and heavy pain.

"Is that what's wrong?" Rose leaned towards Charity. "Do you think Grace is going to take your time with Anson from you? That he might favor her?"

Charity looked directly at Rose for a long moment. Rose felt the cold and shuddered. Charity lifted her cigarette, dragged deep, turned her head back to stare at the boys playing catch across the street, and let the smoke out.

"No," she said. "I don't think Grace is a thief. Or a threat. Although I'm sick to death of hearing how voluptuous Anson thinks she is. According to her."

"Then it's me," Rose said. "You're angry at me." She was reluctant to offer herself as a recipient of the torrent of hostility Charity was able to hurl, dreading the shame that would come when she could not match or evade it. "Why are you angry with me?"

"You haven't a clue?"

"I really don't know."

"You're the problem," Grace said. "The problem we have to fix."

"How can that be?" Rose asked. "What did I do? Everything is going so well. I thought so, anyway. I'm happy. Anson's happy. Why aren't you?"

"I'm going to be," said Charity. "Because we're going to set up rules, and we're going to follow them, or there's going to be hell to pay."

"Anson's talking too much about you," said Grace. "It bugs Charity."

"I don't have any control over what he says," Rose said. "I can't muzzle him. Besides he talks about both of you to me." She couldn't understand the depth of Charity's anger. "Everything he says is nice." And most of the time, it was.

"You don't have to be running out to your yard every time he opens his back door," Charity said, rocking steady, refusing to look at Rose. "And you don't have to be bumping into him at church or the store or having cokes with him at Hunter's."

"She was going to the library and saw you through Hunter's window," Grace said. "She said she waved and you wouldn't wave back."

"I didn't see her," Rose said. "He was there. I was buying a magazine. He offered. I said yes."

"Well, you shouldn't have," said Charity. "Don't you see? That's the problem. This whole arrangement is supposed to be equal for all of us and you've got the upper hand because you live so close to him ..."

"And because you're nicer," Grace broke in, shrugging when Charity glared at her. "Well, she is."

"I'm not going to have you ruin this for me, Rose. Not by a long shot." Charity pointed her cigarette at Rose, jabbing the air with it in time to match her words. "We're going to make some rules."

May Snow

"She thinks he's going to drop us from the deal," Grace continued, "and just keep you."

"Grace," demanded Charity, "*shut up* or I swear to God you'll be living in the street."

Grace made a face at her, then turned away.

"Are you ready?" Charity asked, and before Rose could even answer, she dug in her pocket and whisked out a list. "Number one. No one is to spend time with Anson on off days. Is that clear?"

Rose wondered why Charity's blouse always had to match her pants. There always had to be a leaf or flower or circle or stripe that was the same color as her polyester pants. Sometimes her shoes even matched. And her purse. It was absolutely amazing. Even when she was angry and had come to yell and jam her rules down their throats, nothing clashed. Her colors all matched. Even her hair was perfect. It didn't move. Rose touched her own tousled curls. They were soft and clean and welcomed Anson's fingers. She wouldn't give that up.

"Rose? I asked you a question. Aren't you even listening?" Charity threw up her hands. "I really can't stand this."

Grace giggled and examined her fingernails.

"I don't know what to say," said Rose. "And if I did, I don't think you'd listen."

"It has to be fair," Charity said. "You took him seven casseroles. Who can compete with that? Nobody can feed him as good as you can. And that's major."

"Rule number two," said Grace. "Menus must be approved by all."

"That's just silly," said Rose.

"Not if you don't cook so good," said Grace.

"Look," said Rose, "I won't cook so *much* again. But I can't help it if my food happens to be tasty." They were being ridiculous. And her food was better than theirs. So what? Rose was getting angry. Why not? Might as well have three mad women. "You only cook once every three weeks. What's the big deal?"

"I agree," said Charity. "All menus must be preapproved."

"Fine," said Rose. "Are those all the rules?"

"Number three," said Charity, "there can be no phone calls with Anson longer than fifteen minutes."

That was an easy one. Rose never talked to Anson on the phone. She nodded. So did Grace.

"There's only one more," said Charity.

Rose waited. Charity was looking straight at her. This one, too, must be meant for her.

"No one is to acknowledge Anson's presence without the permission of all of us."

"Enough," Rose said. "This is not a gigantic town we live in. We bump into him over and over. I'm not going to turn my back or pretend I don't see him."

"You saw him today in church, Charity," Grace said. "Remember? I was with you. You chatted."

Charity's nostrils flared and her cheeks grew red. "Not one more word, Grace. Not one." She spoke low and clear. "I mean it."

Grace slumped in her chair.

"You're right," Charity said to Rose. "We will see him and we can't ignore him. But no planned meetings and no long, drawn out conversation. No cokes at Hunter's."

May Snow

"Okay," Rose conceded. She hoped they were done.

"I'll write up the rules and give you each a copy," said Charity.

Grace sat up in her chair. "And if anyone cheats, they're dead."

She looked serious.

✳   ✳   ✳

Rose wrapped her hands around the cup of cocoa Sarah Hunter put in front of her and held it tight. An involuntary shudder traveled her body, protesting the cold that had penetrated and spread and touched every corner and crevice she had, both the known and the secret. The sudden and complete assault took her breath away, holding her in its grip. She was unable to move until it was done and gone in a final, jerking spasm — quick and sharp, up, through, and out. Her shoulders relaxed. Air blew and swelled her lips as it passed them in a long, slow stream from her mouth. The cup was too hot on her fingers. She set it down.

"It is so cold," she said, rubbing her hands together.

"It's the damp," responded Sarah. She stood next to the register talking to Rose while she watched two young boys leafing thorough magazines on the rack behind Rose. George and Joey Turner. Troublemakers. "If the rain would turn to snow, it wouldn't be so bad. It's those hard, pelting drops I hate. Feels like glass slivers cutting right through you. That and the wind." She shivered. "Just thinking about it sends goose bumps right to the center of my bones."

Rose tried the cup again, gingerly enclosing it with skeptical fingers. The warmth was safe and good. She caressed the silky porcelain, savored the feel of it.

"Those boys," Sarah said, shaking her head. "I better see what they want before they smudge every magazine I've got."

She sighed, pushed herself away from the counter, and, hand pressed hard into the small of her back as if to keep herself from doubling over from the strain of movement, walked slowly around Rose toward the floor-to-ceiling magazine rack that stood defenseless against the giggling boys, as they poked and pawed and sampled its wares.

"Sometimes the days are just too long," she said over her shoulder.

Rose closed her ears to the grumbling behind her and watched the leaves and rain pelt the front window. A crimson maple leaf slammed flat against the glass, its points grabbing at the window, seeking to hold on and stay there. It was perfectly formed, veins clear and still full, a king among leaves. Rose watched it cling, sticking there for a wet, precarious moment, and then slowly slide down out of sight, leaving a clear, straight path free of prints for a second before it was filled again by the hammering, drenching rain. Watching it, knowing its feel, she shivered again and turned her eyes away.

The sun, obscured by sodden, dark clouds, couldn't force its warming rays through that mass, and the sky hung heavy and dim. Cars ran along Route 5 with windshield wipers and headlights on.

Rose dreaded the moment she would have to leave Hunter's and scurry to her car. It was parked in front of the library. She sipped her cocoa slowly. She had spent the morning with

May Snow

Grace and Charity, mending books. It would be a long after-noon since she had nothing planned. She could have gone with the sisters to Northridge for lunch and then sat and watched them get washed and trimmed and curled at the Cleopatra. Debbys-Do right next door to Hunter's wasn't good enough for Charity. Rose figured she'd rather be bored curled up on her couch watching soap operas than watch Charity and Grace get prettied up. She'd like to go see Anson, but she didn't dare. It wasn't honorable, and besides, Grace would find out. She had eyes out watching everywhere. She always found a way to know everything.

Sarah was still hung up with the boys. They'd left the mag-azines for the toy display and were trying to decide which baseball cards they already had. Rose heard them arguing. The Turner terrors. They were always in trouble. Probably need-ed a good hugging. God knows, they got enough scolding.

Rose heard a honk outside. The bus was making its daily one o'clock stop. The driver was Sarah's nephew. Thinking to bring his aunt business, he had arranged to make Canadaway a sched-uled rest stop. Looking through the window, Rose saw a woman and two men step off the bus and hurry toward the shop. At the same time, a car hauling a trailer and loaded with boxes on its roof pulled in front of the bus. The driver got out and walked quickly to the public phone outside Hunter's. One hand held tight to his sweatshirt's hood to keep it from blowing off while the other bunched the fabric around his neck to keep the rain out. He needed boots. He was wading through puddles in ragged sneakers. Rose watched the man hunch over the phone, fumbling with coins, while he brushed raindrops from his face. Moving in place from foot to foot, he made a call. Finished, he started back to the car and was hit square in the face with a flying sheet of newspaper. It covered most of his face and nestled against his neck. He stopped. Just stopped still. His shoulders slumped and he covered his face with his hands. Then he yanked the paper off and ran to his car. He got in and drove off in a rush.

Poor soul, Rose thought. I hope he has good heat in that old car. Her head jerked as she caught sight of another figure huddled against the passenger door. A small person. A child. "Oh, I hope he's warm," Rose murmured to herself.

While she was watching the car and its occupants, the three bus passengers barreled through the front door, bringing the smell and sting of the cold, damp weather with them. The men stamped and brushed and shook water from their clothing. They shouted for coffee and hamburgers, then made off for the bathroom. The woman sat quietly on a stool across from Rose. She kept her coat on. She laid her purse on her lap, folded her hands on top of it, and bent her head forward. She looked very tired. It was hard to judge her age. She wasn't young, but maybe not as old as she looked. Fatigue aged a face, deepened wrinkles, sucked out color.

"Not too nice out there," Sarah said, bustling over to her. "I got hamburgers on the grill for the men. You want one too?"

"Just coffee."

"You'll be wanting more than that if you're gonna be on the bus long."

The woman sat silent.

"It's up to you." Sarah shrugged, went to flip the burgers, came back. "Where you going, anyway?"

The woman looked up. Her eyes were a deep blue. "I don't know."

May Snow

Sarah lifted her eyebrows. "Whatever. None of my business." She turned as the men barged back from the bathroom, stepping loud and smelling strong of soap.

"Some kid stuck gum up the spigots, splashed water all over when I turned it on," the larger one said. He laughed. "Did a damn good job of it."

The second man, dressed like the other in denim coat and flannel shirt with white thermal underwear showing at his throat and wrists, grinned. Rose thought his teeth could use a good brushing and leaned away as he sat beside her. He reached across her for a napkin, and she saw that his hands were scrubbed pink. She eased back toward him and watched him start to tear the napkin into strips.

"Nervous habit," he said to Rose. "Name's Ed. That there's Billy. Don't know the woman's name. She ain't too friendly."

The woman looked up at Rose, then at Ed. "June. If you have to know, my name is June."

"June what, then?" Ed challenged.

"Meadows. June Meadows," she said, her voice level, eyes still on his.

Billy let out a whoop and Ed's grin widened.

Rose spoke up before they could. "I like that. Your mother must have had a love for nature."

"You guys got fifteen minutes," Sarah said. She set their hamburgers on the counter.

Martin, Sarah's nephew, came in. "That wind's gonna take every leaf off the trees before it's through. Winter's close."

Sarah poured him coffee and gave him his usual tuna salad on rye. "You just better be looking out and driving careful."

"Don't you be worrying, Aunt Sarah," Martin reassured

her. He took a big bite out of his sandwich and nodded. "Hey there, I hear Johnny Coes died. Old Millie's gonna be having to find a new renter."

Millie Lewis owned the apartments a block down at the corner of Main Street and Monroe Avenue. It had been a busy hotel in the days when Rose was a young wife and Route 5 had been filled with cars buzzing by on their way to Erie and Cleveland or going east to Buffalo and Rochester. Rose remembered selling tomatoes and cukes and corn from a stand by the road. Mr. Dunning had let them put it near the feed store and hadn't charged them a cent. The Amish still came into town from their farms in the hills and sold baked goods there. Only there wasn't as much traffic now — hadn't been since the thruway started up in the sixties and grabbed up all the travelers. With a motel springing up at nearly every exit, not many stayed at Millie's Hotel after that, so she converted her rooms into small apartments.

"Hey, Rose," Martin said. "You oughtta go see Old Millie and grab up Johnny's efficiency. You don't need a whole house no more, not just for one person."

"Millie's not so old, Martin," Rose changed the subject. "Probably not so far from your own age as you'd like to think."

Martin chuckled. "I always did like you, Rose. No matter what anybody says." Still laughing, he wiped his mouth. "Hey there, people, get a move on. We gotta be shoving off."

"I'm gonna get me a magazine before we go," Billy said. He winked at Sarah. "You got any good ones?"

Sarah frowned at him. "What we got is right there." She pointed at the rack. "Right there out in the open."

"Looks pretty messy to me," Billy said, looking at the

paper books and magazines stacked every which way. "They used? Maybe cheaper?"

"They're not," said Sarah. She turned to Martin. "It's those Turner boys. Touched every one of those books. But I've only got two hands and I can't be everywhere at once."

"You got two registers," her nephew said. "Keep to the cooking and hire someone to mind the rest of the store."

"Yeah," agreed Sarah. "But who?"

Martin shrugged and lifted himself off the stool. He blew his aunt a kiss and winked at Rose. "We're off. Let's go, folks."

"I'm staying."

Everyone turned and looked at June.

"If you'll get my bags off the bus, please," she said to Martin. "And if Sarah here will hire me, I'll take Johnny Coes' place at Millie's, and I'll work here."

Rose watched.

Sarah bit her lower lip. She examined June and June stared back. "How do I know you're not a serial killer?" she finally asked.

"Anyone could be a killer," June said softly. "Under the right circumstances. I guess you'll have to take me on faith."

And being a religious woman, Sarah did just that.

5
November

It was a cold, snowy Saturday night and Rose's turn with Anson. When it was time, she walked into the backyard, which was already dark with early night. Anson had lit his outside light, and it sprinkled illumination on her path of snow. She smiled. Her heart was comfortably touched by his thoughtful gesture. She stepped gently on her way, feeling the magic of the clear night and the mystery of fairy dust flashing and dancing under her feet and all around. She walked slowly, a princess in a wonderland — enchanted, wrapped in wizardry.

Anson was waiting at the door to welcome her. She saw him standing with the light cloaking his body like shining armor. A prince. And suddenly she felt shy, lovely, young.

He took her hand and led her in, unbuttoned her coat, slid it from her with hands that didn't touch her body, and draped it carefully over a kitchen chair. Then he bent and held her boots while she pulled her feet from them. Looking down, she cursed them. They were large and flat and ugly. They embarrassed her and brought reality into her dreams.

"They're kind of big," she said, ruining the mood further and instantly hating herself for it. But it was foolish to think they could fit into Cinderella's slipper. And it was the kind of thing she felt she had to say. It was an apology for bringing something ugly to a beautiful moment.

Anson laughed. "They got you here, didn't they? What more do you want?"

"Slim and arched, I guess."

He laughed again. "Sit. I'll get you cocoa and we'll decide what to do tonight."

"I'll get it," she said.

"Sit," he repeated. "My house. My cocoa. My responsibility."

She sat. It felt strange to have a man bring her cocoa.

"Drink," he insisted. He sat down opposite her. "Now, this time you tell me what you want to do. You make the choice. It's been what I want every other time. Now I want to know what you want to do, where you want to go."

"I don't know," Rose said. She didn't want to make a wrong choice. Her happiness this night was simply that she was sharing it with Anson. The place and the circumstances didn't matter. If it was to his liking, then that was her pick.

"You must have some idea," said Anson.

"It's pretty snowy to drive to Northridge for a movie. Or dinner. I could cook."

"Bah," Anson said. "I'm tired of restaurants and I don't want you cooking. Tell you what. You sit. I'll cook...my style."

He grabbed a can of soup out of the cupboard and on his way to the refrigerator turned on the radio. Loud. Country.

"Good, huh?" he said.

Her response was quick and honest, a reaction to the blare. She shook her head fiercely to thrust the twanging notes out of her ears.

"I don't like country music." She was immediately sorry. "Not that it's wrong to like it. Lots of people do."

He laughed and pulled her up, wrapped her in his arms, and jiggled her around a little. "Now it's country. Maybe a little later, mushy stuff. But first we eat."

She wondered if he brushed her breast on purpose as he sat her in her chair. His arm was hard and strong against her, and she hoped Charity and Grace hadn't felt his arm pressed against them in the same way. As she sat and watched him cook, his touch stayed fresh in her thoughts and made her cheeks warm.

He made grilled cheese sandwiches to go with the soup. They ate at the kitchen table. He put the radio on the table and turned the volume low.

"If you listen to the words, it's not so bad," Rose said.

He cocked his head as if to hear her better.

"The music," Rose explained. "Country music. The words are sad, but a good sad. They stir up a satisfying melancholy, give you an excuse to let loose the tears. It roars from your gut."

Anson smiled. "I don't hear the words. Only the music, the strength of the mood that rolls out of it. I like it."

Rose smiled back. "Justified depression. Therapeutic weeping. Sweet rejection. Permission to poke your soul with grief."

Anson shook his head. "Eat your soup, woman."

Rose could sense that his comfort matched hers. "I don't

think I'll ever like it," she said. "But maybe I can elevate it a little on my list of favorites, just because tonight it makes me feel so good."

After dishes, sitting in soft living room chairs, the music changed to golden oldies. Anson took a crude, wooden dog from a closed drawer. It was a treasured gift from his grandson, carved before he had died. He had been a child born with so many problems, ill beyond saving, but loved beyond forgetting. Anson ran his finger over the smooth, dry wood. He held it for awhile, then tenderly placed it in Rose's hands.

"Every now and then I take it out and look at it and remember David and all he gave, all he packed into such a short, hurting life. I remember all he took from that life, found in it, and used. And I wonder why we didn't learn more from him."

While she listened, knowing this was a pivotal moment, a moving to a different place in their unfolding connection, Rose caressed the cherished figure with gentle fingers.

"We have to take what we can from life, Rose. Sometimes it's hard for me. Change. I like to keep my life comfortable. It's easier when you know what's going to happen tomorrow."

He paused, seeming to be searching for words. She wanted to help him, but she stayed silent, sensing his struggle and his need to join his feelings with his words, put them together and know their meaning.

"I want to thank you, Rose, for giving me a new piece of life. I think I was stopped. Not like David, who kept reaching. You made me reach. You made me step further. Forward."

Rose passed the precious carved dog back to him. She kept a hand on his.

"There's a line of life," she said. "It goes on and on. And

everything you've ever had or been or known is on that line. It's taking you to eternity. It needs to be full when you get there. You need to come with riches. Because when you're finally there, all the time there is belongs to you. It's yours to examine and mull over. It's yours to enjoy and to remember all the things you've done and all the people you've gathered. My grandmother gave me a little ceramic cat to keep forever. She said it was to remind me that she's on my line. And if I lose or break the cat, it doesn't matter. Because the cat's on my line, my grandmother's on my line. They're inside me. They're inside my soul. And my soul can't break. These are things my grandmother taught me. And David is on your line, Anson."

"And so are you, Rose."

"And so I am."

They sat for awhile in silence.

"My granddaughter, Louisa, might be coming to stay with me," Anson said. "Her mother's having problems with her. She wants too much from Louisa, more than she can give. She wants Louisa strong and organized like she is, but Louisa just kind of does nothing. She had a job, but she drifted away from it. I think she might need to be in a place where she's more than a shadow."

"Not like David," Rose said.

"David was never a shadow."

"That must be very hard for Louisa, if her mother doesn't see the beauty in a shadow."

"Enough," said Anson, standing and holding out his arms. "I promised you a dance."

They danced on the rug, and when he touched the softness

of her breast, she knew it was deliberate. He laughed when she pulled away.

"How come you're the only one who hasn't talked of bed to me?" he asked.

"The others did? Grace and Charity? Both of them?"

He didn't answer, but he held her tight as they danced. He kept his fingers off her breast.

Finally she said, "Did you sleep with them?"

He only grinned.

"They're on my line," he said.

And that could mean anything, thought Rose. She let it go and enjoyed the rest of the night.

❄   ❄   ❄

The rain had turned to snow. Its fall was gentler, comelier. Rose sat at the front picture window, watching the flakes cover the leaves on her lawn. Her knitting lay heavy in her lap. Occasionally she slipped yarn from one needle to the other, but the weight had grown burdensome, and finally, as she watched and thought, her fingers dropped the needles. She snuggled into the warm wool. Although she looked still and peaceful, her face without expression, within her stirred a troubled force, grinding and spitting doubts and questions, causing her to wonder about all that was happening.

She thought of Anson's hand on the cloth that covered her breast and then thought of Thomas's touch on the same place, only with no fabric to muffle the heat of his skin. And she wondered if Anson had wished no clothing were there on her bosom. She did. God forgive her, she did. Thomas forgive her, she did. She thought, *can you be unfaithful to a man who was dead?* She had promised "till death do us part." And Thomas had died and left her. Did the promise still hold because she was alive? Please, Thomas, help me.

She was frightened. She was feeling too much for Anson without knowing what he was feeling for her. It could be a lot. She sensed that sometimes. But maybe Charity and Grace thought that too. And maybe they were sleeping with him. He certainly seemed to be a happy man. Well, she couldn't sleep with a man who was doing all manner of intimate things with another. At least, she didn't think she could.

Sometimes it seemed that every man on earth, at one time or another, juggled his women. She thought *not Thomas,* hoped not Thomas. *But how could you know?* she wondered to herself. *Look at Forrest. Son-in-law Forrest. Traitor to her daughter. Did they, all those frolicking men, find joy in the pain they caused? Oh Thomas, why did you die? I don't want this turmoil. Where are the days when I looked to the sky and the biggest problem I threw at you was: Do I need new tires? Or, how do I fix the leaks in the faucet? Or, do you want roses or geraniums on your grave?*

Thomas, you should not have left me!

A car drove into the driveway next door. She dropped her thoughts while she dealt with the concrete news close at hand. Peering through the pane, she looked at the car. She'd seen it before. Pulling the same trailer. Outside Hunter's in the rain in October. The driver got out of the car and hurried up the steps to the empty house. A woman, not a man like Rose had thought. The woman moved with jerky steps. Either her legs were stiff and tired or she was irritated and im-

May Snow

patient. While she fumbled with keys and pushed the door open, a young boy, about nine, and an older one, a teenager, got out of the car. The young boy hopped and spun around shaking his body and screwing his face grotesquely. The teenager leaned lazily against the car, chewing his fingernails until the woman came back and pointed to the trailer. Rose could see her mouthing words and knew without hearing they were mean-edged and piercing. She figured the woman wanted to poke the stodgy boy into action and probably would if he didn't move sharp.

The younger boy, black hair messed and clothes askew, saw Rose in her window and stopped, his arms high and legs bent. Rose waved. He turned away quickly and ran to his mother. She gave him boxes to carry and herded him and the older boy — Manley Warner, Rose finally recognized him — back and forth to house, trailer, and car until the trailer and car were empty and everything was taken inside. She gave no slack. They all marched steadily. When they were done, she took money from her pocket and rubbing each bill, counted some out for Manley. He took it, gave the young boy a friendly punch in the arm, and ran off.

The boy shouted something — Rose couldn't hear the words — and started to run after the loping teenager. The woman grabbed the boy's arm, stooped down, and spoke words close to his face. The boy stepped back. His face showed fear. The woman pressed a hand to her mouth, shook her head, then pulled him to her and hugged him tight, rocking him to her.

Rose watched. It was a desperate hug. Another thing to wonder about.

6
December

Rose, Charity, and Grace were squeezed together on a park bench in the village park across the street from Hunter's. Rain and snow gone, the day was unseasonably warm — clothes-hanging-outside warm, sweater-wearing warm. The ladies had spent the morning at the nursing home reading Christmas poems to the patients and writing notes in holiday cards for them to send to friends and family. They were on their way to mail them. They hoped to get them out early enough so there would be plenty of response time for receivers who were too busy or had forgotten those frail bodies sentenced to beds by the infirmities of age.

Choosing to walk and enjoy the bootless, mitten-free weather, they had stopped to catch their breath, rest Rose's legs, and check out June. They had a good view of Hunter's big front window. They had picked a good time. Anson had just gone into the store.

May Snow

"Hey," said Grace, swinging her legs. "Bet he flirts with her."

Charity poked her with an elbow. "He will not. And quit kicking me."

Here they go, thought Rose. She sighed. Some days it was hard to tolerate their childish bickering. "Let me sit in the middle," Rose said, getting up.

"We're only joking," Grace said.

"I'm not," Rose said. "I don't like to be kicked."

"Then I'm not joking either."

"Move," Rose demanded. She shimmied her body between them. "Look, there. He's talking to her."

"She sure wears her pants tight," said Charity.

And looks good, thought Rose. *Firm butt, high up and hard.* She wiggled on her own sagging cushions. Thomas had liked to sink his hands into her soft, spongy flesh. Better than rubbing a steel rod, he said. Ah, but did Anson?

"Look at her put that hamburger down on the counter," Grace said, pointing. "Her boobs are bent right at him."

"Boobs don't bend," Charity corrected.

"Well, they're practically poking right through him."

"She doesn't have too much up there," Charity said, patting her own round mounds.

"I don't think men care too much what size they are," said Grace. She leaned forward on the bench. "Look, now he's looking at her rear."

"He is not," said Rose. "She gave him whatever he's drinking. She's done with him. She's walking back to the grill. He just happens to be looking her way."

"I don't think so," said Grace. "I think he likes her wiggle."

"What happens if he does like her?" asked Charity.

"He can like whoever he wants to," said Rose.

"I don't think so," said Grace.

"As long as he pays attention to our agreement," said Charity.

"He'd better," said Grace. She frowned. "I think I remember the agreement."

Charity reached across Rose's back and patted her sister's shoulder.

"It would seem that three women would be enough for him," stated Rose, bending forward to avoid Charity's crowding arm.

"She's younger," said Charity, moving her arm away from Rose.

"How young do you think?" asked Rose, relaxing and leaning back.

"Maybe sixty," said Charity.

"Pretty young," said Grace. "I don't think I like that. Uh, oh. She's coming back with the coffee pot. He's drinking coffee, girls. Bad. Too stimulating. I think they're gonna chat awhile."

The ladies sat and watched. Rose felt too warm with a sister on either side pressed against her. She wiggled and pushed against them a little, hoping to get a bit more space.

"Shh," said Grace.

"I didn't say anything," Rose grumbled. "Besides you can't hear what they're talking about anyway."

"Shh," Grace said again. "I'm concentrating."

"This is silly," Rose said. "You're both paranoid."

Charity pokedRose to be silent. Rose waited, squirming against them and not liking the feel of their bodies so close.

She'd elbow them a little bit from her, and then they'd slide right back.

"Have you talked with her at all yet?" Rose asked when no one made further comment.

"Not much," said Charity.

"Funny, isn't it? She comes on the bus, and a little boy moves in next door, all at the same time.

"What little boy?" asked Grace, her eyes still focused across the street.

"Look," said Charity. "Now they're laughing."

"Maybe she's looking for a man too," said Grace.

"Could be she needs him as much as we do," said Rose.

"What do you mean, *need* him? We don't *need* him." Charity turned to face Rose. "We did fine without him. He just adds a little extra something. And he gets back as good as he gives."

"Maybe she'd like a little extra too," said Rose, thinking that she did *need* Anson. Or Thomas. Or somebody. Life was too hard alone.

"Don't even think about including her in our time share," Charity said. "Not for a minute. He's stretched thin enough now."

"If Anson wants to see her too," said Rose, "I don't think we'd have much choice."

"There are always choices," said Grace.

"What?" said Rose. "Threaten to stop doing his dishes? Or cook his potatoes. He could care less."

"There are other things," Grace grinned.

"What other things?" asked Rose.

"We've got to decide what to do about this chickee-poo if she gets to be a problem," said Charity.

"We could kill her," said Grace.

"I'm serious. I don't want her barging into my time."

"We could kill *him*."

"Grace!"

"What other things?" Rose asked again. She wanted to know what Grace was hinting at, hoping it was not sexual in nature, but she suspected there was some kind of physical merging involved.

"Rosey, Rosey, you sure are nosey," Grace sang.

"June's too skinny," Charity said. "Men like more meat. Not a lot but in the right places. She does have height, though."

"Rose is little all over," Grace laughed. "Except her feet."

Without her bidding, Rose's feet went under the bench. Her lips pressed tight and her fists clenched. Grace knew where to hit.

"I think we'd better get to know her," said Charity. "Mystery has appeal and nobody knows much about her."

Rose didn't want to talk about June. She wanted to talk about Anson and the liberties they'd given him. *If they were letting him do things she wasn't, then she'd have to wrestle with her conscience and see if she could stay in this conjoined, moral-stretching relationship at all. Maybe she would even let him touch her in a place or two. Just a whisper of a touch, a finger kiss.*

What was she thinking? Somebody grab Thomas and hold him in his grave. He must be spinning. Poor soul. His wife, ever faithful, was turning traitor. But the sin of body pleasure from a source outside the spousal circle seemed to be losing power when

May Snow

marriage wasn't possible and the body still ached to couple. God forgive her. She wanted sex with Anson.

"Are you sleeping with Anson?" she blurted.

"Who?" asked Charity.

"Either of you. Both of you. Are you sleeping with Anson?"

"We agreed," said Charity. "Nobody has to say anything personal unless she wants to."

"Then want to," said Rose.

They looked at her and smiled.

❄   ❄   ❄

They were all altos. Charity and Rose were happy singing the lower, less glorified notes, but Rose knew that Grace, in her heart of hearts, wanted to be a soprano. But Marigold Pentagrast, partly trained as a music teacher, then married and mothered and relegated to church choir director, wouldn't let her. Grace's voice was not meant to soar high, and Marigold would brook no squeaks or straining vocal chords in her chorus. Grace stood at the end of the alto line next to the sopranos and sometimes let her voice slide into their notes with as much cunning as she could muster, but she was always caught, either by the indignant Christi Wells of magnificent trill standing next to her, or by her own traitorous, resounding bellows.

The ladies were sitting in the front pew, watching Marigold run through the solo pieces before the full choir practiced their hymns for the Christmas Chorale. The rest of the group singers had not yet arrived. Rose, Charity, and Grace were early. Grace, as usual, was wiggling in time to the

70

music. Rose sat quietly, eyes closed, feeling the flow of majestic sound filling and lifting her.

"Psst," Charity poked Rose. "We have to talk."

Rose frowned and shifted away from her.

Charity poked her again. "Come on, Rose."

The music left her and she opened her eyes. "What!" she exclaimed, too loud. Marigold dropped her hands and the singing stopped.

"Sorry," Rose said loudly. Marigold lifted her arms in a swift, stiff movement and the music resumed. Grace lifted her fingers to her nose and wiggled them at Marigold's back. Rose scowled at Grace.

Charity tugged at Rose's robe and pointed to the back of the church. Reluctantly Rose got up and followed her. Grace was close behind.

"We have to decide what we're going to do about a Christmas present for Anson," Charity said when they were settled in a back pew.

"Are you thinking we should get him something together?" Rose asked. She didn't want to do that at all.

"We could," said Charity.

"Not me," said Grace. "I want him to open a present from just me alone. Personal and private."

Rose was relieved. She was already too much entwined with them in the pursuit of Anson.

"Personal maybe," said Charity. "but not private. We need to know who gives what. So it's all equal."

"Or else Rose might get him something better than we do," said Grace.

Rose said nothing. Anson's gift had been on her mind.

May Snow

She wanted to see his excitement when he opened it, his joy. She wanted him to understand that with the gift came a piece of herself, an opening of her heart and soul and mind to him — trust and hope. She wanted him to recognize her as special and needed. But she didn't know what the gift could be, and she didn't want Grace and Charity intruding into the selection.

"This is not a time for joking, Grace," Charity said. "Christmas is coming and we have to decide what to do." She looked sternly at Grace, who wrinkled her nose, shrugged, and slumped in the pew. "I've thought long and hard on this. I was hoping we could give him one present together so that we all stayed equal, and I came up with the idea that we could get a picture taken of the three of us and frame it in something nice like brass or fine wood or something. But now you both want to get him a present by yourself, so that idea's down the drain."

"Get a picture of yourself," Grace grumbled. "He could put it in his bathroom. Over the toilet."

"That's it," said Rose. "The perfect gift. We'll each give him a picture of ourselves. Good thinking, Charity."

"I was the one that thought of separate pictures," said Grace.

When Rose, Grace, and Charity were young and growing up on adjoining farms, when Rose found time away from her chores to play with the sisters, when they met at recess and chatted over books, though Rose was closer in age to Grace, it was Charity who was her best friend. Of the three, it was Grace who was the accepted intruder, the added voice mimicking, whining, cajoling her way into their circle of acceptance. She was tolerated, loved from duty and parent

72

command, and loved, too, for the generous hugs she gave when she got her way, her little hands patting their backs with adoration.

When Grace was older she broke away from them. She worked at the five and dime store and met Stan, the peanut man, there. He was a traveling peanut salesman and he was all she thought about, all she talked about. When he asked her to go on the road with him, she was gone in a flash.

Rose and Charity knew she'd married Stan. She wrote and told them. She sent them postcards from all over the country. They couldn't write back. She didn't stay in one place long enough. Then one day, long after Thomas and Maxwell were dead, she was back — a widow too. She'd had no children. She had no money. Charity opened her house and Grace went in. They were a threesome again. There were times when Rose would like to choke the thoughtless, childish words that spilled out of Grace's mouth, but Grace still hugged with patting hands that swelled a heart, and Rose could not hurt the loving child that still was so much a part of her friend.

"You did think of it, Grace, and it was a good idea," said Rose. "And that's what we'll do. Anson will have a picture of each of us."

"We'll go to Northridge together," decided Charity. "To the department store. Everybody wear high necks and pearls. Not too much makeup. Hair like always."

They agreed. It was settled. They were pleased with each other, satisfied. Rose relaxed, sat back, closed her eyes, and fixed her ears on the solo singers praising God with splendid voice.

May Snow

Charity poked her. "I talked to June," she whispered. "She's not so bad."

❄   ❄   ❄

Every year Rose made Christmas cutouts from Great-aunt Lizzie's hand-me down secret family recipe. The cookies were rich with sugar and butter and eggs and sour cream and had just a touch of almond extract to give them a special holiday flavor. Rose sang and sampled as she mixed, rolled, and pressed the reindeer, star, Santa, bell, and angel cutters into the soft, yellow dough. She slid trays in and out of the oven, spread the cookies on racks to cool, then frosted and sugared them in bright, cheerful colors.

It was near the end of daylight when she was done. Aches ran all over her body but she felt good. Christmas baking did that to her. It lifted her, cleared her head for fun and happy thoughts, made her feel young and needing to move.

She peeked out the window at the little boy's house. There were tracks in the yard and strips of green in the snow. He'd made a snowman, lopsided and with only two balls of snow. He had a hat where there should have been a head. Rose smiled. She remembered Margaret and her friends rolling balls in the snow; piling them into round, fat men; hiding behind them; throwing soft, smaller balls at each other; and coming in wet, laughing, and hungry. She'd fed them soup and warm bread and cookies. She'd never seen the little boy next door play with anyone, and his mother was often gone when he came home from school. She wondered if he heated his own soup. Or maybe his mother left him cold sandwiches.

"All little boys need cookies," she said out loud, looking at the festive cutouts spread on her counter and table, icing drying. "And I have cookies galore." She took a plate and piled it high. "It's time to meet the boy next door and get me a name to call him."

She wrapped herself in wool and took the cookies over. On her way, she blew a kiss to the headless snowman.

The boy's mother answered the door. Rose had expected her to be gone, but she wasn't sure which days she was there and which days she wasn't, and she was glad for the chance to talk with her.

"I'm Rose. I live next door. I made some Christmas cookies, and I thought you might like some." Holding out the plate, she smiled, waiting.

The woman hesitated. "Thank you." She didn't take the cookies and she didn't ask Rose in.

"They're for you," Rose said. She thrust the plate closer to the still woman. "It's Christmas, we're neighbors, and they're not poisoned."

"We don't neighbor much," the woman said. She shivered and wrapped her arms around her body. She stood her ground.

The young, dark-haired boy came up behind his mother. He stood there, not speaking, looked at Rose and the cookies, and put his hand on his mother's arm.

"Please take them," Rose said. "It's okay if you don't want to be friends. I'd just like the boy to have the cookies. Please."

"All right. Thank you." Reluctantly, the woman took the plate. She looked tired. "I'll wash the plate and bring it back to you."

May Snow

"Oh, don't bother washing it. I've got lots of time. Maybe the boy could bring it over."

"Wait. Come in. I'll just put them in another dish and you can take the plate now."

Rose stepped into the living room. It was pretty bare, kind of messy with toys and papers strewn about.

"Wait here. Nicholas, you come with me."

Ah, a name. Rose watched Nicholas follow his mother into the kitchen. He turned his head and looked at her while he was walking. She lifted her eyebrows, and he gave her a half smile.

She stood by the door until they came back. A puddle was growing under her feet. She didn't know what to do about it.

"Oh dear," the woman said, following the direction of Rose's eyes with her own. "I should put a rug there. But we don't use that door much." She handed the plate to Rose. It was washed. "My name is Amy. Amy Tanner."

"I guess you've found work," Rose said. "I mean, I see you're gone sometimes. At night. I'm not watching or anything. I just see you go. Sometimes. Afternoons. Late. It could be something else. Not work, I mean. I don't really know. I see you come home. Sometimes. I don't always sleep too well, and I hear your car. The light sometimes shines in my house." She faltered. "It's none of my business, is it?"

"No," Amy said. She sighed and rubbed her cheek. "Anyway, thanks again for the cookies." She moved toward the door.

"I thought maybe I could keep an eye on Nicholas for you. In case he needs something ... or something."

"I waitress. Nicholas knows the number."

December

"He's so little. He might like company sometimes … or something."

"He's nine. And sharp. He knows what the world's about. And he's careful. He knows my number. If he needs *something*, he'll call."

That was the end of the conversation. Rose left. On her way home, she punched the snowman.

❊   ❊   ❊

Three old ladies bearing gifts in shopping bags trod gingerly up Anson's snow-dusted steps.

"Watch those floorboards," Charity said. "They're pretty slick. Grace, if you slip, you could break a leg."

At the top of the stairs, Rose, reluctant to step forward without support, held fast to the rail. The porch showed broom marks, but new snow, wet and heavy, blew across the planks, dropping flakes that stuck and spread. Snow on painted wood spelled trouble. Rose watched with envy as Grace, sure-footed and fearless, pranced across the treacherous path. Charity followed behind, cautiously planting her feet in Grace's footprints, tote bags stuffed in the circle of one arm while the other stretched to catch and save her sister from injury should she fall.

Pointless, thought Rose. *If Grace goes down, she'll take you with her.* Pressing her lips together, Rose grunted and took her hand off the rail. Go for it, girl. Remember, the pioneers had whole mountains to cross. She slid her way along the porch floor, both feet flat against the wood, neither foot lifting, legs stiff, muscles tight. *Thank God their backs are to me,*

77

she thought, feeling foolish. *Please keep upright, legs. I'll owe you big time. A nice warm soak.*

Just as Rose made it to Charity and Grace, where they huddled together at the front door, Grace's finger pointing, ready to jab the bell, the door opened. Anson stood there holding a bucket of salt.

"Right, Anson," Charity said, "harness the horse after the plowing's done."

As the sisters, muttering angrily, stormed past him, Anson took Rose firmly by the arm and guided her across the threshold. She lifted a foot and fell against him. Her legs quivered and jellied. She feared they wouldn't hold her, and she grabbed his shirt with her free hand. "Damn legs. Damn creaky old legs!"

"Relax," he whispered, standing close. "You're okay. I'm here."

She nodded, grateful.

"Rosie," Grace called from the kitchen. "Come help us."

"I have to help them," Rose said, moving away, even though she wanted to stay close to him. He was big and he was strong and she was safe. "They're calling me to help."

He nodded and let her go. He motioned to the door. "I'll sprinkle the salt."

She went into the kitchen to help Charity and Grace unpack the bags and spread out the cookies and crackers and cheeses and little sandwiches. The scent of Anson's freshly laundered flannel was still in her nose. The softness of the cloth lingered on her cheek. She wanted to go back and lean her head against his shirt again, rest safe and close to him. Instead she did what they expected. She set her bags down and dropped her coat on a chair.

December

"Put the presents over there," Charity said, pointing to an old, glass-fronted cupboard. Two fat Santa candles sat on the counter that separated the top shelves from the bottom drawers. The head of one jolly elf was melted. Red wax streaked his curly white beard, and one eye was gone. Both candles were grimy, gritty with dust. Charity frowned and shook her head. "He should throw those ugly things out."

"I told him to get a tree," Grace said, putting Anson's gift, wrapped in glossy red paper with dancing penguins, on top of Charity's green and red striped package. "I don't think he likes Christmas too much. There are absolutely no other decorations in this house. I tried. He said no. What a scrooge. We should sparkle it up for him. Whether he wants it or not."

"He loves Christmas," Rose said, adding her gift. It was wrapped in shiny silver stars glimmering on deep blue foil. She traced the melted edge of the burned Santa — old Santa candle, left over from child-filled family Christmases, when families were whole and each member knew the other as well as he knew himself. If Anson could bring that time back in his heart, in his mind, by putting out an old, dirty treasure, his beloved Santa candles, that had been lit many years ago by wondrous little fingers, to light a way for Father Christmas, wandering in the night, then bless his heart and give him joy. Oh yes, Anson loved Christmas.

"I have an extra gift. Well, actually two," Grace said, putting more packages on the shelf. She turned quickly and lifted her hands, palms out. "Now, don't be yelling, Charity. They're from all of us. For Gossip and Rumor. A squeaky clown for Gossip and a green rubber mouse for Rumor. So what do you think? Good idea or not?"

79

May Snow

"When did you buy those?" Charity asked.

Grace frowned, looked down at the floor, then up at Charity. She shook her head.

She doesn't remember, Rose thought, then let it go. She felt a draft — a quick, cold rush of air that scattered crisp, biting kisses over her skin, through her clothing, up and down her back, circling, mingling, merging with a warmth — and then it was gone. Before Anson stepped into the kitchen, before she heard his voice, she knew he was coming. She turned her face to the doorway, anticipating, ready to smile her greeting. And then he was there, slapping his arms to get the blood moving, stepping briskly in place, his nose red and dripping. His mouth lifted in a broad grin. Her heart ached with yearning. She made ready to step in his direction.

"Great idea," Anson said before Rose moved. He swung his arm around Grace's shoulder and danced her around the kitchen, stopping at the table loaded with goodies. He bowed and presented her with a sweet, round cookie mounded with raspberry jam. "For you, your highness," and he popped it into her mouth. She chewed and curtsied and shoved three tiny sandwiches into his mouth.

"Like a wedding," Grace said and laughed.

Rose felt a hard ball drop from her throat to her stomach. Her bladder quivered and she stood very still, hands clenched together, not feeling the pain throbbing the joints in her fingers. She begged her face to stay empty, but when she could finally pull her eyes away from the tittering couple, they landed on Charity, and Charity's eyes were planted firmly on hers. Rose felt those eyes could see inside her head and know her thoughts, and Rose was ashamed.

December

A gloom, heavy and sedating, spread darkness through her, stayed with her, kept her an outsider to the party that spiraled around her. She tried to break through. She could not comprehend the magnitude of her jealousy, the tremendous sense of betrayal. She knew Anson wasn't hers. He was a shared commodity. It had been an agreeable pact. An equal part of Anson for each. As good as signed in blood.

As Rose stood watching Anson and Grace, Charity handed her a plate. "Hurts, doesn't it?" she said, lifting an eyebrow and shrugging. "Well, pout or play. Your choice."

Rose pressed her lips together and drew air deep through her nose. Anger rushed through envy, breaking it apart, clearing her head. She locked her eyes on Charity and willed her to feel her fury.

"Grow up, Rosie," Charity said. "It doesn't always go your way. Not all men are Thomas." She tugged at Rose's sleeve to emphasize her words. "Don't ruin it. Grace is having a good time. Let her. She needs it. More than you can begin to know."

Rose pulled her arm away. "You think I'm mad at Grace?"

"You're sure mad at somebody," Charity said.

"You," Rose said. "I'm mad at you."

"Why?" Charity looked puzzled.

"You like this," Rose said. "You like me getting put down a peg. It gives you a great big thrill to see Anson ignore me."

"Well, maybe it does a little," Charity said. "Hey, we've tasted it. Now it's your turn. Anyway, lighten up. It's a party. If you're gonna ruin it, tell Anson you've got a headache and go home." She gripped Rose's arm hard. "I love you, Rose, but we've all got a share in this, all of us. And maybe you'd better remember that. This isn't a game. This is life. I'm not about

81

to give up a piece of it just because you're jealous. And you can be damn sure Grace isn't either." She dropped Rose's arm. "You think on it."

Rose sighed. The anger was gone as quick as it came. Guilt, shame, sadness rushed in to fill the new emptiness. She was so tired. This thing with Anson was too much. How could three women share one man harmoniously? Obviously they couldn't. She swore that in her next life she was going to marry a man many, many years younger than she. Let her die first. Then let the old ladies fight over her leavings, and she would watch from above, basking in the wisdom of having lived the whole of her adult life partnered and safe with her mate at her side. She needed to tell Charity she was sorry. She opened her mouth.

"No, don't," Charity said, lifting her hand, stepping away. "I'm going over to Anson and Grace. And I'm going to have a good time. You put yourself together, and then you come over too, and we'll open gifts and sing songs and talk light. But you straighten up first. Then you come over. Until then, I don't want to hear a word from you." Charity pulled herself tall and strutted off.

Chastened and confused by the strength of the passions let loose from within her, let loose on their own without her command, Rose stood quiet a moment to gather the pieces of character that made her Rose. Calm Rose. Reasonable Rose. Fair and just Rose. When she was enough herself, she joined the party.

Anson opened his gifts. He gave them theirs. Live, little kittens. One for each of them. He laughed when Charity wrinkled her nose and bequeathed hers to Rose. Charity tried to convince her sister to do likewise. Grace would not.

Rose was glad to have two. She buried her face in their soft fur, felt their tiny throbbing purrs, and while the others laughed and sang and spoke Christmas joy, a part of her relived Grace and Anson dancing. She wondered how she could have felt such anger over a trivial thing, a simple sharing of holiday happiness. But she could not totally lose herself in the merriment around her. She saw all that happened but could not feel it. She functioned properly, smiled, spoke the right words, but her head was ever thinking, wanting to know the secret of Anson's power. She wondered if the want of his essence, the need for his male presence could cause Charity and Grace, or her, to risk it all, even their friendship. She didn't know. She was glad when the party ended and she could finally go home.

※　※　※

Later she sat in her rocker by the front window and watched the stars shine proud in the night sky. The kittens slept in her lap. She moved back and forth slowly, gently stroking their silky fur. She felt their hearts beat steadily, and it soothed her. She thought God might be sitting on one of those stars looking back at her, and that soothed her too. She felt done in, yet full of tears too tired to fall.

When a knocking fell on her back door, she carefully set the kittens in their box and stood by them a moment until their stirrings stopped and they were still, wrapped in the comfort of soft, woolen rags. The knocking repeated. Harder. She reached and lightly touched a puffing belly. She sighed and dropped a tear. She wiped it and went to the door.

May Snow

Anson was there with snow in his hair and red in his cheeks. She couldn't smile. She was empty, and he was the one who had drained her.

"Merry Christmas," he said with a quiet voice.

She held the door open and he came in.

"The storm's pretty much stopped," he said, brushing moisture from his head. "But I bumped a branch and it poured down snow. Shoulda carried a flashlight."

"Shoulda worn a hat," Rose said and wondered if he had come to give her a weather report. She didn't need it. She had seen the stars. She knew it had cleared. She was too tired to ask why he'd come.

"Merry Christmas," he whispered.

"Merry Christmas," Rose said. She should ask him to sit. She should make him cocoa. But she stood, not moving.

He touched her cheek, just barely. "Smile, dear Rose," he said.

I can't, she thought. And the tears were almost too heavy to keep inside her eyes.

He pulled a package from his pocket, put it in her hand, and wrapped her fingers around it.

She looked at it, looked at him. She had no words to say.

"Open it," he said.

So she did. And when she saw the little carved dog, the tears flowed free.

"I wanted you to have it." He put his arms around her and she leaned into him. He held her for a long time. And when she began to feel again, it came to her what it was she really wanted him to have from her. She pulled away and went to get the perfect gift, the piece of her to match the piece of him that he had just given her.

December

She gave him the little, yellow, ceramic cat her grandmother had given her. And she smiled.

Before he left he kissed her. It was soft and sweet, warm against her lips. He touched her breast and she did not pull away.

She gave him a flashlight to guide his way home.

When he was gone, she sat in her rocker and thought of Thomas as he lay dying and her promise to remain faithful until they were together again. And she wondered if he was sitting on a star next to God, watching her and hurting. And she was sad. Anson had kissed her. It was more than a thought and a dream. It was real. Anson had touched her. And she had welcomed it.

"I'm so sorry, Thomas. I do still love you. But you're not here. Merry Christmas, dear heart. Please love me still."

7
January

Louisa Talber, Anson's granddaughter, moved into his house on New Year's Day. Karen, her mother, his daughter, came with her to orchestrate the transition. Karen had been an obstinate, goal-oriented, single-pathed, loud child, and now she was a forceful, opinionated, cause-driven, loud adult. She trampled his thoughts and ignored his words, so Anson asked Rose to be there for support. It wasn't a scheduled day, but Rose agreed to come. She crossed her fingers that Charity and Grace would not know. Anson and Rose were standing together when Karen barged through the door, dropped her bundles, and motioned Louisa, who was behind her dragging suitcases, to hurry.

"I know this is your house," she said to Anson, hugging him, wiggling her fingers at Rose. "But it's cold out there and you're old. No reason to make you come to the door. So I didn't knock." She stood back and frowned at him. "But you came to the door anyway, didn't you? Here I am trying to

May Snow

save you a step, for what, I don't know. You do what you want to do anyway." She turned to Louisa. "Here now, take this stuff up to your room. Your grandfather doesn't need all this clutter." She turned back to Anson. "Tell her which room, Dad."

Rose, noting Anson's tight-pressed lips and the little throb that had started at the top of his left jaw, took Louisa by the arm and whispered the location of her room. The child, thirty-eight years old, merely looked at her and, when Rose let her loose, picked up some bundles and trudged up the stairs. Rose sighed. She wondered if somewhere in that retreating body there was an inner spark just not bright enough to shine through her skin, laying dormant and waiting for a match to ignite it. Maybe she'd find it here at Anson's.

Rose went back to the living room. Karen was pacing, touching knick-knacks, rubbing fabrics, peering at pictures, fluffing pillows. Anson stood quiet, visibly uncomfortable. Rose pressed a hand against her lips. It would not do for Anson to see her smile now. She knew Karen well. Karen had been Margaret's best friend growing up. She had been an honest and true friend. Not always right and not always thoughtful, but there were no surprises. She said what she meant. She wasn't malicious. She knew no other way to be. Rose had learned to enjoy her.

Karen stopped at the mantle where Charity, Grace, and Rose's photographs sat. "What's this?" she said, pointing at the pictures.

Rose waited, amused. She knew Anson was hoping she would step in and save him. She didn't. She wanted to know how he'd explain three old ladies sharing the mantle with Bernice.

88

January

When Anson said nothing, Karen turned each of the pictures around so only the larger picture of her mother faced forward. She wiped her hands against each other and glared at Anson. After a bit, she strutted to the couch and sat down.

"We need to talk about Louisa," she said.

Anson and Rose sat too. In chairs far apart.

"It's time she got a life. I've done everything I can think of. Got her a job, pushed her into activities, introduced her to people. And nothing happens. It's like God plunked her down and she can't move. She's got a pretty face. Good features — regular, well sized, well placed. But nobody notices. It's like she's just not there."

"She'd make a good spy," Anson said.

Karen gave him a withering look and Rose covered her mouth quickly.

"If she'd just lift her lips," Karen said. "She's got a gorgeous smile. She just isn't perky. I've done all I can. You have to help her now, Dad. She's your flesh and blood too."

Anson looked at Rose. She shrugged.

"Well anyway, I'm going. She's yours. Do something with her." Karen got her coat. She slipped it on efficiently. On her way to the door, she stopped at the bottom of the stairs. "Louisa, get down here and clean up this mess. Now! Before your grandfather trips over your stuff." She turned abruptly and looked at Anson. "And remember, now that Mom's gone, what's left when you're gone belongs to your children."

She opened the door and left.

May Snow

❄   ❄   ❄

Worried that the storm would down the phone lines, Rose called Margaret early to cancel lunch.

The winds were high and blowing cold. Heavy snow slashed against the house, slammed into the windows, swept under the doorway, and wet her rug. She thought if she put her ear to the window glass she would hear the roar of Lake Erie's waves as they rose and lashed and met the rushing wind. She hoped Nicholas was warm in the house next door and enjoying a day off school — the single benefit she could think of from the raging monster assaulting her town.

"Are you all right?" Margaret asked. "Do you need anything?"

"I'm fine," Rose said. "Stay home and wait it out." She eased herself back in her rocker. "How are you doing, dear?"

"I'm fine," Margaret said.

Rose gave her time to say more. If that was what she needed. Wanted. She shivered, pulling her afghan closer.

"Mother," Margaret said finally. "Are you dating?"

It was not what Rose had expected. She thought Margaret would speak of Forrest. "Why would you ask that?"

"My neighbor Janice saw you with Anson in Hunter's. She saw him grab your hand. And keep it. Are you seeing him? Like in the dating sense?"

"Not exactly," Rose said.

"What would Dad think?"

"Your father's dead," Rose said. She pressed the receiver to her ear. There was static on the line and the snow beating against the windows was so loud. *Oh, Thomas, what do you think?*

"But you two never so much as peeked at anyone else," Margaret said.

"You're always telling me to let Dad go," Rose said.

"I mean for you to do your own thinking," Margaret said. "Not to be jumping into an old man's bed."

"With these ankles, I don't think I'll be jumping, " Rose said, smiling. She reached for a kitten and put it in her lap.

"You know what I mean."

Rose said nothing. She wasn't sure she wanted Margaret giving her advice.

"It's just there's so much sex going on all over," Margaret said. Rose could picture Margaret running her fingers through her hair. "Janice's husband told me I've got good legs."

"You do," Rose said, stroking the kitten and rocking gently.

"He's got no right to tell me that. He's got a wife. He should be looking at her legs." Margaret paused. Rose heard her sigh. "I don't know. I guess it's okay, you dating Anson. You're right. Dad's dead. You can't really be unfaithful. I guess. Mom, do you think Dad ever thought about, you know, doing it with other women?"

"How could I know his thoughts?" Rose said. She stopped rocking. The kitten squirmed and jumped down.

"He knew yours," Margaret said.

"Maybe not."

"Oh, Mom, you were always so transparent. Your thoughts were his. Whatever he wanted, you were."

Rose put a hand to the base of her throat, kneading the

loose skin there. "If you think about it," she said, "you'll see what a cruel remark that was."

"I'm sorry," Margaret said. Rose heard the tremble in her voice. "I didn't say it to hurt you."

Rose knew she hadn't. Her daughter was a kind, loving woman with nowhere to park her own grief.

"It's storming so badly here," Margaret said.

Rose nodded into the phone and felt tears rising. A storm was raging in her daughter's heart. "Storms pass," she said softly.

"You know," Margaret said, the quiver still there, "all those years Maxwell cheated on Charity and everybody knew it. Why didn't she leave him?"

"I don't know," Rose said. "Maybe she should have, but a woman just didn't leave a man in those days. Where would she go?"

"What if Maxwell had left her?"

"She wouldn't have let him," Rose said. The words fell without thought. "She would have killed him first."

"That's crazy, Mother."

No, Rose thought. *It wasn't crazy at all.*

8
February

It's true what they say, Rose thought, sweeping the snow off her porch. She waved at Nicholas, who was watching from inside his house. He ducked out of sight. *The older I get, the faster time goes.*

January had passed quickly and February was doing the same. Louisa was settled firmly in Anson's house. She was like an ornament — sitting silent, never changing, always there. Sometimes Rose had an urge to poke her, sink her finger deep into Louisa's skin, make her hurt, feel, respond. She told Charity she was afraid that one day that urge would be too strong and she would reach and push and twist without thinking. Charity told her to put a lid on it. Anson loved that girl. No way would he keep the contract if Rose messed up with Louisa.

Rose saw Charity and Grace at church and choir practice, and, sometimes, the nursing home. A couple times they met and bowled. They sat together at bingo and village meetings,

May Snow

bumped into each other at the convenient mart and Hunter's, but there had been no lunches and only sporadic meetings to go over schedules and report on Anson visits. Rose suspected the sisters thought she might be seeing him more often than agreed upon. She was. She couldn't help it. He came to her house. She went to his. The need to see him was overwhelming. It couldn't hurt the sisters. They didn't need to know. She tried not to think she was cheating.

Late in February, Charity called Rose and invited her to dinner. Days were short and dark came early. Rose didn't like to drive after the sun went down, so she declined. Charity hesitated before she offered a change to lunch. Detecting pique in Charity's tone, Rose wasn't sure the invitation promised pleasure. She accepted anyway.

❄   ❄   ❄

"We need to do some revamping," Charity said, leading Rose to the dining room. There was a platter of sandwiches in the center of the dining room table, shredded carrots shoved in pita pockets that were lightly spread with no fat cream cheese, and a plate of celery and pepper strips. No dip.

"Is that it?" Grace said behind them, looking at the food.

Charity glared at Grace, and Rose wondered if dinner would have been better. Maybe worth the risk of a ride in the dark. But when Charity turned her formidable gaze on her, she quickly said, "Looks good to me," and sat down.

Grace walked out. While she was gone, there was no talking. Charity took a bite of her sandwich. Rose took a bite of hers. They chewed.

Grace came back with a loaf of white bread, a jar of peanut butter, and a dish of homemade strawberry jam.

"Want some?" she asked Rose.

Rose shook her head, lifted her sandwich. "This is good." She wanted peanut butter.

Grace laughed.

"You won't be laughing when you're laying on a stretcher with your arteries all clogged up," Charity said. She chomped her teeth on a pepper stick.

"Honey, you and your dead lungs will be laying right there beside me." Grace picked up a celery stick, held it like a cigarette, and puffed feigned smoke at Charity. She picked up another, held it out to Rose. "Have a coffin stick, Honey?"

Rose bit her lip, hesitated, looked at frowning Charity, but couldn't resist. "Why thank you, don't mind if I do." She took it between her fingers, lifted it to her lips, and turned to Charity. "Got a light, Baby?"

Chin jutting out, eyes squinting, Charity stared meanly at Rose. Then the left corner of her mouth quivered, one shoulder lifted, and she placed a hand on her waist. "Just lean this way, little tootsie, and touch your ciggie to mine." She put a pepper strip in her mouth and bent toward Rose until their veggies touched.

"Look," Grace said. "Three on a match." She had three celery sticks stuck in her mouth. They jiggled as she spoke.

"Enough," Charity said, laughing.

Grace pulled a pita apart, patted the carrots into the cheese, and rolled it tightly. Lifting it high, she toasted Charity. "Behold a new and flavorful, nutritious cigarette."

"No more," Charity said. "We need to talk."

May Snow

Levity was gone. Finger against her lip, Rose motioned Grace to be silent. Charity was going to have her say, regardless, and Rose wanted to hear it, be done with it, and go home.

Grace bent down and picked up her Christmas kitten. She held it in one arm, stroking it and tickling its nose. She leaned close to it and blew softly in its face. Rose watched.

Charity crossed her legs and lit a cigarette. "Are we ready?" she asked.

"Say it," Rose said. "Whatever is bugging you, say it."

"Nothing is bugging me, Rose," Charity said. "Should something be bugging me, Rose?"

Like am I seeing Anson when I shouldn't be? Rose thought. She shrugged. *Let her think what she wants. And, yes, I am. And it's his choice. What should I do? Say no? I don't think so.*

Charity picked a piece of tobacco off her tongue and examined it. "I think we should include June Meadows in our little club," she said.

Rose's head jerked up. "No," she said. "Why would you even think such a thing?"

"That's what we're all about," Charity said. "Too many women. Not enough men. June's a woman — a lonely, hurting woman. We can help her."

"Seems like you know her pretty well," Rose said.

Charity nodded. "That's right. We do."

"You and Grace," Rose said.

Grace scooped up peanut butter and stuck it in the kitten's mouth.

"Don't do that," Rose said. "It will stick in her mouth."

Rose stood, tore a piece of her napkin, and reached to wipe out the gummy food.

The cat snarled and, claws extended, lunged at her. As she pounced, her sharp-edged paws scraped Grace's arm. Grace screeched, snatched the cat with both hands, and hurled her against the wall. The kitten thumped and yelped and bolted.

"What are you doing?" Rose asked. "Are you crazy?"

"Leave me alone." Grace grabbed the table and pushed her chair. It crashed to the floor. She stumbled against it.

Rose reached to grab her. Charity pulled Rose back.

"Let her go," Charity said softly.

"Look at my arm," Grace said. "It's bleeding." She looked at Rose, holding her arm out to her. "It's bleeding." Tears fell down her cheeks.

Charity held onto Rose. "Let her be." She spoke firmly to Grace. "Go clean your arm. Go on now. Go in the kitchen and clean it."

Grace wiped her cheek, turned quickly, and left.

When Grace was gone, Charity let Rose go.

"She really doesn't like cats, you know," Charity said.

Rose shook her head. "I didn't know that."

"Yes, you do," Charity said. "Think back. Remember when Daddy gave you and me each one of Mama Cat's kittens? But he didn't let Grace have one. So she got mad and swung my kitten around and around by his tail until she whipped him dead."

The memory flashed, old and ugly, and Rose cringed.

"Dad laid the belt hard on her legs for that," Charity said. "The only time I saw him beat her. She deserved it."

"She was little," Rose said.

May Snow

"Maybe," Charity said, "but I never did see her really like an animal." She dragged deep on her cigarette. "Take the kitten with you. Grace won't care anymore."

"Who are you protecting?" Rose asked. "Grace or the cat?"

"I would do anything to keep hurt away from Grace," Charity said. "Believe that."

She's warning me, Rose thought, *but I don't know why. Thomas, I think your life must be pretty easy up there.*

Charity ground her cigarette out. She swept a pattern in the ashes with the butt. "Grace and I have been seeing a lot of June lately," she said. "She's really a very nice lady."

Now we're going to speak of topics originally intended, Rose thought. *And she's going to do her best to convince me.*

"So are a lot of other old ladies in Canadaway," Rose said, gently rubbing the knots in her fingers.

"She's lonely," Charity said.

"So were we," Rose said.

"Exactly."

"Why would you want another person seeing Anson?" Rose asked. "There are already three of us taking his time. Plus Louisa."

"I don't mind sharing," Charity said. "We went into this to put a man in one little corner of our lives. He's supposed to add a joy that we can't give each other. I don't need squatter's rights. This is not a single-minded, youthful love we have with Anson. It's a tiny piece of awesome passion to use selfishly, for our own purposes. It's not my whole life. It shouldn't be yours. It's just an extra layer on top of all the wonderful bits of life we put together. Why shouldn't we share that with another woman? Especially when she so desperately needs the feel of a good and gentle man in her life?"

"I can't," Rose said. "There's so little time now. How can I give up any of it?"

"You don't have to," Charity said. "We simply add another time slot."

"And what task do we give her?" Rose asked.

"You know we're beyond that. If there's cooking and cleaning now, it's choice. We've each reached a place with Anson that suits us. June can't touch that. She adds a dimension. She doesn't take. She gives. Why can't you, you of all people, understand that? You're loving and generous, my very best friend, the first to offer kindness to anyone wanting. How is it you can't show compassion for June?"

There's more, thought Rose. *Charity may be a good lady, but she doesn't give away her riches unless their loss will be replaced with bigger bounty.*

"If we each keep to one visit a week," Charity said, "if we offer a variety of experiences, new and interesting experiences, if we keep the covenant, Anson will be happy and we'll all be happy. I'll be happy. Won't you?"

She thinks I'm seeing more of him than I should, Rose thought. *And I am. But I can't tell her. I won't tell her. I am violating the agreement. I'm cheating and I'm breaking my word. And it's wrong. But I can't stop. I won't stop. I don't want to stop. Oh God, Thomas, I'm sorry.*

Rose put her hand on Charity's arm. "I would never want to hurt you," she said.

"How would you be hurting me?" Charity asked softly.

Rose sighed and laid her hand back in her lap. "June is so

May Snow

firm and pretty. She could find another man. I know there aren't many, but she doesn't sag. Men look at her. I don't want to share Anson with her."

"She has no friends," Charity said.

"She could if she wanted," Rose countered.

"We've seen Anson talk with her," Charity said. "She sparks his interest. Maybe it would be prudent for us to control that interest."

She's worried about June, Rose thought. *Maybe she thinks if we toss a young, firm, flexible sacrifice into Anson's web, it will set his juices flowing and we'll all reap frisky rewards. I don't know. I wish we had never started this.*

"I think we have to talk to Anson," Charity said. "It's what we want."

"I don't," Rose said.

"I do. Grace does. We out vote you."

❆   ❆   ❆

The next day Anson took Rose for a ride along Lake Erie. Beyond the edge of frozen waves, which were piled and spread like a miniature mountain range and beyond the bordering shelf of ice, radiant with the meshing of sun and moisture, the water was clear and blue. The coastline of Canada stood sharp on the other side.

Anson stopped at Dew Point, an overlook where young lovers park at dark and explore each other's hearts and bodies while the waters crash and thunder, unnoticed, beneath them. He faced the car toward the lake.

"You've been so quiet," Anson said. "Spit out what you're

thinking." He tapped his fingers on the steering wheel. "I can tell by the look on your face that your head is busy cranking out all kinds of unspoken thoughts."

Rose reached and patted his hand. "It's not you," she said, "if that's what you're thinking." He took her hand in both of his, stroking it with one finger. "At least, it's nothing that you've done."

"What then?" he asked.

Rose looked out at the lake, watched the rhythmic throb of waves as they steadily rolled to the ice shore and broke, lapped at the brittle edge, tasting the frozen brim, and then slipped away to regroup.

"If I watch long enough," Rose said, leaning forward, eyes straining through the windshield, "I become part of all that tremendous power. I am the lake, swelling, lifting, gushing sparkling beads to the sky, thrashing down onto the great gyrating mother body, and splitting into a million laughing bubbles. And nothing else matters, nothing. I'm at peace."

"Do you need that now?" Anson asked.

"I guess I do," Rose said. She leaned back and was part of the world again. All the pounding thoughts and feelings, silenced by the mesmerizing water, rushed back into her head, blasting and bouncing, fusing and breaking apart, all a jumble she could not decipher.

"Because of me?" Anson asked.

"Some," she said.

"Tell me," he said.

"I don't know how to reach into my head and find the words that fit my thoughts," Rose said. "Sometimes feelings are more than words, bigger than words, and when you try to match words with what you're thinking, the words change the meaning of the feeling. And what you end up saying isn't what's inside you at all."

"Try, Rose," Anson insisted. He squeezed her hand.

Rose thought of all the times she had tried to talk of feelings with Thomas. "Don't get mad at me," she said.

"I'll try to understand," he said.

Rose looked at him. She thought she saw compassion. She believed he would try to comprehend the meaning of her words. She hoped she could choose wisely, clearly. She drew in her breath. "Charity wants June to have a turn with you."

Anson smiled. "A turn with me?"

"You know what I mean," Rose replied sharply. "Either take me seriously or let's just stop this."

"I'm sorry," Anson said. He rubbed his thumb gently over her fingers. "I do know what you mean."

"What do you think about June?" Rose asked. She pulled her hand away and clasped it to her other and pushed them tight against her lap.

"Let's sort out what you think first," Anson said.

"I don't know her very well. She gives me a Cherry Coke or a glass of lemonade or a cup of cocoa. I hear her say, 'I wish the snow would stop,' or, 'George Turner, either buy that book or put it back.' She doesn't *talk* to me. And I hate the way her upper arms don't jiggle when she wears short sleeves."

Anson turned his face away, but Rose caught his smile. She stopped talking and focused on the water.

"Rose," he said.

She heard him. There was no smile in his voice. She listened.

"It's hard for me to tell you what I feel for June. I don't

think much about it. She's a good woman. I like to talk with her. She trusts me. I like that. She's had a sad past. I'd like to help her pick up her life, go forward. And, yes, I guess I like to look at her. Maybe she needs us. Maybe we should help her." He leaned toward Rose. "Come, sit closer."

She shook her head. "Not yet." She didn't want his scent or the brush of male muscle perceived through his coat to keep her from the sorting of his words or the ordering of elusive emotions that were casting, shifting, and sliding inside the slopes and crevices of her mind. She needed to fit June and Grace and Charity against the shape of his passion, the fullness of his heart, the stirring of his will. She had to fit herself there. And she had to grab and hold onto Thomas, her anchor. He was spinning away from her.

"Where do I fit?" She looked at Anson with anguish.

"I don't know." He looked down at his hands on the steering wheel. "*That* I think about a lot. I don't know where you want to fit."

"Do you still love Bernice?"

"Yes." He looked out across the water. "But I have a life to live."

"And Charity? Grace? Where do they fit?" She wanted to cry.

"I want a whole life." He gripped the wheel.

"You mean sex, don't you?" she whispered.

"If I asked you to commit to me, to be mine only," Anson asked, "to let Thomas go, would you do it?"

She knew he didn't want her to stop loving Thomas. He wanted her to separate from Thomas. "I promised him I would always keep myself for him. He made me promise on his deathbed."

May Snow

"Oh Rosie, Rosie, what do I do with these feelings I have for you?"

And I for you? she wondered to herself.

9
March

Every year on the first Saturday in March, the children of Canadaway gather at the village green to build the biggest and best snowmen possible. They bring hats and scarves and brooms and sticks and carrots and lumps of coal and cans of spray paint to decorate their creations. Snow is rolled, scooped, and sculpted until the park floor is stripped of white, and round, fat men stand all over the wet, slippery grass uncovered beneath.

Rose was careful to stay on the plowed cement sidewalk that crisscrossed the green. She ducked and laughed as Charley, Charley, full of Barley threw a handful of loose snow at her. The church chimes were ringing *Winter Wonderland* and the high school band was gathering in the gazebo. They would perform later in the afternoon after Mayor Russo had declared every snowman a winner and awarded every child a balloon and a bag of candy.

Sarah Hunter had set up a stand with free hot cocoa and

marshmallows. June was moving through the park passing out Styrofoam cups of the steaming liquid. She bent and offered her tray to a trio of youngsters poking pinecones all over their wobbly snowman.

"Blow on it," June said, laughing. "Careful, eat the marshmallow first."

She looked up and saw Rose walking by with Louisa at her side. June smiled and held out the tray.

Rose shook her head, tried to smile, her lips lifting a little, but she kept walking.

"I want some," Louisa said, tugging at Rose's sleeve.

"Later," Rose said. "Come on." She had brought Louisa with her as a favor to Anson. He didn't know what to do with his granddaughter. She was there in his house, in his space, in his face. All the time. Mostly sitting. Rarely talking. Always watching him. He told Rose he thought he was starting to forget he was duty-bound to love her.

Rose saw Dwight Wilson up ahead. Red-headed, trembly, meek, but nice — Dwight. He was dripping water from a bucket, pouring it over a magnificently fat two-bellied snowman.

"Hey, Dwight," Rose called, pulling Louisa along. "Looks like your snowman's missing a head."

Dwight pointed to two young boys sliding on the wet grass. "It's theirs. I'm babysitting."

"Looks like you're doing all the work," Rose said. "Guess you should get the balloon."

Dwight blushed and Louisa gave Rose a dirty look. Dwight was thirty-seven.

Rose shrugged. Neither had a sense of humor. She turned

to go, but then turned back and looked hard at Dwight. It hit her. Neither had a sense of humor. Compatibility.

"Dwight," Rose said, "this is Louisa Talber, Anson's granddaughter."

"I've seen her before. With Anson," Dwight said. He looked at the ground.

"You've got a red spot on your cheek," Louisa said.

"It's freckles," Dwight said. His eyes continued to stare at dead, winter grass.

"No, it's not. It's a welt. You've got more," Louisa said.

"I ate a strawberry," Dwight said.

"Allergies," Louisa said, nodding. "I know about allergies."

Dwight lifted his eyes. "Cashews do it too. Get me real sick. Only need one little nut to send my head reeling and my tongue swelling."

Rose looked from one to the other, amazed.

Louisa touched his cheek, rubbed her finger over his rash. "Looks like blood," she said. "I hate blood."

"Me too," Dwight agreed.

Rose tapped Louisa's arm. "I'm moving on."

Louisa ignored her.

"I'll be over by the gazebo," Rose said. She walked away, shaking her head.

※　※　※

Rose slowly sipped the single cup of coffee she allowed herself each morning as she watched Nicholas from the window. He came out the side door, backpack in place, bundled against the cold. He moved quickly. He looked around the

May Snow

yard, glancing briefly at Rose's house — she couldn't be sure if he saw her, but thought he probably didn't — then carefully pushed the door shut.

He walked to the sidewalk, turned, and waved at his silent house. Rose could see no curtains move or hand flash in the window. His face was wistful. He didn't smile. He stood a moment and then walked purposefully off to school.

He would be back at three-thirty. If Amy wasn't working, she would be at the door, waving a dish towel and laughing, ready to spread her arms and hug him fiercely as soon as he ran up the steps. They would disappear, entangled, talking and giggling into the house, door slamming tight behind them.

Rose didn't know what they did inside, all alone, but she hoped it was good, solid bonding time for both. She often saw them playing together on weekends in the snow at the playground behind Charity's house. It was heartening to watch their joyous response to each other. Pleasure of such intensity could erase hours of loneliness.

At four-thirty, while it was still light, Amy would come out the side door, check it to be sure it was locked, go to the front door, rattle the knob, push against the door, then hurry to her car in the driveway. Before she got in, she always turned and waved and smiled at Nicholas in the window.

If I touched her cheeks, Rose thought, *they would be wet.*

Rose could see Amy's smile for as long as she could make out her face in the car.

Sometimes Nicholas stayed in the window a long time.

March

❄   ❄   ❄

Rose carefully raised herself in the half filled, claw-footed tub. She clutched the towel bar for balance, shivering a little as she eased out of the warm water and stood straight up in the tub. Bubbles slid sensuously down her sweet-scented body. She flung her head back, let go of the towel bar, and pushed the foam from her neck, gently, all the way down over flat planes and rising soft places, across skin that moved with her touch. She lost herself to the feel, the pleasant quivers that darted, faint and sweet, round and through her body.

She bent and clutched the porcelain tub edge, lifting her leg to swing it over the high, white side. Her hand, slick with rose oil, slipped. Her foot landed, flat and firm, on the rug, shooting pain, saving her from falling, and jerking her back to the place where her body was old.

She didn't want to stay in that place. She lifted a thick, lush, sea green towel from the floor, wrapping herself in its soft opulence, and walked to the mirror. The towel felt rich against her body, luxurious. She savored its pampering touch, leaned into the mirror, and smiled. She wrinkled her nose and looked deep at the lines that cracked her forehead and creased the edges of her eyes. She puckered her lips and creviced her cheeks. *Character*, she thought. *Interesting. My face. Like nobody else's.*

A drop of water ran down the side of her face. She took a fresh towel to pat it. As the cloth touched her skin, she felt Thomas. She heard him scold her, point out her frivolous

May Snow

waste. *Another towel, woman? No need. There's a perfectly good, dry one hanging on the bar from yesterday's bath.*

He had been stingy with towels. One a week. That's what she had been allowed. That's what each of them had been allowed. Why waste a towel, thin it and wear it out, by washing it every time it was used? It didn't get dirty. It wiped a clean body, after all. It just got wet, not soiled. After he died, Rose took some money from his hidden cache tucked under rusty bolts in a can in the barn. She drove to Northridge, her head in a turmoil and angry at Thomas for dying, feeling guilty for taking his money but defiant, wanting to hurt him back. She bought the softest, fattest, biggest towels she could find — towels in colors that grew in the woods and along the beach and on the animals that stalked the jungle and flew among the trees, towels so big they wrapped around her whole body with plenty to spare, towels as soft as pillows.

She never mentioned the towels in her prayers to God or her talks with Thomas. When Margaret teased, she turned away. She threw away the old threadbare towels she'd shared with Thomas and didn't even save them for rags.

Rose looked into her eyes in the mirror — sad eyes, thinking of Thomas and how she was about to defy him again. She didn't want Thomas in her thoughts. She shivered and, not moving from the mirror or shifting her gaze, reached for her robe and slipped it on. She touched her cheekbones with the tips of her fingers and moved them slowly, barely touching her skin, over the skeleton beneath, hard and protecting, then under the eyes, and to the side. She brought her palms to her cheeks, squeezed. Still watching herself in the mirror, she lifted her palms and dragged her fingertips ever so lightly and sensually downward over her cheeks, gently across the line of her jaw, and up and around the shape of her ears. She closed her eyes and felt only the touch, concentrated hard on the feel, sent Thomas away. Her fingers traveled down from her ears to the back of her neck. Her hands met and rubbed and eased away the last of her thoughts. Her head was empty for a long, delicious moment.

Finally she walked down the hall to her bedroom. Daylight was gone, but the glow from a lamp in her bedroom was enough to guide her. She paused at the guest room kept ready for Margaret on the rare nights she stayed — nights when Rose was ill and Margaret worried, nights when the wind howled and lifted snow and flung it with mighty, blocking force into the roads between Canadaway and Northridge, nights when Forrest worked late and Margaret could not face an empty house.

She touched the closed wooden door, rubbed it gently, turned the knob, and pushed lightly. The moon shone bright on the furnishings — a bed, a desk, a chair by the window with a lamp on the table beside it, a large wooden chest filled with quilts and sheets and pillows. No one but Margaret had ever slept in this room.

When Thomas died, Rose sold the farm and auctioned off the animals and equipment. The work was too much for her, the money required to maintain its functions too great, and the memories and need for Thomas too overwhelming. She could not stay there.

She bought a house on Washington Avenue in Canadaway. She moved their furniture and made a new nest where she

May Snow

was not constantly surprised to see Thomas missing from the places he had always filled so fully — the doorway, sucking at his pipe, looking out at his acres; the table, reading comics and honing his knives; the stuffed chair, chin on his chest, snoring at the television; their bed, his side snug against the wall, curled against her, reaching for the treasures he had married. She kept the furniture, but now it was in spots where he had never been and she could keep images at bay. Except for the bed.

Rubbing the back of her neck, she went to Margaret's bed, smoothed the spread, and turned it down. The shadow of Margaret was there. She looked around the room, touched the furniture, felt Margaret's eyes on her.

"Be gone, Margaret," she whispered. She sat in the chair and closed her eyes. "I don't want you here tonight." She folded her hands and waited. "I can't keep you in my heart this night. I need it whole and empty to fill with strange, new wonders. I'll fit you in again. Tomorrow when my heart has soaked in pleasures and sits in comfort, then there will be room for you, sweet daughter. Come back then."

She sighed and got up from the chair. Her legs shook as she left the room. She could not take Anson to the bed she and Thomas had shared. If she slept with Anson tonight, it would be in Margaret's room. And when she walked by that room tomorrow, she feared its lingering traces of Margaret's shadow would drift back, searching for her, knowing her mother had changed.

Would Thomas know? The past was with her too much. It filmed and dulled the promises of happiness waiting this night. She wished she could shake it away.

116

March

When she reached her bedroom, she stood in the doorway a moment, her eyes closed, head down, hand against
the frame.

"Please Thomas, don't be here now," she said softly. "Just
for tonight, don't look. I love you, dear heart, but it's not
enough to be happy only in dreams. I want to feel joy with the
earth underneath me. Let me go, Thomas. Just for a little
while give me freedom."

Oh, God, she thought, *I'm sending them both away.*

She walked slowly to the bed, wrapped an arm around one
tall corner post, leaned her head on it, rubbed the base of her
throat with gentle fingers, and looked upon the snow white
undergarments resting on the bed, waiting in the glow of soft
lamplight to adorn her clean, scented body, to make her ready,
sweet and fragile. Fresh for Anson.

She went to the window, held the heavy drape away, and
looked across the yards to Anson's house. Pressing her forehead against the cold glass, she savored the sharp, taut touch
on her skin. She wondered if he was upstairs in the dark, looking back at her. She blushed and let the curtains drop until
there was only a sliver for her to look through.

Sometimes when she looked through the glass, she saw the
old ladies — Charity, Grace, and now, June — slip in and out
of Anson's house. She didn't mean to spy, but for her a window was an opening to the world. It was a way to see an ex-
panding, changing life. It was a way to touch it, mingle within
it, and she often watched from her windows.

This night was sprinkled with moonlight. It was beautiful. It was as if fairies had painted it for their own pleasure and
then decided to share it with her.

May Snow

She ached to feel light and pure, untouched by memories or obligations, beholden only to the present moment. She had walked many small steps to reach this place. One step forward would erase her options, and that imprint would be stamped on the line of her history for all time.

She could still step back. Retreat. Stay as she was.

She was torn, frightened for her soul — wanting to fully love someone as warm-blooded as she but fearing the wrath of God descending upon her, crushing her, allowing her to dream no more.

No, she thought, *God wanted her happy. It was Thomas who wanted to own her, but God had rules and He wanted her too.* The battle in her heart was too big.

She turned from the window and dressed. In a few minutes, Anson would be here. There had been no promises. He had no right to expect what he wanted from her. But he had held her hand while she walked this path, and surely he knew her struggle.

She took a last look in the mirror. Caught in its reflection was David's carved dog sitting on the dresser. She picked it up and stroked it, taking strength from the will David had left as he fashioned this gift for his grandfather. *Until he died,* she thought, *the child had reached for every moment. He'd wasted no time. But his thrust had been honorable.*

When the doorbell rang, she kissed the dog gently and set him back down. She stood for a moment then, trembling, took off her wedding ring and laid it on the dresser next to David's carving.

She went down the stairs to let Anson in.

10
April

"Don't you think that black skirt is just a hair too short?" Rose asked, scraping mayonnaise off her sandwich. "And maybe a smidgen too tight?"

"You don't like the skirt?" Margaret asked, taking the knife from her mother and putting the top bread slice back on the turkey. "I ordered light dressing. You can eat it."

"Oh, I like the skirt," Rose said, removing the bread and patting it with her napkin. "It's just a little skimpy. I don't like mayo, Margaret, light or otherwise."

They had been shopping nonstop all morning and most of the afternoon for clothes to cover Margaret's new body. For the life of her, Rose could not understand why her daughter stretched and sweated every day, struggling to change her soft, shapely body to look like a boy's. Toned, Margaret called it. Well, Rose called it defying nature. Growing muscles where they didn't belong.

Exhausted, they had stopped at a restaurant just outside

May Snow

Buffalo on Lake Erie's shore. Rose was more than happy to stop. She swore they had shopped in every store at every mall in the city.

"Did you like anything I bought?" Margaret asked.

"I liked everything you bought," Rose said.

"Then why did you keep asking me if I really wanted such a low neck and do I really need a push-up bra and do I really think that blouse is quite right?"

"It's real silk, Margaret," Rose said, lifting her arms and chopping the air to emphasize her chagrin. It was hard to be tactful when she was so tired.

"Forrest can afford it," Margaret said, clenching her teeth. "It's a beautiful blouse. It drapes smart."

"You can't even wash it," Rose said. She took a tiny bite of her sandwich and wrinkled her nose. The dressing was too creamy.

"And Forrest can afford a great, big cleaning bill," Margaret said, frowning. "Of course, he might have to give up some other expenses, like business lunches. *Some* business lunches."

Rose sighed and looked at the lake through the floor-to-ceiling glass. It was a clear, bright day. The spring sun dipped through the clouds and skipped diamonds over the water. She wished she could sprinkle Margaret with that sparkle. She put her sandwich down and took Margaret's hands in her own.

"You need to talk to Forrest," Rose said.

Margaret pulled her hands away and shook them, fingers splaying, at Rose. "I can't." Her shoulders slumped. She dropped her hands in her lap. "Forrest doesn't talk."

"Sweetie, if I could help you, I would." Rose wanted better words but couldn't find them.

April

"I know you would," Margaret said, wiping a tear. "And I'm okay. I don't mean to yell at you. I can't seem to help it. I don't yell at anybody else."

"Maybe you're getting even for all the yelling you got when you were little," Rose said, smiling a little, knowing Margaret's pain needed to scream and that she could soak it in without judgment. "I love you, Margaret."

Margaret sniffled and nodded. She swallowed deep. "You never yelled at me. Dad did. Maybe we should talk about something else." She took the tissue Rose offered. "How's Anson?"

Rose took a bite of her sandwich, chewed it carefully. Margaret was watching her. Pictures of Anson swelled in Rose's head. She willed her face not to betray her, not to send signals of recent ecstasy — sex, raw and lusty, mighty sex. She did not want her face to shout her sins to Margaret.

"Mother, when you get that blank look, I know there's something you're trying to hide."

Rose had to steer her daughter to safer pastures. "Louisa has a boyfriend," she said. "Dwight Wilson. You should tell Karen when she calls you."

"That's not it," Margaret said. "I can tell. What don't you want to tell me? Something about Anson. That's it, isn't it? You and Anson. You're a thing."

"Not exactly."

"Not exactly! What does that mean? Oh! You're not sleeping with him, are you? What would Dad say?"

"He'd tell you to mind your own business," Rose said.

"Yeah, he would say that," Margaret laughed. "And he'd be right." She leaned across the table, laughter gone. "I don't know if I want you to be sleeping with Anson, but whatever's going on between you two, don't please him like you did dad, like I did Forrest." She lifted her chin. "Like I'm doing now. Today." She dropped her eyes, paused, then looked steady at her mother. "It eats you up until you're gone. Poof. Nothing there. You have to make up a whole new person from scratch. Don't do that."

11
May

May first dawned flower-sweet and warm. Rose awoke early and hung her wash while the ground was still soggy and cool from the morning dew. She moved barefoot in the fresh spring grass, sinking a little with each step, feeling earth and moisture between her toes. The sharp sensations of skin on soil made her feet feel young, ready to make adventure.

She hooked the line with the clothes pole Thomas had made her from a broken branch the year she was a bride. She pushed it high and tight. Sheets and towels cracked in the stiff breeze.

She lifted her face to wash it with sun. Closing her eyes, she stood quiet and listened to the crisp flap of her clothes and the soothing rustle of strong, growing leaves gently slapping each other and birds whistling, calling, singing. She drew in air slowly and released a deep, contented sigh.

A door slammed across the yard. She jerked and turned to see Nicholas, brandishing a purple paper cone, jump down his side door steps. Rose stepped forward to greet him, then stopped when she saw him glance furtively toward her house. He darted across his lawn to the corner of hers where a large clump of daffodils grew. He obviously didn't see her behind the blowing sheets.

He stooped and grabbed a fistful of stems and shoved the flowers, petals upward, into his bright paper cone. He patted them tenderly, then rushed back to his house and up the steps. Jumping up and down, he hung the flowers on the doorknob and furiously punched the doorbell. He spun around, hurried down the steps, and crouched behind an old maple tree. Stealing peeks at his door, he waited several minutes. Rose waited too.

Nothing happened. Nicholas's shoulders slumped. He walked away slowly.

Rose ached to go to him, but she feared it would shame him for her to see his hurt. She stayed silent by her wash.

Then, face stoic, Nicholas turned and bounded back up the steps. He pounded loudly on the door, scurried back to the tree, and huddled behind it, clutching at the thick, strong trunk.

The door opened. Amy looked out. Her hair was mussed. She clutched her housecoat at the neck. Rubbing her eyes, heavy and swollen, she peered toward Rose's house. She shut her eyes and shook her head fiercely. It was apparent to Rose that she saw nothing amiss. Stepping back into the house, Amy reached for the doorknob. Her eyes widened. She looked down at the flowers, dew-fresh and sun-yellow, and she smiled.

Lifting the cone high over her head, grinning, she shouted, "Nicholas! Nicholas, my love, where are you?" She planted a bare foot on the first step, slowly, looking one way, then the other. Then she moved faster and was down the steps and running on the lawn, checking behind bushes and trees. "I'm going to get you, Nicholas. And when I do, I'm going to smother your face with kisses. Wet, juicy, mother kisses."

Nicholas stood laughing against his tree. He covered his mouth with his hands. His body shook with suppressed laughter and his feet moved up and down.

Caught up in the drama, Rose watched, enchanted.

When Amy did find Nicholas, as she lifted him and whirled him, she did indeed smother him with loving mother kisses.

She sat him down, patted his bottom, and sent him on his way to school. He turned at the end of the driveway and waved. She was still there to wave back.

He looks so happy, thought Rose. He skipped off and Amy went into her house, the flowers caught close to her chest.

By noon Rose was tired. Spurred by spring's invigorating energy that fooled an old lady into thinking she was younger, she had spent the morning doing little jobs, tasks ignored during heavy winter months, tasks that stretched dormant muscles and grated over-worked joints. She had reached for dishes in high cupboards, bent to wipe corners rarely seen, searched the back of closets, sorting the bounty and straightening the keepers. She had put her shoes in a line and wiped the keys on her piano. She meant to bake, but her back and her legs made her sit for a minute, and when she sat her whole body told her it was time to quit.

She called the cats to her lap and cuddled and played for a while. "Oh my, you've grown so big and heavy. So pretty, my little Christmas babies." She blew in their faces. They scrambled over her, rubbing against her when she stroked them and backed away when she tickled their whiskers. She took a ball of yarn and threw it. They jumped down and ran to get it. She threw another, then several. The strands were all over the rug. She laughed as the kittens pawed and rolled the balls and tangled the colors.

"Ah, pretty babies." She pushed with her arms and lifted herself from the chair. "Oh, babies, it hurts." Her back bent, and she grabbed her sides to push in the pain. "But look at all the chores we got done. One more. Only one. Then we can watch soap operas the rest of the afternoon."

She opened the kitchen door, and the cats scooted out. Toe against heel, she pushed her shoes off and set her bare feet down on the steps. The wood was sun hot. The feel was sleek and pleasant.

The cats were gone. Out of sight. Off to explore. They would be back when their bellies wanted milk. Rose wished them happy hunting and put them out of her thoughts. Sliding her feet across a patch of dandelion blossoms, velvet-smooth against her soles, she gave herself to the scent and sound and feel of living earth, soaked it in, and wallowed in its bigness, its complete goodness.

She plucked a towel from the line and pressed it, sweet and fresh, against her face. *Better than candy*, she thought.

She was not prepared for the hand that tapped her shoulder. Jerking away, she twisted her body and pain tore through it.

"Oh I'm sorry," June said, stepping back. "I didn't mean to frighten you."

"Oh my," Rose murmured as she stumbled and, arms outstretched, caught her balance with hurtful, ankle-stabbing, little steps.

"Let me help," June said, reaching out, now stepping forward.

Rose waved her away. "I'm all right. Just give me a minute. Stupid body, anyway. Too old. Doesn't know enough to stay supple. Here, we can go sit over there for a bit." She motioned toward two, old, wooden, lawn chairs tucked in a cluster of maples and oaks. "No, don't help me. Go sit. I'll get there."

"I'm only here a minute," June said, walking backward.

"Please." Rose thought her legs would burn away beneath her. She saw herself rolling to the chair, charred stubs sticking straight out.

June shrugged, turned, and ambled toward the chairs.

Envious eyes on smooth, tan legs under very short shorts, Rose followed. *She doesn't have any vein bumps*, Rose thought. *She can't be that young. Has to be surgery.*

June sat, crossed her legs, and squirmed back into the deep, wooden, lawn chair. She reached in her purse, pulled out a pack of cigarettes and her lighter tucked in the cellophane, and held it out to Rose.

Rose shook her head. "I don't smoke."

June nodded. "That's one of the few things I do know about you. I meant, do you care if I do?"

"It's okay. If that's what you want."

June lit her cigarette, puffed. "It's what I can choose to do now. If I want."

Rose watched and waited and wondered at her remark. Acrid wisps of smoke rose and dissipated in the clean air.

"It's a nice day," Rose said finally.

"Anson and I are going on a picnic. I brought stuff."

May Snow

"I knew it was your day," Rose said, thinking she didn't want to be reminded, wanting to forget. June really made it hard to find a way to like her.

"I thought you might come with us," June said, taking a baby food jar out of her purse. She opened it and ground her cigarette out on the glass bottom. She smiled at Rose. "I really don't like them." She put the jar, cigarette inside, back in her purse.

"Then why smoke them?"

"Freedom."

"From what?" Rose asked. June ignored her question. "I'd really like you to come with us." She swung her crossed leg, and Rose watched, thinking it probably didn't hurt when she bumped that firm hip. Or when Anson rubbed that silky calf. Not a trace of hair on it, not a ridge or purple line. Unconsciously, she smoothed her dress and felt the lumps hiding under it.

"I just don't know you very well, Rose," June said. "And I want to. Charity and Grace think you're wonderful. Even when they're scared you're stealing their share of Anson, they talk about you. The good things you do. The way you put others ahead of yourself. How you feel people's happy times and tears. And care. Only they hope your morals will stamp out your selfish, wanton needs. Those are Grace's words. She's really meaning to say she thinks you want Anson, but you're a woman of principle and maybe you don't dare mess up and cross God. So I know them pretty well, but I hardly know you at all. Not the inside you. The you behind your words. And words can fool. They don't always speak real. There aren't enough of the kind that grab the soul and say what it is." She bent forward. "So come with us. Humor me. Make Anson happy. And I do make good egg salad sandwiches."

Rose was confused. The old ladies held tight to their time with Anson. They didn't share. They monitored each other. They wrung every moment, squeezed their hours to the very edge. June's offer was preposterous. Suspect. But June seemed a woman grown beyond saying what she didn't mean. Rose guessed her to be honest. As far as she went.

Tilting her head back, Rose squinted into the tree behind June. She searched for the bird singing loud somewhere in the branches. The sun was bright, shining through the leaves, blinding her. She couldn't find the bird. She dropped her eyes to June and blinked as bright spots shot before her, then faded. She rubbed the hollow at the base of her throat.

"It seems peculiar to me," Rose commented, "that you would ask me to come along with you and Anson on your scheduled day."

"Why is that?" June asked.

"None of the rest of us would share the alone hours we get with him. I wouldn't. There aren't that many."

June lifted her eyebrows and smiled.

Rose pressed her lips together. *She thinks I'm cheating,* she thought. *She thinks I'm seeing him more than I should. Well, let her say it then. And what do I say if she does? You're right, wanna make something of it? Or do I lie and say I don't cheat? Or do I cry and say I'm sorry when I'm not? Only I am, sort of. They're my friends and I'm deceiving them. Or not deceiving them, if they've guessed. And I think they have. What a dilemma. I want Anson. And I want them. I guess I want it all. Including Thomas.*

May Snow

She pushed her fingers hard into her neck. God, what do I say if June attacks me?

But June didn't. Instead she bent forward and put a hand on Rose's knee. "You need to understand something. I don't need Anson the same way the rest of you do. You all look at him as a potential lover or husband." Rose frowned and flinched in her chair. "For me," June continued, "he's something I've never had — a male friend I can trust. He puts me on his level, takes me seriously, makes me an equal person. He blows air into my soul. I don't always need to be alone with him to feel the strength he gives me." Looking directly into Rose's eyes, her hand tight on Rose's leg, June spoke clear and firm. "And you need to know that I will not let you take his friendship from me. You can have what's rightfully yours, but you cannot make me an orphan."

Suffering from the pain inflicted by the squeeze of June's hand, Rose wondered at June's choice of words.

"You're welcome to come with us. I meant it when I said I want to know you better, be your friend. It might be easier for you if Anson was there to help us."

The pain was growing fierce. Finally, Rose could bear it no longer. She winced and pulled her leg away.

June lifted her hand quickly, looked at Rose's face, and covered her mouth. "Oh," she whispered through her fingers, "I hurt you. I didn't mean to."

Rose touched June's arm. "It's all right. I'm okay. I know you didn't mean to hurt me."

"And I didn't mean to ruin our chance for friendship. Please. Come with us, Rose. Please. Give me a chance."

"Shh," Rose said. "It's really okay. But not today. It's better

May

I don't go today." *I'm not ready to watch Anson admire you with me there.* "You go have your picnic with Anson. Maybe next time. Ask me again."

June nodded and rose. "Maybe next time," she said softly.

Impulsively Rose stood and hugged her. *She doesn't sag much,* Rose thought, feeling June's firm upper arms, but at least she's not sleeping with Anson. I don't think so, anyway.

❄   ❄   ❄

After June left, Rose took down her clothes and folded them before piling them in the basket. Then she sat back in a chair and rested her eyes a moment.

When she awoke, Dwight and Louisa were putting together their own picnic in Anson's backyard. She waved but they didn't notice her, so she sat quietly and watched. The day was getting warmer. It felt good to just sit.

A bee or bug or moth must have started buzzing around Louisa's head. She suddenly stopped her trek across the lawn and wagged her hands furiously, batting at the flying culprit. Prayers and pleas flew out of her mouth. Hopping helplessly around her, Dwight poked the air with a banana.

I know this could be dangerous, Rose thought, *and I know I shouldn't find this funny, but I've never seen that girl move so much or talk so loud. If something bites her, I'll go help, but the poor, scared bug is probably long gone.*

Finally Louisa grabbed the banana from Dwight and threw it on the ground. She stomped her foot and pushed him away.

"A lot of good you did," she cried. "Get that blanket down so we can spread out the food. And don't put it in the sun."

135

May Snow

Rose watched and smiled. No question who was in charge. A new side to Louisa. Energy never suspected. Power enjoyed.

Rose frowned as Louisa took the sandwich Dwight handed her and scowling, shoved it back at him. She grabbed another from the basket and ate it. It looked the same to Rose as the one she had pushed back at Dwight.

Dwight ate without talking or smiling. When Louisa's pout was over, she moved close to him, ran her fingers up and down his sleeve, and whispered in his ear. He didn't resist.

I guess someone always has to rule, thought Rose, looking up to Thomas. *It seems that way. Only it's not very fun to watch after a while.*

She went in the house, poured milk for the cats, and put it outside. Then she sat in the living room and watched soap operas for a bit. But she couldn't get inside them. They didn't fool her into thinking they were real and she was a part of their story. Not this afternoon.

So, she went out on the porch and watched the boys play ball in the park across the street.

❄   ❄   ❄

That night a cold wind from Canada swooshed across Lake Erie, dropping temperatures, bringing back a bitter touch of winter.

Rose shivered in the early morning hours and pulled her blankets close. She heard a patter on the windows, but the telling sound did not register in her conscious thoughts. She was too tired and wanted only warmth and sleep. Huddled in soft wool, she drifted into delicious slumber.

May

Light streaming through the windows woke her. She barely remembered the cutting cold that had awakened her in the night. Pushing off her covers, she checked the brass clock sitting on her nightstand. It was too dark to read, so she lifted it close to her face. Puzzled, she put it back down. It wasn't yet dawn, but her room was brushed with streaks of glowing white stretching from the window. The room lurked dim, not dark. She could see the shapes of tall treetops and perching birds outside the glass. There was too much light. It was too early to see so much.

The room was chilly without covers. She pulled a blanket off the bed, wrapped it around her, and bare feet on carpet, padded to the window.

She looked out in wonder. Snow mirrored and reflected light in the bright fullness of a whole round moon. It sparkled and danced and covered every line and every contour of every configuration within the scope of her eyes. Sugar snow. Wet and heavy and laced with light. May snow.

Rose shuddered. There had been May snow the year Mattie Cow dropped a sick calf and the illness spread throughout the barn and they lost their entire herd. And it had snowed in May the year that Margaret fell from the tractor. And snow had reached into May the year the buds froze on her father's grapes and there was no crop. And it had snowed in May the year she thought Thomas might be having an affair, breaking his sacred promise and her heart, while she stood silent and unsure.

The snow had looked wondrous those years too. Unbelievably beautiful. But snow in May was wrong.

Rose stood at the window, senses sharper in the night, and shivered.

May Snow

❄   ❄   ❄

The day stayed cool, but the sun came out and melted the snow. Still uneasy, Rose called Margaret to make sure all was well with her. No one answered the phone. Unsettled, she pictured Margaret ill and unable to call for help, or worse, beaten by Forrest and lying in a pool of blood even though Forrest had never raised a hand to wife, children, or family dog. Or maybe Margaret had given up the ship and struck out for calmer waters without thinking to say good-bye.

"She's shopping," Rose said aloud, tapping the phone with restless fingers. "She'll call me later."

She went around to all the windows, peering out, finding nothing to keep her at any one of them. She took a bag of flour out of the cupboard, set it on the counter, stared at it, and pondered what to bake. She put it back in the cupboard. Scrubbed the sink. Polished the kettle. Took the burners off the stove to scrub. Frowned at them. Set them back in their recessed wells.

Sighing, she threw a heavy sweater over her shoulders and trudged across the soft, wet yards to ask Anson if he wanted to do something. Anything. A ride, a walk, a board game. It was nobody's scheduled day. He had free time and she needed some of it.

Anson didn't want to go anywhere or do anything. His legs had ached all night — varicose veins — and he wanted to be alone.

Rose pictured him crawling on his knees because his legs wouldn't support him, alone, trying to get to a phone. She told him she should stay in case he needed her. She didn't tell him something bad was in the air. He wouldn't believe her. He asked her to please go, as he ached and didn't want to entertain. She said she wasn't company. He said *go*. She told him to take care of himself, be careful, and not to bump that vein sticking outside on his ankle. He gave her a face that said, *I can't take anymore*, and she left.

May snow meant trouble.

When she got back to her house, she called Charity. "Let's go to a movie in Northridge."

"I'll call June," Charity said.

"I suppose you could," Rose said, thinking June better leave her alone. She was in no mood to make friends. "Who's going to drive?"

"Me," said Charity. "Be ready."

They decided to go to dinner first. Driving toward Northridge, they discussed where they would eat. Charity wanted to go fancy — plush chairs, hot plates, interesting co-diners. Noting the chagrined expression that whisked across June's face and knowing her own purse was not overflowing, Rose suggested a cheaper place closer to the theater. "Then we could park in one place and walk from dinner to the movie. Saves a lot of trouble."

"Are you suggesting it's difficult for me to maneuver the car in and out of tight spaces, so parking just once is easier?" Charity queried.

"I'm suggesting my ankles hurt and it's hard to get in and out of your car," Rose said.

"I suppose you've got a point," Charity said. "But I really

was looking forward to something elegant. And I've got real diamonds in my ears."

"You've always got real diamonds in your ears," Grace said, looking in her compact mirror. "Or emeralds or amethysts or pearls or whatevers." She sucked in her cheeks and tilted her head. "And they don't make you any prettier."

"I'm not very hungry," June said. She sat in the back seat gently stroking her purse, a subdued beige imitation leather, a dime store pocketbook.

"The portions aren't big," Charity said. "Just the choice."

"I don't have a lot of money with me," Rose said, thinking Charity could be a tad more tuned in to June's obvious plight. "And what I've got, I don't want to use up filling my stomach with just one meal."

Grace giggled.

"All right," Charity said. "You're not dressed for exquisite dining anyway."

❄   ❄   ❄

Walking into the lobby of the theater after dinner, discussing the choices of movies, they spotted Dwight and Louisa in a heated argument off to one side of the line.

"Uh, oh," Charity said. "Doesn't look like they're too happy."

"Let's get close and listen," Grace said. "Come on, Rose."

Rose shook her head and stayed in line.

"Leave them alone," June said. "He's not hurting her."

Rose lifted her eyebrows. Another strange choice of words.

"Actually, if it came to fists, Dwight's the one I'd worry about," Charity commented. "Looks to me like he's the wimpy one."

May

"Dweebie Dwight," Grace said, smirking.

"Shh," Rose said.

"He can't hear me."

"Everybody else can," Rose said.

"No they can't."

"She's right," Charity said. "Don't embarrass me."

"Look, she's pouting," Grace said, ignoring Charity. Dwight and Louisa were heading to the back of the line. Louisa, tight-lipped, walked stiff. "Looks like she doesn't like the movie he chose."

"Grace, they'll hear you," June said.

"No, they won't. They're in their own little world."

As they passed the whispering group of old ladies, Rose observed Dwight's face, miserable and defeated. Louisa, red-faced and grim, marched with stubborn strength beside him but was far enough away that he could not touch her, even accidentally. Rose knew that before they reached the booth, Dwight would cave and Louisa would have the ticket she wanted. Rose hoped she would have the grace not to gloat.

Putting her fingers to her throat, Rose rubbed gently. *Oh, Thomas*, she thought, *forgive me, but I think I know how Dwight feels.*

❅   ❅   ❅

Rose answered the phone.

"Don't say anything. Just listen." It was Margaret. "Forrest left me. He's gone to live with this woman person he works with. I don't think he's ever coming back."

"Oh, Margaret," Rose whispered.

141

May Snow

"I told you, Mother, don't say anything. He's going because I'm a weak-willed, non-person. I've got no thoughts or
ideas or dreams that are just mine alone. They're all entwined
with him. All I ever live for is to please him. That's what you
taught me. All those years I watched you doing and thinking
whatever Daddy wanted and whatever Daddy thought and I
hated your weakness. Then I went and did the same thing and
I turned into this weak, leechy nobody."

"Oh, Sweetie, you're somebody."

"No! He said he's too tired to be leaned on anymore. This
ugly Ashley person — he says she's strong and can take care of
herself and doesn't need him for validation. She's mighty in her
own right and doesn't sap him of strength. Sap him! I never did
that. I *gave* him everything. *All of me.* He said she just wants him
because he's fun to be with. She doesn't ask for anything. He told
me I wore him out and he's got nothing left for himself."

"Margaret…"

"Mother, you taught me all wrong." Margaret was crying.
"I did the best I could to make him happy, and it wasn't
enough. And now I've got nothing. *I am nothing.* How could
you do that to me?"

"Sweetie, I love you."

"I'm hanging up now. Don't call me back."

"Margaret."

"I failed, Mother. Just leave me alone."

※　※　※

When daylight faded and shadows ruled, it was not unusual
for Rose to creep across the yards and visit Anson. Or he, her.

May

It was their secret. No one else should know. Their intent was not to cause pain. Rose went to Anson's only if Louisa was out of the house, and when Louisa was at home, buried in her room or skulking about poking into cupboards and attic and hidden corners, Anson went to Rose's house. On those nights, he told Louisa he liked to walk in the evening, to saunter along the street alone, to contemplate in peace. He told Rose that Louisa was not particularly interested in what he did, more in what he had. He was sure she didn't guess his little strolls took him straight to Rose's door.

As the evenings grew warmer, Anson and Rose took to sitting in the dark on her porch, rocking, speaking softly, laughing low. Sometimes they pushed their rockers close and, arms entwined, shared armrests.

Dusk had settled as they sat one May evening, relaxing after a sweet session in Margaret's bed and watching Nicholas play in the shadows, darting and twisting, as if chasing monsters they could not see.

Rubbing Anson's thumb with light fingers, Rose licked her lips, then asked softly, "Do you sleep with the others?"

"Why do you ask?" he said without moving. His thumb stayed pliant beneath her hand.

"You can if you want to." Rose held her breath. Anson said nothing. Hesitantly she threw out the words that she had hoarded in fear lest he give the wrong answer to the question implied. "We're not committed."

"I am." His answer was simple. "For now."

She couldn't let it drop. "Then you're not sleeping with them?"

"I'm not."

May Snow

"Did you ever?"

Anson stopped rocking. "Rose, you shouldn't ask that."

"You can...sleep with them. If you want to." Rose stilled her chair too. "We've never talked about loyalties in bed."

"I'm not sleeping with them now." He patted her hand. "Let it be."

"They want to?"

"Yes."

"June?"

"Sometimes. June. Mostly Grace."

"How do you stop?"

"I think of you."

❄   ❄   ❄

Nicholas always waited until dark to come out of his house and play in the yard. All the other little boys who played ball in the park across the street every night after supper were gone by then. Nicholas chased shadows alone.

Rose watched him from her window, lights off so he could not see her. Sometimes he seemed a carefree apparition flitting among the bushes and trees then he was the conquering hero, knees bent, back hunched, arms stiff and straight out from his body — a lethal weapon — charging unseen adversaries. And sometimes he crouched under a tree, very still, pathetic and wee.

Every night before he went in, Nicholas foraged in the garbage cans outside Rose's garage. All manner of treasure could be found in those cans. They were receptacles for all the out-grown, unwanted, not-needed belongings the townsmen donated for sorting and disbursement to those who would pick and choose and transform their bounty to a prized find. Ordinary garbage did not go in those cans. Grace was chairwoman for the church's charity bin, and this was her collection center.

And every night Rose watched until Nicholas was safe in his house. Sometimes it was very late.

One night Rose left a bag of cookies by the garbage can. Nicholas took them.

"Anson told me he thinks it's time for Karen to come get Louisa and take her home." Charity stirred fake sugar into her coffee. "He's tired of getting asked what everything in his house is worth and who's going to get it when he dies."

Rose smiled. "I think she's coming out of her shell."

"I think Anson would like to stuff her back in." Charity lifted her cup and sipped. "Mmm. It's always so much better when someone else makes it."

Nodding, Rose pushed her marshmallow under the surface of her cocoa then licked the melted goo off her finger.

"It's good to be alone with you for a change," Charity said. "It's been a long time since we've had a chance to chat."

"It is nice," Rose said. She lifted the core of the marshmallow with her spoon and slid it into her mouth. It spread, warm and squishy, over her tongue.

Rose had been sorting clothes from the garbage cans when Charity called and suggested they meet at Hunter's for coffee and then maybe drive into Northridge to hit some early yard sales. They could be by themselves. Grace was helping with the toddler story hour at the church, and June, taking advantage of her day off, was catching up on her laundry and cleaning.

"I hope Grace doesn't forget she's supposed to go to the church," Charity said.

"Why would she? She's never missed before that I know of. Has she?"

"Maybe a few times," Charity mumbled. She wadded up the empty sugar packet and dropped it on her saucer.

Rose stirred a tunnel in the middle of her cocoa.

"Oh, oh." Charity poked Rose and jerked her head toward the door.

Looking up, Rose saw Dwight and Louisa come in and take seats at the other end of the counter. They picked up menus and studied them.

"Watch," Charity whispered.

Sarah Hunter stood in front of the couple, ready for their order.

"I want a bacon, lettuce, and tomato sandwich and a cola." Louisa handed up the menus. She pointed at Dwight. "He wants a hamburger. Well done. Cola for him too."

"Tuna salad," Dwight said.

Louisa scowled, pushing her chin into her neck. "You always get hamburgers."

"I want tuna."

Louisa looked up at Sarah. "Give him a burger." She turned to Dwight. "You know you like it better than tuna. Nobody likes tuna better than hamburgers."

Sarah waited.

Lips pressed tight, eyes on the counter, Dwight shrugged.

146

Louisa nodded. "Give him a hamburger. With onion."

Rose glanced away so she would not witness Dwight's embarrassment. She caught Sarah's smirk and ignored it.

"Hey," Charity said, leaning close to Rose and grinning. "I think the shell's cracked too bad to ever get her back in."

Rose looked back at Dwight's red face. She saw the lines that showed his passage from youth to an older age deepen, white and lengthy, along his nose and chin. Louisa chatted, unaware, beside him.

Charity jabbed her. "What do you think?"

Rose sighed and nodded.

12
Mid-May

Every year near the middle of May while the beach was still closed and empty, Rose, Charity, and Grace walked to the end of the breakwater and threw branches of lilacs, deep purple and fragrant, into Lake Erie. When they were young they had stood on the cliffs further down the beach, heaving their flowers down to the lake. Then they had run, barefoot and spry, to the sand where they clasped hands and walked into the water — three happy girls, singing and laughing, heralding the return of warming sun.

That was long ago when Rose's limbs carried her sturdy and swift without twinge or caution. Now, anxious to get back to the beach after throwing the flowers and beginning their journey, Rose struggled to make her legs hurry as she fought their stiff, painful resistance.

Charity's muscles were still strong, and they took her without battle to the edge of the water where, shoeless in the sand and squirming restlessly, she waited for Rose and Grace.

May Snow

Grace, circling her way merrily in a self-imposed ritual dance, was almost there.

Standing by Charity, serene and still, was June. It was Charity who had asked June to come. She was one of them now. Rose didn't want her there but could not say it. The others wouldn't listen, and it was mean. So this year, four of them threw flowers. Four of them raced to the beach. And June was the first one there, even before Charity.

Grace, close behind, ran through the sand. She grabbed June's hand and Charity's, tugged at them, urged them into the water. Charity held her back. "Wait for Rose."

Forcing her legs to go faster, Rose's toes sank in the sun-cooked sand. She felt the cool wind rolling in with the waves, pushing her hair back and lifting her skirt. It smelled clean. She laughed and pushed against the sand, liking the feel of the warm grains sliding over her feet. Reaching Charity, she clutched the hand her friend held out and, whooping and hollering, they drove into the water together.

Grace was the first to break into song. Rose and Charity caught the melody and shouted it louder. They slid from one song to another. Sometimes in unison. Sometimes each singing a different tune. Somewhere along the way, as they splashed and frolicked and chased lilac petals in the cold, sloshing water, June opened her mouth and let her own music spill out. They sang every song they could think of.

Exhausted from their vivacious celebration of the great, golden sun and its powerful water child, the women dropped into beach chairs that were lined up facing the lake.

"Oh, how it sparkles," Grace said, fondling a wet lilac branch.

Rose lay back in her chair and watched the sun flash on the

moving water. It was bright in her eyes, vivid and clear, the line of the water meeting sand and sky sharply defined. She squinted, wanting to see it true, not dimmed by dark glasses. She felt at ease, peaceful.

"Listen. Hear the waves lap," June said softly. She sat, leaning forward with her head tilted and a wondrous look on her face.

She feels the magic, Rose thought and smiled.

"Time for the feast," Grace said. She reached under her chair and held up a foil-wrapped sandwich.

They each did the same. June, watching them, did as they did.

"Hold it high," Charity said. "A toast to our Creator for the bounty bestowed by Him for our nourishment."

Holding their sandwiches high, the old ladies shouted in unison, "Hail, God, thank you for your tasty gifts." June mouthed each word a spit second after the others had said them.

"Now eat," Grace said, giving direction to June. "It's a tradition. You bring your favorite sandwich, a tribute to life, and it's required that you savor every bite."

"I brought bologna," June said. She made a face.

"That's fine if you like it," Rose said, opening her own sandwich — peanut butter and banana on cold, toasted rye. Sniffing the burst of aroma from the rich, oily peanuts, she grunted with pleasure. "It's supposed to be whatever you like best, no matter how foolish. Next year you'll know." Surprised that she was pleased with the thought, she put her tongue on the creamy spread oozing out of the edges of her sandwich, rolled it into her mouth, and gloried in the taste.

"I forgot to tell her it should be her favorite," Charity said.

May Snow

"Mmm." She bit into the mix of cream cheese and shredded carrot on date nut bread she'd packed for herself.

"I bring the same every year. See," Grace said, displaying her thick, sloppy spaghetti concoction. "It is *so* good."

"Yuck," Charity said, as part of Grace's sandwich dripped on her arm.

June laughed.

Rose couldn't remember having heard June laugh with such joy. It was a good sound. Feeling relaxed, she rested in her chair, sank into its webbing, closed her eyes, and lifted her face to the soft, warming sun while she chewed.

They were quiet while they ate and rested. Wrapped in the sweet comfort of sun rays and sand, they listened to the waves roll over the lake, slap the beach gently, retreat.

"Look," Grace said, pointing skyward. "There's a big, wooly teddy bear. And a fat pig is chasing him." She pulled her skirt high over slim calves and hefty thighs, bunching it over her soft, round belly.

"Put your skirt down," Charity said.

"There's nobody here but us to see," Grace said. "And the sun feels so good. Besides the skirt's wet and sticks to my legs. Oh, look, my pig's breaking apart."

All eyes looked up to the clouds, puffy and white, shaping and reshaping as they sailed across the sky.

"I see an old man," Rose said. "Just his face. He's calling somebody. See his mouth get bigger and wider?"

"If it's a man, he's sure to be yelling, not calling," June said.

Rose twisted sharp to her voice, but June said no more. The others seemed not to hear, paid her no heed.

"Yelling at who?" Rose asked, bending forward.

June shrugged and turned her body away.

"The only thing I see is a great, big cauliflower," Charity said.

"You have to loosen up your mind and pretend there's magic in the clouds," Grace said.

"I don't see anything," June said. "Just clouds."

"No men yelling?" Rose said and felt ugly.

June bit her lip. She said nothing.

"Well, I see a baby," Rose said, changing her focus to uncluttered and kinder thoughts. "He's sucking his thumb."

"There's an elephant with a big, swinging trunk," Grace said. "Up there, Charity. You'll see it if you just look for it."

"Where?" Charity asked.

"There." Grace pointed. "How can you miss it?"

"Well, I don't see an elephant," Charity said. "Just a big blob with a thingy hanging down."

"A thingy?"

"Yeah," Charity said. "A penis. That's what it looks like."

Grace giggled.

Rose smiled. "Maybe it does at that. What do you think, June?"

"I think the thingy is disappearing," June said. She laughed.

They watched the strip of vapor dissipate, scattering wisps of vanishing cotton.

"Hey, Rose," Grace said, tilting her head and lifting her eyebrows. "Do you remember what the *real* thingy looks like?"

"I know it's prettier than a cloud," Rose said.

"Not always," June said.

"When you close your hand on it, it doesn't melt to nothing or pass through your fingers," Grace said, grinning.

"Indeed not," Charity said.

No one spoke for several minutes.

"It's a smart thing we did," Charity said, lighting a cigarette. "Deciding to share Anson."

"I thought I remembered the feel of a man's skin, rough and hard, with its heavy smell, pushing sturdy against my own, protecting me," Rose said. "But I didn't. Anson's arm against mine is stronger than memory." She touched a finger to her neck and pressed gently. "Yes, we did a good thing bringing Anson close to our lives."

"We did," Grace said. "But I wish there were more of him. Then we could each have our own."

"There aren't," Charity said, stretching her legs in front of her. "Too many women. Not enough men. They die too young. We're stronger. So we share. I don't mind. I'm willing as long as I get my time."

"Oh, I'm willing too," Grace said. She lifted sand, let it sift through her fingers, drop on her legs, and slip over their slopes and dips in glistening, beige rivers. "But I truly want my share. I don't want any of you taking something that belongs to me, and if one of you is seeing him more than we agreed, that means he's got more time for us than we scheduled. And if that's so, I want my piece of that time."

"It's hard to be exact," Rose said.

"So, it's hard," Charity said. "We agreed."

"Are you thinking someone's cheating?" June asked.

"Why should you care?" Grace said, pulling petals from the flowers in her lap, crushing them in her fingers, and releasing their sweet, musky scent. "We pushed you right into your share of Anson. You got more than you ever bargained for."

Mid-May

Maybe not, Rose thought. *If she'd waited and played her cards right, used her own rules, not ours, she might have won the whole prize. Her body could have put a whole lot of want into an old man if she had gone after him full force. Not anymore, though. It's too late. I think.*

"I know," June said softly, speaking to all of them. "And I'm grateful. But you're always so worried someone's going to step across the line and get a little more than the rest of you. I can't understand why you're so hung up on that. It seems to me that every one of you should be pretty happy with her own piece of Anson. Enjoy what you've got. Don't be looking for trouble. You'll just end up hurting each other."

"Fair is fair," Charity said. She pulled hard on her cigarette. "We made the rules together, and we agreed they were the same for everybody. If they're going awry, we have to fix the pact." She picked a piece of tobacco off her tongue and looked at Rose. "Don't we?"

"How would we fix it?" Rose asked, looking straight at the water. Her stomach quivered. She was walking a tightrope. Anson held one end. Her friends, old and dear, held the other. She needed them both. And nothing she did should be hurting them. She was cheating. It was hard to hide that from herself. But she wasn't taking anything from them. They still had their time. And that hurt *her*, the wonder and worry of what they were doing in the hours they were alone with the man she slept with, the man to whom she had sacrificed her deathbed promise to Thomas. Didn't that make it even? Wasn't her cheating offset by her pain?

"Kill the agreement," Grace said, getting up and stretching.

155

May Snow

Her skirt fell, wrinkled, to her knees. She twirled and swung it out.

"Sit down, Grace," Charity said. "Twist your back all out of shape later if you want to. Not now."

Grace grinned and wrinkled her nose, swung her rear at her sister, but she sat down.

"Ending the pact won't work," Charity said, scowling at Grace. Then she turned, directing her gaze toward Rose. "If we did that, the cheater would win."

"Wrong," Grace said. She shoveled her foot into the sand, lifted her leg, and the sand spilled over it. "I'd win. And I'm not a cheater. Without the stupid rules, I could see him every day, all the time. Morning, noon, and night delight." She brushed the sand off her leg. "Hey, not a bad idea. Let's do it. Let's just end this silly agreement right now."

"We would have to agree that nobody sees Anson anymore," Charity said. "That's the only fair way. But that wouldn't happen, because the cheater would have already dug her way into Anson's favor, and if she wouldn't honor one agreement, why should she honor another?"

"So we can't fix it," Rose said. "We leave it alone and keep going."

"We could all move away," Grace said, squirming in her chair. "My skirt's getting me itchy."

Charity glared at her.

"Or we could all die," Grace continued. "We could do it now. All join hands and walk into the lake. Just keep going until our heads are under water and the ground drops beneath us."

"Grace!"

"Or Anson could move," Grace continued. "Only he never

would. So we could all push him into the water, hold him down until there was no living, breathing Anson left to share anymore. Sounds good to me. We'd all be equal then."

"Why are you all doing this?" June sat with her knees drawn close to her chest, her arms hugging them tight. Her face was pale.

"She's right," Rose said. "We need to stop this."

"Does it bother you, Rose?" Charity asked. "Why would it — are you cheating, Rose?"

Rose blushed, said nothing.

"I can tell," Charity said.

Still Rose stayed silent. Her stomach was churning. Her head, full of feelings, searched for words.

"Say something."

She was guilty. She was sad. She was angry. She was justified. She was hurt. She looked square at Charity. "You should trust me."

"Say you're not cheating."

"I shouldn't have to." *I can't. She's right. I am seeing him too often. But she's my friend. She shouldn't be attacking me.*

"You can't because you're guilty," Charity said. "Well, you can be sure of this. We'll be watching you, and if you are cheating, if you ruin this for us, *you'll be sorry.*"

The sun was still hot, but the day had lost its warmth.

13
Late-May

Rose sat on her porch in the dark. She was waiting for Nicholas to come out and play. It was a sweet night, smelling of fresh-cut grass and lilacs. She rocked gently, enjoying the calm.

When Nicholas came out, she called out to him. She asked him if he liked the cookies.

He stopped and looked in her direction. Cupping his hands around his mouth, he shouted, "My mom says you eat dogs."

He ran out of sight behind his house. She didn't see him again until very late when he slunk around the corner, crept up the steps, and went into his house. He didn't look toward her house, and he didn't go near the garbage cans.

❄   ❄   ❄

When Rose, scrubbing the woodwork around her bedroom window, happened to glance through the glass, she saw Grace wending her way down Anson's driveway. Balloons were tied to her arms, her belt, her purse, and the silk scarf around her neck. Her step was light, and as she moved quickly from side to side, the bright rubber spheres bounced against her body and flapped in the air.

While Rose watched, Anson came out of his door. He looked at Grace and burst out laughing. She grabbed his arm and, smiling and chattering, pulled him down to the grass where she opened her purse and yanked out a big bottle of liquid soap and two magic wands. She shoved one into his hand, dipped the other into the soap and waved her arm wide. Bubbles fanned from the wand in a cascading rainbow of transparent circles. They lifted and soared, and Grace, body big and old, chased after them on legs that still ran young. Anson clapped his work-worn hands and urged her on. She danced back near him and reached for a bubble drifting over his head. He raised his hand and pinched a balloon fluttering on her arm and against her breast. Rose saw the sudden explosion and flinched. Their joy was not easy to watch. It hurt her. She felt selfish and sinful and was shamed by it.

She had to get away. She left her cleaning as it was, moved quickly down the stairs and out the house, and, careful not to look at Anson's house, got into her car and drove.

She didn't feel the pain in her legs until she was out of town driving on country roads. She had pushed them too hard, too fast, and now they hurt. But not more than the pain in her heart.

She drove down roads with new plantings of tomatoes and corn on either side, past acres of deep-hued grass, and great barren fields — rich brown, heavy with strong and musky scent, broken in rows, open and ready for seed. She

went through a shaded tunnel of locust trees, sunlight flashing through tender new leaves, blossoms dropping like snow.

She stopped by a pasture and watched a grazing herd of
cows for a long time. She sighed and longed for legs that
could ford a ditch, scale a fence, and run her across bristly
grass and lumpy soil, taking her close enough to those magnificent beasts to brush their fine, silky hair; stroke their juicy,
wet muzzles; lay her head down on their thick, sturdy necks;
and let their calm patience soak into her center.

She drove slowly past the house where she and Thomas
had lived. Their farm home. The house had new siding, and
their straight, prim porch rails had been replaced with fancy
spindles. New shrubs spread along the foundation, and young
maples were scattered around the yard, but the forsythia,
blooming full and yellow, a flowering line where grass met
field, was her own, planted when Margaret was a baby. And
the irises circling the mail post were hers too. She looked with
longing and sadness, wanting a time long ago when everything she did had purpose, kept her family whole and happy.

She passed the pasture, now a mass of tangled brush and
seedling trees, and saw Thomas running along the creek,
chasing cows to the barn to be grained and milked. She passed
the hay fields, now rowed with grapes, and saw Thomas mow-
ing the ripe grass, baling it when it was dry and hefting those
bales as the sweat streamed down his sun-cooked face and
shining, straining, golden muscles. She saw herself toting him
a glistening wet bottle of cold beer and laughing while he
stood on the sharp hay stubble and took it all without pause.

She turned down a dirt lane, a path well known, that
would take her to an old and stunted orchard. Sour little ap-

ples, misshapen and hard, still grew there. The shape of the trees was menacing. Gnarled limbs pointed outward like arthritic fingers eager to poke the intruder's secrets and soul. Stunted twigs grew in twisted knobs that jutted from their joints. The trees were like trolls, threatening terrible things to the trustless who trampled their territory. But Rose had faith in the sweet, tiny blossoms and the ancient, sinewy trees. She had waited every year for the tangy, crisp fruit they bore in the fall. She was never disappointed.

Slowly driving along the lane, watching what she passed, Rose saw Dwight sitting at the bottom of one of the apple trees. Back firm against thick, jagged bark and knees bent with feet planted wide, Dwight plucked buttercup petals off a long, branching stem while he gazed straight ahead.

Rose stopped the car and got out. She lifted her hand to Dwight. He didn't wave back. She walked out to him and saw his face was lined with tears.

"Why, Dwight, dear boy." She reached and touched his cheek.

He shook his head, pushing her hand away. "Not a boy, Rose," he said. "I'm not a boy."

"I know," she murmured, and ignoring the pain, dropped to her knees, rolled onto her bottom, and sat with him under the tree. She took his hand and pulled it to her lap, stroking it.

"Not a boy, but a man," she said. "A man in trouble. You know, Dwight, I'm old, and I've known hard times. Sometimes, I can draw from old hurts and understand another person's pain, and sometimes, I can help them." She patted his hand. "Why don't you give me a try?"

Dwight drew in air and let it out slowly through puffed lips. He pushed his head back against the weathered tree, squinted at the sky through scraggly warped limbs and leaves, and snuffed with a loud snort.

"There's nobody in this town who understands the real me," he said. Rose squeezed his hand. "Everybody thinks I'm this piece of debris left over from a broken-up family, picked up by a pitying uncle, and kept because he's a nice guy and doesn't know what else to do with a gawky, personality-poor, stupid-inheritance, me. So he's stuck with me. And he gives me a job in his hardware store and a place at his table and he talks kindly to me, but never about real stuff. What he tells me is that I stock the shelves good, keep the dust away. He never asks what I'm thinking, if I want more, do I dream, am I happy, does it bother me because people laugh at my red hair? I'm his dog. He pats and feeds me. I fetch and pad softly around his store and house. He's fond of me. But he's still the good master and I'm still the pet rescued from the pound. His shadow. For thirty plus years now." His chin sank to his chest. He shook his head slowly.

"Why don't you move on?" Rose asked gently. "Find a place of your own?"

"How do I do that? I don't have any money. Do you know how I ache to be out of Canadaway? Into a place where I've got some power and nobody laughs. I'm stuck in a hole, and it's like I belong there. If I scratch at the sides and try to dig out, somebody comes along and kicks dirt in my face, pushes me down. Not because they mean to, but because they don't see *me*. What they see is a blob that doesn't think or feel. Like I'm a nothing. And they're wrong. That's not me. I am something."

"Of course, you are." Not wanting to shame him, Rose kept her gaze straight ahead and focused on buttercups growing thick in the orchard.

May Snow

"When I met Louisa, I thought something special was happening. She listened to me. She laughed with me. She gave me a chance to crawl out of the hole. But she's not the same anymore." He moved his hand away from Rose and scratched it. "She stopped listening to me and only hears herself now. What she wants. What she feels. What she needs. She thinks she can get it all from me. Power. Control. Admiration. She's jerking me around. And people are laughing." He dug at the side of his neck. "You figure it out. Here's Anson with all you old ladies prancing around him, and all I've got is Louisa making a fool of me."

Rose shifted her buttocks on the damp, grassy soil. Her bottom had grown numb, and as she lifted one side, then the other, gripping pain exploded. She gasped, drew in her breath, counted, and it slowly loosened its hold. When the ache was gone and the prickles subsided, she stole a glance at Dwight, hoping he had not noticed her pain. She saw red, staining blotches spreading across his face. "Oh."

He looked at her. "What?" he asked.

"Your face." She didn't want to embarrass him, but she feared he might need more help than she could give him. "You've got red spots. All over."

"Oh," he said, scratching them. "It's strawberries. I stole some jelly for my toast. I shouldn't of. I'm allergic. Not bad though. They'll go. It's cashews that'll really get me. Make my lips puff and throat swell. Even just a little piece of that nut will do it. Kids used to sneak and stuff cashews in my peanut butter sandwiches in school to make me sick. They thought it was funny. I can't tell the difference in taste and they knew it." He grimaced. "See, I've always been somebody's joke."

Rose patted his knee. "You think about it too much. People don't have as much time to dwell on you as you imagine. They're busy with their own lives. Their touch on you is short and shallow. Keep your eye on those who love you."

"Not many of those," Dwight said. A tear slid from his eye. He hit it soundly, brushed it away. "Damn strawberries."

"I think Louisa loves you," Rose said.

"She has a damn poor way of showing it."

"Love might be new to her too. Maybe she has to learn to work with it, make it pleasurable."

"I've been sitting here a long time thinking. And I gotta let her go." Dwight yanked a buttercup out of the ground, roughly peeled petals from the stem. "I'm more than a bag of skin and guts to jerk around every which way. I gotta stand up to her. Gotta get rid of her, move on."

"Talk to her first," Rose said. "Tell her how you feel. Give her a chance."

"Maybe … maybe not."

❄   ❄   ❄

Rose stood in the dark by the garbage cans waiting for Nicholas to come out. When he did, she set a bag of cookies down by her feet.

"I don't eat dogs," she shouted. "I like dogs. I would never, never, *never* hurt a dog."

His shadow didn't move.

Leaving the cookies, Rose walked back to her house, went inside and closed the door behind her.

14
Early June

Several days later, in early June, Rose was crouched on a special rolling seat with tall handles for pulling herself up. Forrest had made it for her during a sympathetic time when her pain concerned him. She was planting impatiens against the back of the garage. Suddenly she heard a commotion behind her. Turning, she saw Dwight running down the driveway away from Anson's house. Louisa was at the top of the steps, bent forward, fists on her waist, spittle flying, shouting at his fleeing body.

"Don't you ever come back here. Not ever." She stamped her foot, grabbed her hair, and shook her head vehemently. Not able to contain herself, she circled the stoop with short, quick steps. Stopping, she picked up a pot of young, straggly geraniums, lifted it over her head, and brought it crashing down on the wooden floor. Then sagging against the house, she buried her face in her hands and sobbed.

May Snow

Rose watched it all — trowel in one hand and flowers, dripping dirt, in the other.

Dropping her hands, Louisa turned to go back in the house. Before she went through the door, she stopped and scanned the driveway and yards. She saw Rose. She looked hard at her, bent over the railing, gathered saliva on her tongue, and hurled a mighty stream of spit from her mouth at Rose.

Rose watched the spittle fly, falling short of its target. *I don't think I should have told Dwight to bare his heart,* she thought.

Louisa shook her fist at Rose and retreated into Anson's house.

Sighing, Rose returned to planting flowers. She figured Thomas was up there shaking his finger at her. *Stay out of other people's business, Rose. Or pay the price.*

❄   ❄   ❄

"I think Louisa is mad at you," Anson said into the night air. His chair creaked as he slowly pushed it back and forth with one foot. The other swung free, leg crossed over his knee.

Arms press tight against her rigid body, Rose rocked steady and made no comment. *Obviously* Louisa was angry with her. She'd spit directly at her. That could not be construed as a friendly action.

"Dwight told her she was acting bossy and he'd had enough."

There was a long silence. Rose waited for the blame to fall on her.

"He said you told him to tell her that."

Rose stopped rocking. She gripped her hands together. "Not exactly."

Anson chuckled in the dark. "She sure was mad."

"She spit at me."

"No way she could have reached you."

"I wonder what she would have done if I'd spit back."

"Why didn't you?"

She heard the laughter in his voice. "I should have."

"Two spitting women. That's some picture."

Rose smiled. Just a little. Anson pulled happiness from her even in her anger.

"She'd win," Anson said.

"I don't think so."

"Her mouth is younger. Yours would dry out too fast."

Rose relaxed her body, rested her arms on her chair. "You're probably right."

"What a pretty night," Anson said, breathing its calm in deep.

Rose nodded and looked up at the stars.

They rocked in rhythm. Anson reached out and pulled her hand into his lap, moving his thumb gently over her palm.

"We could go upstairs," he said softly, leaning towards her.

She touched her forehead against his. That position was uncomfortable, hurt her back. She sighed and slid back into the familiar easing curves of her chair. "The energy in this old body is sadly lacking tonight."

"I know," he said. "I'm pretty tired myself."

"Sometimes it's nice just to let the thoughts lay sweet in your head."

He patted her hand. "No problem with my imagination."

May Snow

"The mind can be more agile than the flesh," Rose said, squeezing his hand. "Especially old flesh."

He pressed back, then tenderly placed her hand back in her own lap. They stood and embraced. He kissed her cheek and smiled. "Maybe tomorrow."

She smiled back and nodded. "Good night, dear Anson."

He struggled down the steps. She knew his body was stiff from sitting so long. He rarely complained. She heard him mutter, "That boy should be in bed," as darkness folded around him.

He sees Nicholas, Rose thought. She slipped back into her rocker. She was tired, and it was soothing to rest in the chair, melt into the quiet glide of silky night.

Nicholas slithered across the lawn, slid past her field of vision — a graceful shadow in the moonlight. He threw a ball onto the roof of his house, waiting impatiently, jumping, stretching, kicking his legs, then caught it as it rolled back down. He tossed it up again. His movements were fluid, flowing in and out of dark shapes, passing mysteriously through pools of light falling from windows and street lamp.

He ran off into blackness. She couldn't see him any more.

Suddenly out of the dark, she heard a shouting. "Thank you for the cookies."

She waited.

"I know you don't really eat dogs."

She closed her eyes and rocked.

❄   ❄   ❄

"I miss the children so much," Margaret said.

Early June

"I know," Rose said. She pushed the bowl of chicken salad, Margaret's favorite, loaded with apples and grapes and nuts, closer to her daughter. "Please eat a little, Sweetie, you've grown so thin."

Margaret shook her head and held up her hands, palms out. "I thought they'd always be near me."

"I know." Rose put a spoonful of salad on Margaret's plate.

"You're so lucky to have me so close. You can see me whenever you want to." Margaret, hands folded now in her lap, looked at the chicken. "Why is it whenever I see you lately, it's over a plate of food?"

"We all need to eat. Even you. Especially you. Try it, dear heart. It's just how you like it."

"Nothing is how I like it any more."

Rose, appetite gone, put her own fork down.

"Emily's so far I never see her children, my grandbabies," said Margaret. "They should be filling my life. Like mine did yours. Beck's so wrapped up with grad school. And Robert's wife keeps him all to herself."

"I know," Rose said. "Life's so different now. So fast. So many things to do. There's no time to touch the ones you love except in thought, and that's hard when you need more. But they do love you, Margaret. Tell them Forrest is gone. Tell them you're hurting. Give them a chance to give what is in their hearts, all that love you helped put there. You'll all be better for it." She speared a chicken chunk with Margaret's fork and held it out to her.

"I can't tell the children," Margaret said, ignoring the fork. "I can't tell anyone. I shouldn't have told you. And there's more. But Mother, I can't tell you. Especially you. You can't know."

May Snow

"What can't you tell me?" Rose asked softly.

"I don't want to tell you."

"What, Sweetie? What don't you want to tell me?"

"The words just won't come out." Margaret raised her hand to the table, squeezing her napkin. "I can't make them come out."

Rose put the fork down. She covered Margaret's hands with her own. "You have something to tell me, Rose said quietly "and there is nothing you cannot say to me. Nothing you cannot share with me. Nothing I cannot help you bear."

"I failed." Tears rolled down Margaret's face. "I wasn't the perfect wife you taught me to be, wanted me to be. Forrest left me. And there's more. I'll tell you, but don't say anything, don't ask anything. She's pregnant. Forrest's whore is pregnant and he wants to marry her. He wants a divorce. He called me and told me and he sounded so happy and he didn't care when I cried... when I begged. I failed. I failed him and I failed you. And I don't want anyone to know."

"Oh Margaret."

"I'm sorry, Mother. I couldn't keep him. I'm sorry. Oh God, it hurts so much."

"Oh, Margaret, my baby." Rose ached for her child.

Margaret pulled her hands from her mother. "Don't give me sympathy. You don't understand. It's always been perfect for you. You were such a good wife, Dad never needed anyone else. Well, I tried and I failed. And I did the right things. Everything you taught me. Everything you did. But it didn't work for me like it did for you, and Forrest is gone. Forever."

"I love you, Margaret." She didn't think her daughter could hear more. Not now.

Early June

"I told you. You wanted to know, so I told you. But I don't ever want to talk about it again."

Rose went to her daughter and held her. Margaret cried in her arms.

"Never," Margaret wept. "Never!"

❄   ❄   ❄

Fingers entwined, Rose and Anson sat on a bench on the beach at The Point facing the water, watching the circus strewn out before them. Frisky children romped around bodies spread out for tanning, filling their sand pails, dumping them, and filling them again. Serious swimmers dipped and skimmed among the wave-jumpers and splashers. Timid wee ones ran in and out of the water's edge. Tall sails, crisp and white, danced majestically in the far water, and closer, motorboats pulled strong-legged skiers shearing the water and laughing children clinging to rubber rafts. Playful drivers bounced their boats on waves, smashing into the swelling water as it beat their boats with mighty, jarring thuds. Jet boats zipped and raced and crisscrossed the lake. The colors of swimsuits splashed bright, and laughter and shouts echoed loud.

It was Rose's scheduled day, so it didn't matter who saw her sitting alone with Anson. She smiled sadly and wiggled her bare toes in the sun-baked sand.

"Margaret isn't doing too well," she said. Cool lake breezes ruffled her hair, rippled the soft down on her face, kissed her bare neck and arms. She pulled her skirt up over her knees and rubbed the top of her thigh, taking pleasure from the sun's heat on her skin. "She thinks it's her fault Forrest left."

Anson dropped sand on Rose's thigh and grinned. "Shall I wipe it off?"

"I don't know what to do for her." She pushed his hand away.

Anson pulled a foot, which had been buried in a grainy cave, out of the sand and rested it on his knee. He draped his arms over the bench. "Watch the water, Rosie. It'll relax you."

"I don't need relaxing. I need advice."

Anson chuckled. "I love you, Rosie Celador. No way will I give you advice."

"If you really do, then you'll help me."

"If I really do, I'll keep my thoughts to myself."

"What's that supposed to mean?" She looked sharp at him, ready to release Margaret's hurt that was now hers against this man. Sweet as he was, he was still male. A Forrest. "Do you think different than me?" It welled up and out and she couldn't stop it. "Isn't this important? Can't you try to help me? I help you with Louisa. I always give you straight answers when you ask about her. Louisa's no picnic, you know. At least Margaret has some personality."

"Hey, hey, calm down." Anson dropped an arm around her shoulders and grazed her arm with barely touching, pacifying fingers. "I just don't want to say the wrong thing. Set you off. Who knows," he said, laughing, "I give the wrong advice, maybe you'll spit on me."

Forgetting aching joints, Rose jerked away from him. "This is not funny. And it's not trivial. This is my daughter and she's hurting."

"No, it isn't funny. I'm sorry, dear Rose." He slid his large hand to the back of her neck and rubbed his thumb in circles against her pliant skin. She tipped her face to the sun. His hand moved into soft curls as he gently cupped her head, moving his fingers, stroking her tension, easing its sting. The sun was hot on her throat. She closed her eyes.

"I'm not mad at you, Anson," she said.

"I know."

"I'm sorry I yelled."

"Sometimes it's hard for an old man to know the right words."

"You talk more than most," Rose said.

Anson smiled and dropped his arm back over her shoulders, moved closer to her. "Is that good?"

"That way I know what you want. I don't have to guess." She leaned into the strength and comfort of his body. Her eyes were still closed. "Although I am a pretty good guesser."

"And what is it you think I want?" Anson asked.

"Right now you want me to relax."

He pressed her close, a loving squeeze, then relaxed his grip. "And are you?"

"Right this moment every bad thing is pulled tight in a ball and tucked in a corner and I can't feel it."

"Good."

"But it's there. And balls bounce easy."

"I do love you, Rose. I'll keep it quiet."

She opened her eyes and watched a toddler — his fat, little legs running in short, quick steps along the sand as he clutched his diaper in a vain attempt to keep it around his waist.

"If nothing ever rolls in my head again," she said, "it's the same as dying."

May Snow

Anson shook his head.

"Do you like me better happy?" Rose asked, wondering if she was pushing too far.

"I like you any way."

"Margaret says I always did what Thomas wanted, that my life's goal was to pleasure him. Regardless. Sometimes she makes me feel like nothing."

"It's not wrong to please someone."

"Did Bernice please you?"

"Yes."

"Did you please her?"

"I tried."

"I don't think Thomas tried to please me. I think he thought if he was happy, I was happy."

"Were you?"

"I thought so." She strained to remember. "I'm not sure." She thought awhile. She felt drained, as if she could not move. "Do the others please you?"

"The others?"

"Charity and Grace and June?"

"In different ways."

"How?"

"June does whatever I want. Charity does what I want if she wants it too. And Grace? Grace just is."

"She amuses you."

"She does."

"Which way do you like best?"

Anson squirmed against her. "Rose, you're fine the way you are. Just be you. That's what I want. Just for you to be you."

"You like them too."

Early June

"They're good people... Rose, do you want me to stop seeing them?"

"I don't know. Maybe I do." She heard him sigh. "But I'm not sure."

Holding Rose firm in the circle of his arm, Anson gently patted the soft flesh above her elbow. "Margaret will be all right."

She turned into him and rested her head on his chest. She had touched his heart and forced words to flow, and she knew he could pull no more from the fragile corner of guarded feelings. He had given more than Thomas ever had. For that she should be grateful and let him move to safer ground.

"I pray for that," she said.

"Louisa sits and mopes." He took the move further.

Rose smiled and nestled closer. His arm tightened. *Safe words*, she thought. *Let them spill and move us to a more shallow place.*

"She says she might go home," Anson said with a confident voice. He moved his arm along her back, rotating his shoulder.

Rose heard his soft moan and eased away from him, straightened her back, held the pain until it faded, then slumped a little against the bench. Anson's arm dropped clumsily to his lap. She saw him wince and touched him briefly, a wordless thanks for ignoring his own discomfort to lighten hers.

"Says she hates Dwight, can't stand his guts," Anson said, lifting his arm and pumping it up and down. "Then two minutes later, she's crying in a corner missing him."

"Look." Rose poked Anson and pointed. "That's Nicholas over there with his mother."

Amy lay on her belly in the sand, no towel under her, while

May Snow

Nicholas poured sand over her legs and outstretched arms. She looked like she was sleeping, but just as Nicholas covered the last bare spot on her legs, her arms jerked up, her legs kicked, and sand flew from her limbs. Nicholas bolted, stumbling on the heavy, gritty floor. Amy jumped up, chased her giggling son, and hugged him fiercely when she caught him.

"What can I do?" Anson asked. "About Louisa."

"Bring Louisa down to the lake and tell her to relax," Rose said absently, watching Amy and Nicholas with hands joined run into the water. They jumped over the breaking waves, fell backward into the water, and kicked with frenzied glee.

"I thought you gave me straight answers."

Rose glanced at Anson's pouting face and burst out laughing. Pressing fingers tight against her lips to hold in further chortles, she shook her head helplessly.

"Now who's making light of serious stuff?" he asked.

"It's a lovers' spat, Anson," Rose said, breathing deep, biting her lower lip. "Not a break up of a deep, abiding relationship. She'll survive. Just let her be."

"I don't know. She was different with him. More like Karen." Anson flexed his fingers, spread them on his thighs. "It wasn't always pleasant, but she was showing a little initiative."

"She was leading Dwight around like a bull with a ring in his nose. And she had a mighty tight hold."

"She was pretty forceful. I'll admit that."

"She was humiliating him, and he didn't like it." Rose flexed her own fingers. It hurt. She laid them gently in her lap.

"What did you tell Dwight that made Louisa get so mad?"

"I told him to talk to her." Rose turned her hands palms up to feel the sun. "I guess she wasn't willing to listen."

Early June

"Usually it's the woman who does the talking."

Rose twisted toward him. "Doesn't have to be."

"No, I don't suppose... Bernice talked a lot. But she never forced me to cater to her every whim."

"Like Louisa did Dwight?"

"It wasn't right... it was disrespectful."

"Did Bernice cater to your every whim?"

"I hope not."

"Would you know?" Rose looked out across the water. "Margaret thinks I was the perfect wife. She used those same words... catered to his every whim. I don't know. Maybe I did."

"You were a good wife."

"Is that what a good wife is? Is that what you think a good wife is, Anson?"

"Margaret will be all right, Rosie." He took her hand.

Maybe, Rose thought. *Maybe she'll be all right. Or maybe she'll be like me.*

❄   ❄   ❄

Rose sat on her porch, slowly rocking. Her eyes were on the baseball boys gathering their gear in the field across the street, watching them as they hurried to beat the dropping dark and the scolding words of worried moms. She marveled with admiring envy at their painless, endless motion. Not one stood still. They hopped, skipped, and feigned miraculous, imaginary plays. They punched and poked and clasped each other, ran uncharted paths, and patted butts like the big league players. And all with noise. Their young vocal cords stretched to full volume. Their feet stomped the ground and moved the soil. Their hands thumped a partner's back and slammed against another's hand with the cracking sound of brotherhood.

They were gone in a rush. There. Then gone. And the quiet they left was so big.

Margaret filled her head again. She had tried three times to call her. There had been no answer.

Rose closed her eyes and rocked steadily, counting the whoosh of rocker rolling on wood. She thought only of the numbers and the same, same rocking sound. Nothing else. Until Margaret was gone. She drew a deep, thankful breath, but she couldn't keep the void from filling. Charity came into that hole. She was sharp in her mind, as clear as she'd seen her, just awhile ago, walking up Anson's driveway and staring at Rose's house all the way until she disappeared through his door. Her face was hard and ugly. It looked like hate. Her dear, dear friend. And now Charity was in Anson's house. Laughing with him. Glad Rose wasn't there with them. That couldn't be. Charity had to be sad too, sad that their friendship was crumbling.

She pressed her thumb and forefinger hard against the bone beneath her eyes until the pain she felt was on the outside of her head and easier to bear.

The sky was full of stars. She thought they would make a beautiful chorus if they could sing. She wondered if Thomas could be a star, if he was up there straining to make her know his twinkle, guiding her to his sparkle and away from Anson's.

A whisper of fur brushed through her legs and was gone. Smiling, she bent and peered at the dark porch floor. She sensed rather than saw the sleek animal body that swept across the veranda, leapt through the railing, and landed with a soft thud on the grass.

"Good hunting," she murmured, settling back, rocking.

She saw that Nicholas had quietly sat himself on her top step while she was watching the cat. She gently rubbed the hollow at the base of her throat and waited.

"My mom doesn't know I play in the dark," Nicholas said.

"I know," Rose said.

They were silent awhile, absorbing each other.

"Aren't you ever afraid in the dark?"

Rose paused her rocking a moment, then started again. Slowly, steadily. "Sometimes... are you?"

"Sometimes... there are worse things."

Rose let the words sit a minute. She didn't want to lose him. He was so little. She didn't know how ready he was, what he was looking for. Comfort? Advice? A friend?

"I guess worse would be walking down the road with the last bunch of bananas in the world," she said, "and an ape suddenly appears."

"I mean real stuff," he said, turning and looking at her.

"Like being alone?"

"Yeah, that," he said softly. "Hurting."

She bit her lip. "A sad hurt, Nicholas?"

"No. Like body pain. You know, when it *hurts.*"

"You mean when you fall or have an earache. Or someone hits you."

He twisted his body away from her. "Yeah. Real stuff. Like that. Stuff that *could* be." She heard his feet tapping. "I didn't say it *does* happen."

She waited. She didn't dare touch him.

May Snow

"My mom doesn't let me play with the other kids after school."

Rose waited for more.

"But that's okay."

"It must be lonely."

"Sometimes I take walks at night down by the lake."

"Oh, Nicholas, that could be dangerous."

"I don't go alone... Louisa goes with me."

He jumped off the step and ran across the yard. "Don't tell my mother."

❄   ❄   ❄

By the time Charity, arms filled with dewy, pink peonies, walked into the church basement, Rose had the coffee made and was spreading pastries on a platter.

"I'm not late," Charity said, pulling cut glass vases out of the cupboard. "The coffee would have been perking by Bible study time without your help. And these flowers would have been sitting up on the altar long before Pastor Russell opened his good Book and said his first prayer. You needn't have worried, Rose. *I* always do what I say I'm going to do."

"I know," Rose said, and she did. Charity was a woman of her word. Stubborn, inflexible, and honest. "I just thought I'd help. Yesterday in the park, Grace didn't look so good. She said she didn't think she'd be in church today, so I figured you could use an extra hand getting all this stuff together."

"I could have called someone from the youth group if I needed help."

"It wouldn't be like you to ask for help." Rose moved all the pink-centered cookies together. "Grace looked very tired."

"I'm taking these up to the sanctuary," Charity said, lifting the flowers she had jammed into the vases. She didn't mention Grace. "If you want to be useful, push the chairs in a circle. And put the Bibles out."

"Those vases are heavy and awkward." Rose put the plate of pastries down and reached out to Charity. "Let me take one."

Charity closed her eyes and sighed. "Your legs hurt. No call to go up more steps than you have to. Now hurry with the chairs as best you can. I'm late. And it needs to be done quick before everybody comes barreling in."

"It probably wouldn't hurt if everyone picked up his own chair and put it down where it belonged and then walked over to the shelf and picked up a Bible and a cookie and a cup of coffee using his own feet and hands."

Charity smiled. "That's true. But I don't want any tongues wagging about me and my failings, so I'll just run these up and you push the chairs, and I'll stay the lady who gets everything done."

Rose watched Charity, her arms taut, muscles firm, vases safe, walk toward the door.

"Charity."

Charity turned, eyebrows lifted.

"What would you do if Anson chose one of us and pushed away the rest?"

"You mean if he chose you?"

"If he chose *one* of us."

Charity shifted the flower-filled vases in her arms. "I would be the worst enemy you ever had, Rose."

May Snow

❄   ❄   ❄

Rose hung up her robe, slipped quietly out of the chatter-
filled choir room, and eased through the empty sanctuary to
the vestibule where Deacon Eddy, straightening pamphlets
on an ornate table donated by Charity, lifted a hand in greeting. She waved and stepped out the open church doors into
the sun to the sweet peal of the tower chimes. Most of the
congregation were done with their weekly touching of each
other's lives and had gone on to Sunday dinners, drives,
naps, golf, lazy freedom. A few still lingered in small groups,
not quite ready to separate, talking low, laughing, willing to
include her in church-inspired fellowship.

She paused at the bottom of the steps. Anson was at the
corner of the churchyard talking with George and Anna
Strang. They stood in the shade of a massive controversial
oak. The old tree had spread thick, roped roots under the bordering driveway, powerfully pushing at its cement, cracking
it, tarnishing the image of the stately, immaculate brick house
of worship. There were parishioners who wanted it chopped
down. Charity and Grace and Rose stood together in firm op-
position. The tree was old and alive and full of history — a
point of agreement for the three old ladies struggling to keep
love. A bond.

Rose sighed. Anson's back was to her, but Anna had
caught her eye and waved. Rose waved back.

"Handsome, isn't he?" Charity said, stepping down behind
her. "Even from the rear. That straight back line. No give
there. Pure elegance. Put gloves on his hands and no one
would guess he was a farmer."

Early June

"His hands are beautiful." *They touch strong,* she thought. *There's a history of support and protection in each crack and callus.*

"You're a romantic. They're work worn and bulge with veins. Same as his legs, and I think we should go over and say hello, don't you?"

"Is it in the rules?"

Charity turned to face Rose. "This is not a child's game, Rose. The stakes are high for all of us. You can be sarcastic or you can be nice. I don't cheat. I play by the law of the rules. Cheaters lose. That will never be me."

"Are you the definer of cheating?"

"The rules are simple. You play by them or you don't. If you don't, blame yourself for the chaos you create."

"He sees us," Rose said. "Since it's allowed, I'm going to speak to him."

"I'll go with you."

Rose shrugged and pulled her arm away from Charity. "Whatever you want."

"A bit touchy, Rose?"

"I'm just tired of your constant insinuations."

"Just tell me direct they're not true." Charity touched Rose gently on the arm. "Do you honestly think it pleases me to think ill of you?"

Rose bit her lip and patted the hand on her arm. Then she lifted her face, looked forward, and smiled.

They didn't have to go to the tree. Anson came and stood before them. "Ladies."

"Anson," Charity replied. She tilted her head and grinned. "Hot, isn't it?"

Anson looked amused. "Good weather to sweeten the hay."

May Snow

Rose stood awkwardly, hoping Charity would not shame her, accuse her in front of Anson and the others.

"What do you think, Rose" Charity asked, lifting her eyebrows. "Isn't it hot?"

"I like it," Rose said, thinking she would not let Charity best her. Shame be damned. She'd done nothing wrong. She'd taken nothing not given freely. She'd caused no harm. "It cooks energy into my body."

"Oh, a feisty sausage you are," Charity said, laughing. She winked at Anson. "Careful, she'll clog your arteries."

"I'd say she's more like a sweet sugar cookie," Anson said.

Charity frowned. Rose, anger deflating, vigor dropping fast from her body, wanted only to go home.

"I'm driving up to Niagara Falls with George and Anna," Anson said. "Gonna have a picnic. Plenty of room for both of you. You're welcome to come."

A robust guffaw spewed out of Charity and she slapped her chest. "An Anson sandwich. You in the middle and Rosie and me, one on each side."

"And a free dinner to boot," Anson said. "Food seems to be heavy on your mind."

"No," Charity said. "Thank you for asking, but Grace is home feeling poorly and needs me." She pinched Rose's arm where Anson could not see. "How about you, Rose? Are you accepting?"

Looking at neither of them, Rose shook her head. She rubbed the spot Charity had pinched. The pain from it was behind her eyes, trying to close them and fill them with water. Charity was taunting her. And so was Anson. Pushing to spill her guilt before she was ready. She would not do it.

"I have to go," she said, backing away from them.

"Can I drive you?" Anson asked.

"Go with him, Rose," Charity said, challenge in her eyes. "I don't mind. It's only a ride to your house. Of course, I can't speak for Grace and June. They might not approve a bend in the rules."

"That's enough, Charity," Anson said.

"Enough of what, Anson?" Charity's lips pressed tight, and a deep, white line sank on either side of her mouth. She stood straight and still.

"You've been friends for such a long time," Anson said, reaching and touching her cheek.

She didn't move while he touched her.

"I'm not going with him, Charity." Rose could bear no more. "I'm walking home. In the warm sun. All by myself."

Charity didn't look at her. "I'll see you tomorrow," Charity said to Anson. "I'll bring dinner."

When she got to her house, Rose fixed a bowl of cereal and ate at the kitchen table. By the time it was half gone, it felt like food had filled her body to the top of her heart and another bite would drown her.

She went upstairs to lie on the bed she had shared with Thomas.

Before she put her body down to rest, she looked out the window toward Anson's house. Louisa and Dwight were tangled on a blanket on the yard, whispering close, biting and nipping, tickling and laughing, poking each other. They had on skimpy bathing suits. Rose saw Dwight cup a breast. Louisa threw back her head and laughed. Rose climbed up on her bed and cried.

May Snow

❊   ❊   ❊

It had rained so hard the grass was spongy and the dirt slick. Rose stepped carefully, seeking hard and firm spots so her feet wouldn't slide and upset her. Anson was not there to hold her arm and walk her back from his house to hers, to keep her upright and balanced. Just as they were leaving his house, his phone rang. It was Karen. Rose, understanding his need to announce the remarkable reconciliation of Louisa and Dwight, waved good-bye and started the treacherous trek by herself.

Walking through the yards, she pretended she was in a rain forest and must keep an eye out for low-swaying snakes and jutting roots and parrot eggs. She'd never seen a parrot egg. She wondered if the shells were washed with many bright colors. As her feet sank in soggy soil, she smiled and hoped exotic bugs were not buried in the mud that squished through her toes. Even though she kept her eyes centered on the ground, prudently fearing the painful twist of a stiff ankle, she saw the rain-sweetened leaves and flowers and air and soil with her ears and nose. It was a delightful journey, and she was a trifle regretful when her foot connected with the tar of her blacktop driveway and the jungle was gone.

Sometimes it was hard for Rose to let fantasy go. She stood a moment, eyes down, letting imagination fade and reality emerge.

When she was ready, in sync with orchids turned to impatiens and parrots to robins, she lifted her eyes to the world she lived in. And at the end of her driveway, facing her, staring at her, were her two best friends and June.

Early June

She lifted her fingers to her mouth, pressed them tight against her teeth to stop their trembling.

"Charity," she whispered. "Grace." She reached out an arm, fingers spread to gather and hold them.

They stood without movement.

She took a step forward.

They turned and walked away.

Rose put her hand to her mouth and stifled a cry. It wasn't her day to see Anson.

She ate no supper that night. Her soup sat cold in a bowl in front of her. Every so often she dipped her spoon and stirred it, lifting a bit to her lips, but before her mouth could open, the spoon was gone, dropped back to the bowl, her fist still tight around it.

Finally she took the bowl to the sink and set it, full, onto the porcelain. She looked out the kitchen window over the sink across the yards to Anson's house. She saw his lights go on. Dark was settling in.

Still she could feel nothing but a deep, draining weariness. Absently rubbing her throat, she dragged her feet across the linoleum, knowing the way without light, seeking the plush comfort of her couch and the warmth of her thick, knit afghan smelling sweet of soap and fabric softener and clean air and just a hint of kittens.

She huddled in the corner of the couch, pushing back thought. She was unable, unwilling to feel, waiting for her body's fatigue to spread and weight her eyes, close them, and chase away consciousness.

Sleep didn't come. She sat a very long time, barely awake, wanting to drop over the edge, but every time she tottered close to the chasm that would sink her to an empty dark void, remembrance jolted through her — brief, sharp, painful. Three friends. Charity, Grace, and June — standing in her driveway, staring at her betrayal. Each time she saw them, clear and shocked and hurt, she blew out her breath as if punched in the stomach and willed emptiness to fill her again.

Finally she pushed away the afghan, crawled out of the cushions, stumbled to the stairway, grasped the rail, and heaved herself up the steps on slow and heavy legs.

Fully clothed, she fell on her bed. Her shoes were lead weights dragging her down. Sleep came. Guilt and sadness faded in its wake.

In the middle of the night, she woke, sudden and complete. The house was still. She listened carefully. Her heart beat fast. Her head was clear. She couldn't remember a dream or a noise. But something had caused her to come awake fast. She lay frozen, fists against her chest, waiting to know what it was.

Rushing force hit hard and swift against the side of her house with a terrible thud. Bits of stone and gravel rained down on the windows.

She jumped from her bed. Pain clutched her body, protesting the rapid, violent motion, but it couldn't stop her. She moved quickly against it into the windowless hall, crouched close to the wall, and covered her ears.

The pounding continued. Dreadful thumps and thuds that made her shake. She couldn't look to see where they came from, and her body would not slide from the spot where it cowered to get to the stairs, to her phone, to help.

She was guilty. The ladies knew. And God was punishing her.

Early June

When it was quiet, she slipped to the floor and slept.

In the morning, when she was able to haul herself out and into the bright sunlight, she stepped onto her front porch and into a puddle of thick soil, heavy with water. Mud. Piled in heaps all over the floor. She gasped, reached for her throat, and looked up. Her house was covered with circles of brown sod, like child-drawn suns, streaking rays of stone and dirt.

She sat in a rocker and covered her head with her arms and cried for a long time.

❄   ❄   ❄

Rose hired Manley Warner to clean her house and porch. She caught him smiling when he thought she wasn't looking, but he was a nice boy and made no comment, asked no questions. He took her money and thanked her. She hoped he would not say too much to others.

Rose saw Grace and Charity at the convenience store. They looked at her and through her, didn't smile when she did, didn't answer her lifted arm with a wave, moved slowly and silently to another aisle.

June kept her eyes lowered and her mouth closed firm when she served Rose a cherry cola at Hunter's.

Rose found her choir robe scrunched in a corner, too wrinkled to wear. She sat in a pew and watched while the others sang, then carried the robe home to press.

She called them. They hung up when they heard her voice.

She complained to Anson in soft and weary voice.

"Of course they are angry at you," Anson said. "They

May Snow

know now what they only suspected before. Just let it be, let it wither."

Rose sighed, propped her elbows on Anson's table and dropped her chin into her hands. "They're still coming to see you." She rubbed her cheeks. "Regularly. I watch them from my window. They never look my way."

"Yep," Anson said. "They keep coming."

"Why aren't they mad at you?"

He shrugged, put an ice cube in his mouth, sucked on it awhile, and dropped it in a napkin. "Cold," he said, rubbing his teeth with his tongue. "I think they are mad at me. They asked for more time." He squeezed lemon into his tea, ran the fruit over his tongue, puckered his lips.

"And?" Rose said. She wanted to grab the lemon, toss it away.

"I refused."

"One at a time?"

"Nope." He bit lemon pulp and chewed. Rose's mouth filled with saliva. "All together last night. Defensive as hell. Tight-lipped and stiff as a bull's horn. Outraged at my complete disregard for an honorable agreement."

"They're angry," Rose said. "At you too."

"I don't think they'll be back."

"Then it's over. No more sharing." Rose sat back in her chair.

"Could be." Anson got up, stumbled over Gossip, and hit his leg against the chair.

"Careful," Rose said, rising quickly. "Watch that vein. Don't hit it. You'll burst it."

"You worry too much," Anson said and poured himself another glass of tea.

Early June

❄ ❄ ❄

That same night Anson came to her house. He held her in the hallway, then took her upstairs to bed.

And after they were done, they stayed together into the night, bodies close and touching.

Rose thought he slept, so she let herself drift to the pleasant edge of slumber.

"Rosie, will you marry me?"

She opened her eyes. The room was dark. She could see only black.

His heart beat steady under her cheek. Her hand rested on his bare stomach. She spread her fingers to show that she'd heard.

"I love you, dear Rose," Anson said.

She rolled away from him and sat on the edge of the bed.

He lay still behind her.

Then she slid off the bed and walked to the window.

The sky was lit with moon and stars.

She looked toward Anson's house and wondered where they'd live.

She looked toward the sky and wondered how far it was to heaven.

"Rosie?"

One star shone brighter than the rest.

"I don't know," she whispered.

15

June

Monday

On Monday morning, Rose, still in her full-skirted granny nightie, opened the front door to let the cats out. She stepped onto the smooth, clean porch; stretched her arms to embrace the sweet morning; and drank deep of the fresh, flower-scented air. The wood was warm under her bare feet and the sun was hot on her face.

"Ah," Rose sighed. "A good day."

Across the street the boys were starting to gather for play. She glanced at Nicholas's house, wishing some magic power would whisk him out his door, whirl him to the center of the forming ball game where the guys would slap him on the back, pull his cap down over his eyes, and toss him a bat. But no warlocks lurked about, conjuring spells or mystic happenings. Nicholas's door stayed shut, and he moved in secret somewhere hidden behind it.

Rose sighed and shook the thought away. This day would be lived glorious. No bad reflections, worries, or memories.

May Snow

She turned to go inside and ready herself to enjoy it. Who knew how many days were left? This one she was going to make good.

A paper cone hung on the doorknob. She had not seen it coming out. She squinted as light reflected on the gold foil trim. It was a fancy cone. Shiny paper with glittering swirls of silver and gold and hanging tassels. And spilling from the opening were dead pansies, velvet purple turned black, withered and wrinkled and ruined.

Rose's hand flew to her throat. As she stood and stared, a solid ball grew and swelled against the inside softness of her belly and spread and stretched and filled her with a stiffness that made her hard and strong and angry.

Skirt billowing around her, she swung the door open. It hit the side of the house with a mighty bang, and she didn't care that it probably dented the siding.

She marched to the phone. She knew whom to call. It was old ladies who remembered that May baskets used to be love gifts from suitors, and that the one consistent, romantic treasure from Thomas was a spectacular, flower-stuffed paper cone hanging on her doorknob every May Day. Well, this wasn't May, but the message was clear. And she was tired of it.

"Don't hang up," she said as Charity answered her phone. "This has gone far enough. We need to talk."

"You're right."

"The four of us."

"Yes."

"Today."

"No," Charity said. "June is working."

"You name a time."

196

"Thursday. June's day off. We'll come to your house."
"That's fine."
"I'll call the others," Charity said.
"Thank you."
"No," Charity said. "Don't thank me."

16
June

Tuesday

On Tuesday morning when the sun shone orange in the eastern sky and enough dark lingered to paint clean, black strokes on the edges of trees and houses and telephone poles, making them stand sharp and clear against the horizon, Rose crept out of her house. She slipped into her car and drove slowly, carefully up Washington Avenue, turned left on Main, right on Clover Lane, and on to Grimmers Pond. There she stopped and watched the sun finally push away the last of night.

She stepped out onto the dew-damp grass and walked to the edge of the water. The smells of earth — the dirt and flowers, crushed pine, wet wood, mint, animals out of sight but their ripe and rank scent faint and barely tainting the air — touched her nose with welcome pleasure. She looked across the water and up to the sky. She was at a place that felt like home, and the feeling was so intense, so joyous that she could not stop the tears.

May Snow

She closed her eyes and let the years drop away, let them go until she was at a place of light and emptiness. Then she smiled and called a young Thomas to her. Naked in the water, he swam and splashed and teased, until she was in there with him, young and naked as he. And he reached and touched her for the first time. And she shivered with the splendor of it. Quietly, for a long time, she stood by the water feeling those young lovers, seeing them, happy and loving, safe in her head, living again.

And then they were gone.

Hugging herself, she opened her eyes and looked to the clouds.

"Thomas, are you there?" she whispered. "You were my rock, sweet husband. You set my sails in the right direction. You held my hand when the world trembled around me. Oh, Thomas, our souls are entwined." Tears flowed and they were sad. "But, dear heart, I am lonely and I can bear it no longer."

She searched the sky for a sign that he heard. The sun was hot on her face and the wind rustled the leaves around her. The water lapped the bank gently and birds sang. The clouds were big and puffy and moved and broke and joined again above her. It was all as it should be on a common day.

There was no answer from Thomas.

Impatiently, she wiped tears from her face. More came and she shook her head.

"I'm sorry," she shouted and then sighed, shoulders drooping, brief anger gone.

"Good-bye, Thomas," she said softly. "I have to go for awhile."

June, Tuesday

She lifted her hand and waved. "See you later, dear heart. Wait for me. I love you." She turned, walked back to her car, and drove home.

When she got there, she walked straight across the backyards to Anson's house. Before she knocked, she glanced one last time to the sky, without words with a straining sensation directed to God, willed Him to put her together with Thomas. Then she closed her eyes and let herself empty of that wish, put it away, so she could say the right words to Anson, have room to pull him inside her and be happy.

He opened the door as soon as she knocked. She saw pleasure in his face, and as she reached and touched his cheek, she saw concern spread over it.

"Rosie, dear Rosie, are you all right?"

His gentle voice closed around her fragile emotions. She bit her lip and forced a smile. "I'm fine," she whispered.

He took her hands in his and rubbed his thumb over her palm.

Lifting her chin, gazing steady into his eyes, Rose spoke. "I went to Grimmers Pond. I said good-bye to Thomas." Her lower lip trembled and she took a deep breath. "It won't be for always, Anson. When I die, I'll be with him."

Anson gathered her in his arms. "I know," he said. "I'll be with Bernice."

They stood quietly wrapped together, giving and getting comfort.

"Come in now," Anson whispered in her hair. "We need to talk."

She shook her head against his chest. "Not yet." She wanted time to sort and settle and let the pieces fall where they belonged. She wanted to sit in her rocker, quiet and alone, and let her heart ready itself for Anson. Thomas lingered too strong in her center. She needed a few gentle hours to shrink his hold and tuck him in a waiting place.

"Later?" Anson said, rubbing her back.

She nodded, still pressed tight to his body.

"For lunch?"

She shook her head. She didn't think she could eat. There was so much inside her. "After lunch."

"You'll be ready?" he asked.

She tilted her head back, closed her eyes, and opened her lips. He bent and softly kissed her mouth.

"I'll be ready," she said and smiled.

He came for her shortly after noon. Without knocking, he stuck his head in her kitchen door.

"I had a tuna sandwich," he said. "It goes down fast."

Rose laughed and held up the sandwich she was eating. It was tuna.

"See, we should have had lunch together."

"I wasn't sure I could eat," Rose said quietly, lowering her eyes.

"But you can." He sat next to her, took her hand, rubbed soothing circles over her knuckles. "It's all right, you know. Thomas and Bernice are up there relieved, happy they can go play angel games without worrying about us. We'll see them when it's time, Rose. Till then, hey, it's you and me and whatever our old bones will let us do."

She tilted her head and winked and blushed when he grinned.

"It's all good from now on, Rosie girl. No more clutching at old memories. No more hiding. No more secrets. No more guilt."

Rose put her sandwich down. "No more hiding." She pushed her plate away. "But I don't know what that means. Do I get you and lose my good and old and dear friends?"

"They'll understand," Anson said, bending toward her. "Give them a little time. Anger fades."

"It's more than anger. It's heavier. I hurt them. I didn't mean to, but I did — right to the core, deep and sharp and brutal. I'm not sure they'll ever forget."

"I wasn't that important to them."

"My trust was."

"They've lived a lot of years. They've been hurt worse and got through it. And they've loved you a very long time. They'll forgive."

"I don't know. Their anger has turned ugly and they frighten me." She rose and took her plate to the sink. Anson followed, put his arms around her, and pulled her back against his belly.

"I don't think they'll hurt you," he said. "Maybe with words and maybe pranks, but they won't injure you."

"You mean my body? They won't injure my body?"

"Yes."

She turned and faced him, stiffened in his arms. "But what about my heart?"

"Hearts heal."

"And what about theirs?"

"Theirs will heal too."

"I think the scars might be too big."

Anson dropped his arms. "Rose, I don't know what to say

to you. There are no guarantees. Either you're willing to go forward or you're not. Choose." He walked toward the kitchen door.

She didn't follow him. He was not Thomas.

"I did choose," she said, standing her ground. "You. But I have a right to think and wonder and be afraid. And I can speak my thoughts if I want to."

He stood in the doorway a moment, then nodded. "You do. And I'm sorry. I'm scared I'll lose you."

"You won't. Not if you don't want to."

"Maybe when the preacher says, 'Do you take this man?' you'll say, I can't. I can't have both and I have to take my friends."

"If that was going to be my choice, I wouldn't have thrown integrity to the winds and snuck to your house on the days I was honor-bound not to." Her face was white and her back straight. "I can rationalize and I can close my eyes, but I know what lives deep within me. There's a mirror in there just waiting to reflect and show me all those times I walked to your door and you walked to mine when we had promised *friends* we would not do that, when we let *friends* think we were beyond reproach. And we were indignant that they should question our honor. I've killed something I hold dear and it will never be the same with them again. If I wanted, and I don't, I don't think they would let me choose them now. But, dear Anson, I truly wish I could have both."

"I know," he said and came and held her, his large, rope-veined hand spread across the back of her head, pressing it to his chest. His other arm was tight around her, his body swaying gently along with hers. "I could not bear to lose you now. I can't be without love again. It's so lonely."

June, Tuesday

"I'll be with you, dear heart," she said, moving with him, eyes closed, following his step in a dance without music.

Later they walked down to the lake and threw bread to the gulls. They didn't speak of friends again. Then they went back to the ballpark across from Rose's house and sat on a bench and watched the boys bat and chase and run bases. Their arms pushed tight together, their feet pressed against each other's, and her hair brushed his cheek as she bent to his words. Their eyes touched. They shared smiles, and gentle fingers grazed on willing skin.

At last, signaling silent agreement, hand in hand, they departed the solid, common world and went to Rose's spare bedroom where they soared from a tender, giving love so sweet it drew tears from them both.

Reluctantly they parted for awhile. He wanted to take her someplace special for dinner, and she wanted to wear a prettier dress.

She put on the same pink, flowing garment she had slipped on with hesitation and hope the first night loneliness and growing love and sweet desire had led her to lay her body next to his, to join with Anson in a completeness she had only felt before with Thomas. When Anson came for her, he gazed silently, then stroked the silky fabric. He winked. She blushed. It pleased her that he remembered.

He drove her to Caroline's by the Lake — a small, elegant restaurant with flowers everywhere and a glass wall facing the water.

They sat and watched the sun fall into the lake. Magnificent colors exploded through the clouds as the sun dropped, spreading orange across the rippling waves, hesitated, then

May Snow

slipped down into the water. The sky was dark and silent. Then stars began to twinkle, first one, then another, then many, and a new beauty was born.

"To you, Rosie." Anson lifted his champagne glass and toasted her with beer. Their waiter had lifted his eyebrows, but he brought the golden liquid in a fluted glass as requested.

"And to you, dear Anson." Rose lifted her glass and toasted him with real bubbly.

He smiled at her. She tilted her head, lifted her chin, and smiled back. He nodded, put his glass down, and picked up his fork.

"Your face is so happy," Rose said.

"Even behind my face, I am happy." He pointed with his fork. "This smile that will not leave is no lie."

"It will be there so long, it will freeze into place. Tomorrow and tomorrow and tomorrow."

He frowned. "Not tomorrow. Tomorrow I'm taking Louisa back to Karen. It's time. She's been with me too long. When she's gone, then I can smile forever."

"Does she know?"

"That she's going to see her mother tomorrow? Yes. That she's going to stay there? No."

"What about Dwight?"

"He can go too. Karen won't care."

"Oh, Anson." Rose lifted her hand in frustration. "You can't just toss her out. You have to prepare her."

"She wants me to give her money to buy Dwight a business. She teases and teases. I can't stand hearing it anymore and I won't argue. She's going home."

"Why not give her the money?"

June, Tuesday

"After I'm dead, she'll get money from me. Not before."

"She's in your will?"

"Yep. And she knows she is. But she's afraid I'll live too long and Dwight will run away before she can lock him in her clutches with a great big ego gift he can't resist."

"Dwight's a good man. He just needs a little confidence."

"He's a boy that didn't grow up." Anson flattened his potatoes and spread corn on top of them. "He needs to break away and take a stand. Like he almost did. Or come back on his own terms. He doesn't need to be leashed by Louisa and I won't help her do it."

"He'd work hard, make a solid contribution, turn a business into his own." Rose watched Anson divide his potato-corn concoction into sections. "Anson, are you playing with your food?"

He looked at his plate and frowned. "This is the way I eat."

She smiled and shook her head. "See. Every man does boy things. You have to look beyond them. Give the money to Louisa with stipulations so she can't control Dwight. Better yet give Dwight the money. Or loan it to him. Keep her out of it. Help him get to a place of respect on his own. He can, you know. He wants it really bad."

Anson ate the middle section of his potatoes. He sawed a chunk of steak and stirred it in gravy, put it in his mouth, and chewed.

Rose waited.

He swallowed. "Could be you're right," he said. "I'll think on it." He speared a piece of meat and pointed with it. "But Louisa goes home. I liked her better moping in a corner. All this nagging, whining, and teasing is just too much." He looked at Rose's plate, still full. "Eat, girl. Put some roads in those potatoes."

"It's been a long time since I did that." Rose thought of Margaret in her highchair, bibbed and laughing, her spoon an airplane, dipping and scooping vegetable rows and soaring to her mouth. When Thomas came to the table, the playing stopped.

"Sweet lady, you will be doing a lot of things you haven't done in a long time." Anson lifted his beer and winked. "And you'll love each and every one of them."

Later in the car they drove with the windows down. The warm air was blowing, soft and gentle, on their skin. They cruised the lake to the pier. It was empty except for a couple of men fishing near the edge of the boat dock. Legs hanging down over the cement, backs bent, they sat motionless on plastic pads, staring into the water. They looked content, as if they needed nothing more. They didn't move as Anson swung onto the pier and his headlights brushed over them.

He drove to the end of the pier and parked under the amber glow of a lamppost. Water lapped rhythmically against the concrete pilings and a faint, fishy smell drifted pleasantly in the air. Rose could see waterfowl. Ducks and geese, the rich greens and grays and blacks and whites of their feathers darkened by the night, appeared and disappeared. Caught by the light of the pier lamps and the flashing beams from the breakwater, Rose watched them ride the moving, low-peaking waves.

A soothing moan broke uncontrolled from the center of Rose to her throat and escaped into the night. Anson turned to her, slipped his arm around her shoulders and drew her into the nest of his body. She pressed her face into the warm scent of him, and he rested his cheek on her apple-sweet hair.

"I love you, Rose Celador," he murmured into her softness.

She brushed his chest lightly with a slow, circling hand. "And I, you, Anson Stone. With all my heart."

They sat, barely moving, rubbing and touching with feather fingers.

After awhile, Anson tenderly withdrew Rose from his arms and rested her in the cushions of the car. She stretched her legs, sank back, hugged herself, and grinned.

"Old bones might need regrouping," she said, "but they sure know how to store and appreciate good feelings."

"They do." Anson flexed his fingers, pushing his arms straight in front of him. "Stiff they might be, but their ache holds the pleasure of a good woman's touch."

"Are you as happy as I am, dear Anson?"

"Happier."

She snuggled deeper into the cushion. "Not possible."

He turned on the radio, found a station with music remembered from a time when they were young. He looked at her and smiled.

"Your eyes are closed," he said.

"Mmmm."

"And *your* face is happy."

She nodded, smiling, eyes still closed. "For the rest of my life as long as it's with you."

"It will be, sweet Rosie. I promise."

She heard him get out of the car. She thought it was to wrestle the kinks from his legs. She listened to his footsteps move away from the car, pause, then come back to her side. He

May Snow

opened her door, reached across her, turned up the music, took her hands, and tugged.

She opened her eyes, looked up into his.

"Come," he whispered.

He helped her out of the car, folded her in his arms, and they danced in the lamplight at the end of the pier.

17
June
Wednesday

Rose awoke on Wednesday morning feeling no worry, satisfied, and just a trifle smug. Dream memories had already left, but she knew those sleeping stories had been good. She'd come awake with lips still lifted. Obviously, last evening's pleasures had spilled into her dreaming moments, pillowing her sleep, multiplying her happiness. She lay awake in her bed, relaxed, resplendent with the contentment of a woman valued.

Sighing, reluctant to move into the day and tarnish her pure and joyous remembrances with flawed reality, Rose rolled to the edge of the bed, pushed herself to a sitting position, then stood. She caught her breath as her legs, stiff sticks, wobbled and fought the weight she made them carry.

"Damn trunk legs," she mumbled. Just a few moments before, in dreams and thought, they had held her with ease, dancing her lightly, swollen-free and painless.

She shuffled to the open bedroom window. Already the

morning heat ate away at the lingering cool of night. The sill was warm to the touch. Rose braced herself against it, shrinking the load on her legs. She looked toward Anson's house, wanting a glimpse of him before he left with Louisa. But it seemed too bright out, too late for him to still be there. She had slept too deep and, she smiled, too nice.

After she dressed and ate a banana, she called Margaret. The phone rang and rang while she paced, impatient, with pulsing thought, urging her daughter to answer. But Margaret didn't, so Rose went out to the porch to rock and think about her troubled daughter. She needed to tell her that she, dear child, was a good person, not guilty and not deserving of pain. She needed to tell Margaret that she could get through each day and that the days would get easier. Eventually they would be hurt-free, and finally it would happen, calm and joyous and welcomed. But Margaret wouldn't talk to her. Rose couldn't find a way to reach her child. She couldn't set it aside. It was a scar upon the happiness that had come to her. She closed her eyes and hung her head — chastised to realize that she resented Margaret's anguish touching her own bliss, shamed that she was so selfish she could not allow her child's grief to be first in her heart.

The sun grew full and bright at the top of the sky. Rose's face was hot, her body sticky and too heavy to lift against the mass of fire-filled air. She ought to go inside and make cookies for tomorrow's meeting. *Sweeten up the ladies when they come,* Rose thought, *sugar their mood, keep their mouths filled so they can't yell when they hear that it's just Anson and me from now on, when I tell them I want them to bless us and love me again.*

She wiped her face with her apron and flapped it to stir the

June, Wednesday

air. Numbers ran through her head. She decided she could afford bakery cookies if she bought day-old and kept to the cheaper gingersnaps or shortbread. Maybe it would be cooler tomorrow so she could bake.

Rose wondered if Anson had made Louisa pack up her stuff. Maybe they'd fought. Louisa probably cried. Wouldn't have moved Anson, though. He'd just close his ears and lead her to the car, pile in her stuff or leave it for later, wouldn't matter. As long as he got Louisa back home to stay.

Rose wished she could call Charity to ask her what she thought about Anson pushing Louisa out. They'd have quite a time conjuring up possibilities. And Grace. Grace would have them in stitches with all the stories she'd make up. Probably act them out too. All the parts. Anson and Louisa. And Dweebie Dwight. Grace's name for him. Not hers. Actually Rose liked Dwight. Ah, but it would be fun to be in sync with the old girls again. Maybe she should have just played by the rules. Kept it simple, not so heartfelt. Then she could have had everything. Charity and Grace. June, too, she guessed. And Anson. And Thomas. She'd still have Thomas. She sighed, closed her eyes, rubbed her throat. But she wouldn't have had last night.

The heat sapped her energy. She was hungry, but her body wanted just to sit and languish in the sun. Her arms lay like lumpy stones on the armrests of the rocker. She crooked a finger and winced. Better to let it rest. She looked at it lying there lifeless and had a perverse desire to lift it again. Instead she closed her eyes and listened to the rhythm of her rocking. Soothing. Taking her into herself. Inside her head she was floating.

She should call Margaret. The thought flashed and she

pushed it out quickly. Not now. A picture of Anson appeared in her mind. He bowed and he whirled her, twirled her, dipped her deep. Their old bodies bent painless, supple and free. She smiled. Her chin fell on her chest and she dozed.

She tried to call Margaret again after she awoke. Then and several times later. Margaret didn't answer. Rose tried not to feel punished.

The day seemed endless. The heat grew too thick to sit long on the porch. It poured into the house, eating all energy in its wake. Rose turned on fans in the living room and kitchen and wandered from window to window. The fans whirred valiant and steady, but they gave little comfort. Their breeze was warm. Her lungs struggled in the hot, heavy air. When her legs tired and shot pain, she would sit for a few moments. Then she would get up and circle the windows, peering for sight of life and interest.

Twice she saw Amy slip out of her house, drive off in her car, and come back with bags. Once Nicholas was with her. Amy yanked him sharply when he lingered by the vehicle staring across the street at the boys playing ball. It hurt Rose to watch.

Stopping in the living room, Rose stooped by the front window, leaning into it to see past the porch to the ball field. Someone had brought out a hose, and the boys dropped balls and bats and mitts to run, in tee shirts and shorts, laughing and yelling, through the gushing water. *Nicholas should be there*, she thought.

Many times she looked out the kitchen toward Anson's house. There was no sign he had returned. With or without Louisa. She wished she had a long, winding telescope that would reach to his chimney, dip down deep, peer through the hearth, then send tentacles to every room, peeking and prying, telling of his presence or lack thereof, revealing evidence of Louisa residue. Or she wished she had a pair of good healthy legs that loved to run in the heat and could scoot her, undiscovered, in and out of his house.

But he'll call me when he's back, she thought, rubbing her back. *He has to be missing me as much as I want to see him. Unless it's too late and he thinks I'm sleeping. He's too much a gentleman. Better he was selfish and pounded on my door no matter what the time.*

Finally the sun gave up its punishment and went to bed. The night air was cooler and sweeter. Rose sat for awhile on the porch, ear cocked to the phone for Anson's ring, and let the still, fragrant darkness comfort and soothe her, wipe away the day's misgivings, and give her a measure of peace.

Looking into the night one last time, hoping to see Nicholas and bid him a 'good night and be careful,' she leaned over the porch rail, drawing deep of the clean air. She couldn't see him. She thought she should check on him, but she felt so tired. Her worn-out body needed sleep and wouldn't wait much longer.

She could see Anson tomorrow.

She called in the cats and went upstairs to make ready for bed.

Standing at the window in her nightie, so weary but needing to see her love, she sighted Nicholas huddled by the garbage cans. He was staring, quiet and still, at Anson's house. She followed the path of his view and saw nothing. Anson's house was dark and silent.

May Snow

She smiled and imagined Nicholas, crouched and ready to spring, tracking a rabbit or a big-eyed alien, or maybe he was a lion stalking his supper or maybe a leaf waiting to drop from a limb. Oh, dear youth.

She went to bed. Sleep came quickly.

18
June

Thursday

It was still hot. Rose sat on the edge of the bed with her head down, legs hanging, groggy from a night of half sleep, hours spent dozing in a place that allowed neither rational, clear thinking nor deep, replenishing slumber. She rubbed the back of her neck, wiped her sweaty hands on her damp nightgown. Pulling the cloth from her body, she slid her legs down the side of the bed. Her feet hit the floor flat and shaking. She stood shuddering as air, false cold and dead, rushed between her skin and the wet cloth of her nightdress. "A shroud," she whispered, "for a corpse." Shivering in the heat, she tugged it off and dragged on a dry, cotton robe.

Walking stiffly to the window, she raked her fingers through her hair, pulling it away from her slick, clammy face. She looked across the yard to Anson's house. It stood quiet in the shimmering sun. No sign of life. *Smart,* she thought, *still sleeping.* She looked with longing at her tumbled bed. There

May Snow

was too much to do. Her house had to be perfect for the old ladies, Anson-worthy, beyond reproach. If Charity raised her eyebrows or pursed her lips, it wouldn't be from cobwebs or smudged silverware. She wanted them to concentrate on words and feelings. No distractions to sidetrack them from the friendship repairing she meant to do. She sighed and went to take a shower.

She felt better after she'd showered and washed the night's sweat from her body. She dressed quickly, drawing in her breath and forcing her stiff fingers to open and close even while they sang their pain.

She drank aspirin in her orange juice. She fed the cats. She told herself the movement would oil her joints and make them run smooth. She rinsed her glass and wiped the counter. Stared at her cupboards. The ladies would expect goodies. There were flour, sugar, and vanilla in the cupboard, and eggs and sour cream in the refrigerator. She shook her head. Too hot. She swept the floor. She hoped the aspirin would kick in fast. She was moving too quickly. There was no time to rock on the porch and let the morning come slow while her body eased into the day's needs.

She went outdoors. If she got to the bakery on time, she could get some good day-old stuff. She looked toward the garage and pictured herself sinking into the car's soft cushions. Closing her eyes. Sleeping. She sighed. The air smelled good and the walk was short. Besides, it hurt to get in and out of the car.

Head full of tasks — sweep the porch, iron the napkins, surface dust, and vacuum — she set off down the sidewalk.

June, Thursday

While Rose was in the bakery picking unbroken gingersnaps out of the day-old bin, a siren pierced the early morning quiet, flooded the bakery with crescendoing blare, peaked, then faded.

"Oh dear," Rose said, shaking her head. "I'll bet it's another poor soul at the nursing home off to the hospital. Or worse, the morgue." She handed her bag of cookies to Jerry, her bakery friend. She'd watched him grow from a toddler in his father's shop, to a worker after school and on weekends, then a partner, and now, since his father had left to bake cookies at a retirement settlement in Florida, the sole owner of the bakery.

"Could be," Jerry said, lifting her bag onto the scale. "They're pretty old over there." He weighed the cookies and put them on the counter. "Sometimes, it's better."

"To die?" Rose said. "Why would you think that?"

"You know, pain and all." He stuffed a few extra gingersnaps into the bag. "Come's a time, you gotta face it. Life's not gonna get better, no more sun and kisses, dreams dead. So why hang around miserable? The old death angel's not always an enemy, you know."

Rose looked hard at Jerry Sullivan, still relatively young, muscles still firm, stomach just a little paunchy, and wondered if he ever thought beyond easy truth. She reached in her pocket and handed him money. "Do you really think the old don't dream?"

"Well, yeah," he said, smoothing the bills. "Dreams are looking ahead. The old got nothing good coming, so they look back to the good that was. Memories. That's what they've got. All the things that happened before." He put the bills in the register, took out coins. "After awhile it's gotta get depressing rehashing all that old stuff."

"Do you think I'm old, Jerry?"

"Well, I dunno," Jerry said. He rubbed his forehead. "I mean you're not like those old people in the nursing home. You get around and do things."

"I'm old, Jerry."

"Yeah, but you still can do stuff."

"And I still dream and want and wish." She took the change he offered, picked up the cookies. "And sometimes I do it sitting down in a rocking chair. Sometimes it's a little hope for a finger to stop throbbing. Sometimes it's a big hope to see all the paintings in Rome. Sometimes it's wishing every person I see on that day will give me a smile. And I'm going to keep right on dreaming even when they strap me on a stretcher and take me for my last ride to the hospital."

Jerry sighed. "Hey, my mouth sometimes drops out words before my head filters them."

Rose patted his arm. "Don't be embarrassed. You didn't hurt me or make me mad. I just want you to remember, nobody ever stops wanting the next piece of life or hoping it will bring something wonderful and new. No matter how old we get or how much we can't move, there's more to have."

She hoped she'd taught him something, but if she hadn't, it really didn't matter. He'd learn. You had to live it before you knew it.

"Kiss the youngsters and tell Alice I said hello." Rose picked up the cookies and smiled. "Thanks for the extras. You're a good boy, Jerry."

June, Thursday

"Hey, it's nothing. You come back soon. And don't you be thinking you're so old. You still got plenty of spunk."

God, let me keep that spunk, she thought as she hurried along the sidewalk. *Even when my legs won't bend anymore and my fingers swell. Just let me keep thinking and dreaming. And thank you, God, for Anson, my sweet, unexpected dream boy, wrinkled and welcome. Now give me back my friends and I'll feel touched with bliss. But first give me strength to put a sparkle and shine on my house as good as Charity always does.*

She stumbled. Pain shot through her legs. She gritted her teeth, counted, and kept walking.

The church chimed nine o'clock. There was time to stop at Anson's, give him some cookies, get a fortifying kiss. She could have it all. Her dream. She'd make the old ladies understand it was right. She hadn't set out to hurt them. Fate meant her to have Anson. She concentrated on planting her feet firm on the sidewalk, away from cracks and lumpy cement.

She got to her driveway and raised her head. She looked past her garage, across the yard to Anson's house. He should be up by now. Her foot lifted to start that welcome journey when she saw the ambulance.

She thought it was there in error. She'd heard the siren. It was for the nursing home. It had to be. Not for Anson. That couldn't be.

Then fear rushed through her heart. The coroner's car was there too. Alarm flashed, sharp and quick, across her mind. The old ladies had found a suitable punishment for her evil, cheating time with Anson.

"My God, they've killed him."

May Snow

She dropped her bag and ran on hobbled legs. She didn't feel their pain.

She didn't knock. The back door was open. So many people hovered in the kitchen. She pushed through them. She looked for Anson. She didn't expect to see him up and moving. But that's what she wanted. She prayed for it. *God, let him be alive.* Over and over. But someone was dead. The coroner's car was there. *Maybe he was only hurt. Or Louisa. Maybe she had come back with him and she was hurt. Or dead. How could she wish for that? Oh God, she did. No, she didn't. Nobody should be dead. Oh, please, especially not Anson.*

The coroner, Willis Redman — old friend, dear friend, wouldn't-let-Anson-be-dead friend — was in the living room sitting on the couch by a huddled, weeping bundle. Louisa.

Louisa was alive.

Rose kept her eyes on Louisa. She would not look at Willis. If she didn't meet his eyes, he couldn't tell her what she didn't want to hear. But she couldn't stop from moving closer. Damn legs were floating, would not turn her away, walk her back to yesterday.

"Rosie." Willis stood and took her by the shoulders. He spoke low and she didn't want to hear the gentle command in his voice. "Look at me, Rosie."

She tried to pull away, but he wouldn't let her. He was one of the Friday boys. The guys Anson fished with, played cards with, ate their slimy oyster stew with. He would know what Anson thought and felt. They were the old men, like she and Charity and Grace were the old ladies. He would know she was Anson's love. And he would show her pity. And if he did she'd know that Anson was gone. Dead. Up there with

Thomas. Well, she didn't want to hear those words drop from his lips and she didn't want to see his eyes watered with sadness. So she kicked him. Hard. And turned away when he dropped his hands in surprise.

She went to the stairs. He must be in the bedroom. But they wouldn't let her up. Stanley and Ed, who'd eaten fresh berry pies in her kitchen and had chased Margaret with dead mice, now grown into volunteer firemen and full of authority, blocked her way and refused her pleas. She liked them better when they dropped the mice and ran when she yelled.

"Rosie, Rosie." Strong arms from behind came around and held her. "Reach down deep, sweet lady. Get yourself together."

"Let me up there," Rose said, struggling to be free.

"Not yet," Willis said. "Breathe deep. I don't want you leaving us too. Now, relax."

"I don't want to," Rose said. Her legs ached. She couldn't handle that too. Damn them. Straining against Willis' grip, she cursed their betrayal and forced them to bend and flex and give her more power. "Let me go!"

"Stop it, Rose. You're seventy-three years old, not a child. Be sad if you want. God, I'll help you cry. But settle yourself and face what you have to."

She couldn't get away. She rubbed her forehead, pushed the heels of her palms hard against her skin. She wasn't strong enough. She wasn't strong at all. All she had was gone. No strength left, only tumbling pain. She sagged against Willis and he lessened his hold and turned her so she faced him.

"You okay?"

She nodded. She looked into his eyes. "It is Anson, isn't it?"

May Snow

"Yes," Willis said. He met her stare.

Her heart hurt. "And he's dead?"

"Yes." Willis stroked her arm.

"Let me sit down." Her head was light, its weight sliding down, pooling in her stomach.

He led her to a chair and eased her gently onto its firmness.

"My legs are so jittery," she said.

"Can I get you some water?"

She held up her hand. "I'm all right." She bit her lip and sighed deep, began to pull together the buried bits of power and determination that lay within, waiting ammunition for threatening times. "What happened?"

"He broke a vein in his ankle. We think he bumped it in his sleep. The skin was stretched so thin there that the vein protruded and was vulnerable. It broke and he bled. Profusely. He wouldn't have felt anything, Rosie. No pain. He just slipped deeper into sleep."

"He died."

"Yes," Willis said.

"How could he have bumped it?"

"I don't know for sure. There's a stool by his bed. Maybe that's what he hit. There's blood all over it."

She winced. "You said he was sleeping."

"It looks like he got up, went to the bathroom. He must have bumped it. It broke. He crawled back in bed and went to sleep."

"He would have known."

"He was half asleep and it wouldn't have hurt."

"He was careful."

"Things happen." Willis took her hand.

She jerked it away. She saw the pain in his face and was sorry. But only for a moment. He wasn't the dead one.

"How do you know it was an accident?" she asked. "Maybe somebody poked that vein. Lots of people have seen it. Everybody knows he couldn't bump it or he'd be in trouble."

"Everybody?"

"People close to him."

"People close to him loved him. You know that. Be reasonable, Rose. Nobody wanted to hurt Anson." He shrugged and smiled ruefully. "You're safe, Rose. There are no murderers running around the neighborhood."

"People get mad and do crazy things." Rose saw Willis' face tighten. His cheeks pulled in and his eyes narrowed. She knew he was losing patience. There were other places he needed to be. He was kind and he liked her, but she was keeping him too long. He probably thought she was foolish, disoriented in her grief, old, but he was wrong. There was no confusion. She was old, but she had lived much, felt much, and she had stored so much despair and pain and everything else in the bucket of her body, that she could reach in there, take what she needed right now, and save the rest for another time. She could cry later, but now she had to sit straight for Anson. She held Willis by his sleeve, bunched it in her hand. "There were people very angry with Anson."

"Nobody came in and killed Anson." He took her fingers and gently released them from his sleeve, one by one. "He had an accident and died."

"You don't know that. Think about the other. Just consider it. Someone could have hurt him."

He lifted a finger to his lips and shushed her. "Calm down,

May Snow

Rose. Let it be. No one came in and attacked Anson. Louisa heard nothing. Nothing was stolen. No sign of a break-in. Anson had been warned to watch that vein. A terrible thing happened. He bumped it and it broke. Just let it be, Rose. Let it go."

Rose rubbed her throat. She was cold. It could have happened that way. He could have gotten out of bed sleepy and groggy, bumped the vein, broken it, not known it, fallen into bed, snuggled into sleep, all the while bleeding painlessly. Leaving her. Her body slumped. She put her hands in her lap, clasped them tight together, and watched her knuckles grow white.

Willis left to join Stanley and Ed at the foot of the stairs. They were bringing Anson down. She didn't look. She didn't want to see him helpless, body maneuvered to someone else's time and movement, face covered so he couldn't breathe.

She heard Louisa sobbing on the couch. Dwight should be there with her. He was over by the fireplace looking at all those pictures of Anson's women. She wondered if Karen had been called. Or Greg, Anson's son, far away in Oregon. Never came back much. Resented all those years he'd worked so hard on the farm. So long ago. Couldn't let go of the bitterness. Must have known Anson loved him all those years he didn't come. No need to make the trip now. Anson wouldn't know. She exhaled. Yes, he would. Anson would know. He'd be up there watching. Up there with Thomas. And Bernice. She looked up at the ceiling. Nothing there. Stark white paint. No heavenly shadows. Heaven was a nice thought, but God forgive her, she wasn't there and didn't want to be. Not yet. Not until she knew which of the old ladies had killed Anson.

June, Thursday

"You can do whatever it is you do up there," she murmured, eyes uplifted, talking to a wall, hoping her words got through the plaster and soared to Thomas, Anson, and Bernice, up there with God. "You wait for me. And I'll do what I have to do down here. Watch over me and help me know what happened in this house last night. I love you so." She wasn't sure if she was talking to Anson or Thomas or God.

The house was emptying. Rose waited quietly in her chair. Firemen, sheriff, coroner, neighbors, friends, church brothers and sisters, the faces of Canadaway shuffled out, patting Louisa's shoulder, shaking Dwight's hand, nodding at Rose as they passed by. Shaking her head and rolling her eyes, Nettie Hinkle whispered that she'd be back with broom and bucket to clean "the little mess upstairs." Clare Biddle said she'd be back too with food to keep poor Louisa nourished in her time of sorrow until her mother saw fit to come and take care of her. Behind their backs, Laura Morrisey wrinkled her nose and winked at Rose then went to comfort Louisa with strong arms and soft bosom.

The house was almost still. Its soul was gone with Anson's leaving. Louisa's soft crooning, interlaced with Dwight's sharp tapping on the fireplace mantel, drifted in and out of corners, around tables and lamps and chairs, seeking to fill the hollowness of a barren room. Rose could feel the sadness of the house, its mourning. Death left a flat and final hole.

Reluctantly, Rose struggled out of her chair. Her legs had borne so much this day, and she wasn't done with them yet. She made them move, aching, in small steps across the room, up the stairway, down the hall to Anson's bedroom.

The smell, ripe and heavy, met her at the doorway. Rank

animal odor. Anson's blood. Spilled and spread from his dying body. It was in her nose before she saw it.

Tears stung swift and sharp. She bit her lip and walked into the room.

The sheets had fallen from the bed. Rumpled and bunched and shoved on the floor at its foot. Spattered and streaked with the stains of blood drained from her Anson. Blood was on top of the bed, the mattress, and the pillows. It was on the rug and the stool and the mirrors. The walls. And the curtains. How could it gush so far?

Except for the sheets, all was in place. Neat. Tidy. Except for ugly red splashes all over. She trembled and turned away.

As she walked out, her eyes fell upon the top of his dresser. The little, yellow, ceramic cat she had given him was gone.

❄   ❄   ❄

Although it seemed as if hours had passed, it was only eleven o'clock. Rose sat at her kitchen table, holding her head in her hands as she rubbed both sides of her scalp, hoping to sooth it's ache.

She heard the soft chimes from her living room clock dance through the house as if the world had not stopped, and she marveled that time endured and persisted onward, pushing her to move with it when a part of the world had dropped away, could not hear the tick, and was done. She resisted it. Pushed her palms hard to the sides of her head. But she couldn't keep it away. The awareness forced her forward into the next moment. And the next.

Slowly she pushed herself up from the chair where she had

dropped when she came home. It was the nearest to the door, and her poor, aching legs could go no further. They demanded care and rest. It seemed as if they had carried her for hours, and yet, it was only just past eleven. She gave them some time and then raised up on them again and burdened them, trembling and shuffling, to take her to a softer chair by the telephone where she could sink and let her thoughts swim where could she close her eyes and give herself up to the powers that had changed her life. She prayed for acceptance so she could start taking control back. Time would take her forward, with or without her permission, and she wanted the direction to be hers.

She sat for a very long time. In and out of conscious thought, she let her spirit drift. She felt, sometimes, that Anson touched her, stroked her soul, warmed her heart. And sometimes, it was like he had never been and she was alone and cold and the world was stark around her. Then she longed for the time before Anson when Thomas had held her, given her comfort. But he too had left her. When she could bear those moments no longer, she took herself to happier times, old and good times, and love spilled over her, and she savored the sweet memories let in by her hurting heart.

She was not aware of time.

When finally the ache in her soul crystallized to bearable reality, she drew in the segments of her being and made herself whole. She opened her eyes, a solid person, ready to function amid her sorrow and pain.

The first thing she saw was a spider web hanging from a corner of the ceiling.

She looked at the clock.

Dinnertime had passed.

May Snow

The old ladies had not come to see her.

Charity would have frowned at the spider web.

But they had not come as they planned. Anson had died and her friends had not come to her house.

Because now there was nothing to negotiate.

Anson was dead. They would not marry. There was no reason for her friends to be angry anymore.

But they had not come.

She wiped away a tear. Silly eyes. She should get the cookies from the driveway and throw them out. No need for them now.

Let the spider web be. It belonged to the spider. He'd worked for it. It should stay there. It was a work of art, a statement of being. No harm could come from a dangling bit of filament.

She sighed. She had to get herself ready to go across the backyards and meet the mourners. Share the circle of grief. Console the core of its center, Karen and Louisa, while she danced on the outside edge, the secret wife that never was.

❄   ❄   ❄

Rose went into Anson's house without knocking. No one would notice. She wasn't a stranger there. She knew her way.

The scent of vanilla assailed her. There were candles everywhere. Squat stubs of creamy wax sat on counters and tables, mantel, windowsills, stovetop, steps of the stairs. The smell was mellow, hinting of times past, of grandmothers and sweet sleep and soft hands that took worry away. It almost covered the stench of blood.

Margaret was there. She sat on the couch beside Louisa,

holding the pale girl's hand. She smiled when she saw Rose, but her lips trembled, and Rose felt her compassion like a well-chosen gift.

Nettie Hinkle came up beside Rose with a tray of sandwiches and doughnuts.

"Did you see all the food in the kitchen?" Nettie said as she offered the tray. "Might as well eat some. There's plenty."

Rose shook her head.

The fishing buddies were there in a bunch, mostly quiet, sometimes touching briefly as if to assure each other it was all right to still be alive. There were neighbors, chatting and chewing, but red-eyed and careful to keep their sounds low. Karen, pale and determined, hovered among them. Louisa had stopped crying.

"I cleaned up the room," Nettie said. "As best I could. They'll have to get a carpet cleaner in. A professional."

"Did you clean the insides of the dresser drawers too? Under the handkerchiefs and underwear?" Rose asked and was instantly sorry. With so much sorrow hanging thick, there should be no room for cruelty.

Lips pulled down, eyebrows up, Nettie jerked her head to one side and back and stepped away with an angry, "Humph."

"I heard you," Margaret whispered beside Rose.

Rose grimaced and shook her head. She hadn't seen Margaret come across the room. "She does enjoy prying."

"Anson would have laughed," Margaret said, sliding an arm around her mother's waist.

"It wasn't kind."

"No, but there's not a whole lot of kindness in this world anyway, is there?"

May Snow

"More than cruelty, I would hope." Rose watched Dwight leave his spot at the hearth to sit with Louisa in the place Margaret had vacated. Her eyes strayed to the mantel. The only old lady sitting there, glassed and framed, was Bernice. Rose and Charity and Grace were gone. Her lips curled in a half-smile. Karen held the reins now and she could pull them any way she wanted.

"Louisa said you were here this morning," Margaret said.

"I was." In a rush it was all there in her head. The whole sad morning. She pushed the picture away.

"I'm sorry. It must have been hard." Margaret pulled her mother closer. "I love you… you didn't see him, did you?"

"No." The morning would not stay gone. She saw it clearly.

"Good. It wasn't something you should see."

"I saw the room."

"They shouldn't have let you."

"It was bloody and smelly. And if they had let me, I would have gone up there while he was still there, and I would have held him and stroked him and breathed love into him and made him alive. But Willis wouldn't let me go up. And when they brought him down, he was all covered, his face was hidden and he was dead and what could I do? I didn't want to see him anymore."

Margaret rubbed her mother's shoulder. "Oh, Mother."

Rose leaned her head against Margaret's head. "Don't listen to me, child. I'm just being foolish."

"You should sit down. Are you hungry? I can get you something."

"No." Rose shook her head. She rubbed the base of her throat. "Have you seen Willis? I don't think he's here."

"He came and went."

"Do you know when the autopsy will be?" "They're not doing an autopsy," Margaret said. "Please, come sit down."

"Why not?"

"Karen doesn't want one."

"Isn't it the law?" Rose rubbed harder.

"Ha!" Margaret said. "Tell that to every man who ever committed adultery. That's a crime on the books too."

"But how will they know why he died?"

"He broke a vein, Mother."

"But how will they know if it was accidental if they don't do an autopsy. They have to. It's the law."

"I told you," Margaret said. "Karen doesn't want one. He was an old man. It was his time to go. Willis doesn't do an autopsy on every old man that dies in his own home."

"He should."

"Oh, Mother. This is a small town. Look, I have to go now. Will you be all right?"

Rose nodded.

"I can take you back to your house."

"No."

"I can't stay with you."

Rose saw Dwight get up from the couch and go toward the kitchen. "I'll go over and sit with Louisa for awhile."

"I'll help you."

"No, go. I'm all right." She turned to her daughter. "I love you, sweet girl. I'll be okay. I made it through your father's death. I'll get through this."

Rose felt the brush of Margaret's lips on her cheek and leaned into her daughter for a moment.

May Snow

"I'll call you," Margaret whispered.

When she'd gone, Rose made her way to Louisa and sank on the couch.

"Hi, Rose," Louisa said. Rose's eyes stung in sympathy as she looked at the girl's swollen eyes. "Grampa's dead."

Rose took her hand.

"Lots of people loved him," Louisa said. "You did. They just keep coming. Nettie cleaned upstairs. I don't think Mother was too thrilled. They've brought lots of food. He had so many friends. And he was so old..."

"Louisa," Rose interrupted, "did the old ladies come yet?"

"Who?"

"Charity and Grace. And June. Did they come?"

"No."

"Have you heard from them? Did your mother?"

Louisa squirmed next to her. "I don't think so."

"Don't you find that strange?"

"Maybe," Louisa said. "They used to be here all the time. Like you."

"Why do you think they're not here now?" Rose asked.

"I don't know." Louisa blew her nose and looked around the room. "Why do *you* think they're not here?"

Rose inhaled deep. She planted a seed. "Maybe they're guilty."

Louisa pursed her lips. "Guilty of what?"

Rose shook her head. "I don't know," she whispered.

19
June

Rose sat very still in a straight-backed chair by the stairway, watching the horde — a human wave of flowing, probing limbs — move through the kitchen and dining and living rooms. It was the custom in Canadaway between viewing hours at the funeral parlor for friends and neighbors to gather at the home of the deceased to offer support to the surviving family members. Rose had not viewed the body yet, but she'd brought a tuna-noodle-pea casserole to feed the house crowd, and she'd offered comfort to Karen and Louisa and Greg. Greg had come alone, all the way from Oregon, without wife and sons to mourn or apologize or reflect or drop guilt or stand empty beside his father's coffin. Rose wasn't sure what he was feeling. She wondered where his family was, but she didn't want to ask him. Neither did she want to be at Anson's house. Her own home promised peace, but she couldn't dishonor Anson's love with her absence, so she sat, silent and still, at the edge of the motion and watched.

May Snow

Across the room Charity, Grace, and June sat in front of the fireplace under the mantel that no longer held their pictures. They were perched on hard, folding chairs similar to Rose's own. Grace's body, squashed between Charity and June, sank and rested in the empty spaces unused on their chairs by their slimmer bodies. They looked connected, a tight trio, and when Rose looked their way, she saw six joined eyes boring through her.

Rose lowered her head and studied her hands. They lay motionless in her lap. Gazing intently, she watched them grow, separate from her body, fill her head. They became separate, living entities waiting for her command. Revenge and compliance struggled in her brain. She willed her fingers not to move, and at the same time, dared them to lift and point and fling fire at her traitorous friends.

When Rose looked up she saw Amy come through the archway carrying a box of doughnuts. Nicholas was pale, his eyes darting in every direction. He hesitated, and Amy grabbed his arm. Rivers of blood gushed under his skin and pushed against her fingers, leaving swatches of deep pink when she let go.

Rose stood up quickly, instinctively, meaning to go to him, rescue him, but Amy pushed her son in another direction, toward the old ladies. Rose followed.

She couldn't get to them. Nettie stood in her way.

"I see you finally got up from your chair," Nettie said.

Rose looked at her and said nothing.

"I'm not being critical," Nettie persisted. "You got bad legs. So you sit. That's sensible. But you need to stretch them once in awhile. That's what my doctor says, anyway."

"Nettie, I do not sit my life away," Rose said, stretching to see around that woman.

"Looking for Karen?" Nettie asked. "I think she's in the kitchen. Poor dear. I've been trying to get her to eat something. She needs a good hearty meal. Roast beef and potatoes. Not this mishy-mushy casserole stuff I see on the table."

"Nettie, I brought a casserole," Rose said.

"I know." Nettie smiled and moved on.

Rose sighed. An overwhelming urge to laugh assaulted her, and she stepped hard with bent ankle to kill the urge with pain.

"Rose!"

Rose turned. Helen Bond, church sister and fellow nursing home volunteer, called her over as she hefted her ample body from an overstuffed chair.

"Come sit here," Helen said. "I saw you way over there." She patted her chest. "Didn't think I should shout out over everybody, but now that you're here, take my seat. It's closer to the girls." She pointed to Charity, Grace, and June. "I have to be going anyway." She pulled Rose's arm. "You okay? Haven't seen you with the girls much." She shook her head. "Isn't it awful about Anson?" She guided Rose to the chair. "You sit now, closer to your friends."

Rose sank into the soft cushions. She sensed the quiet that descended next to her where the old ladies sat and where Amy stood.

Helen smiled. "Now isn't that better?" She wiggled her fingers at all of them and waddled away.

Rose waited, eyes downcast. When the silence stayed too long, she lifted her head and looked at the old ladies. She saw Grace's bold grin and June's weak smile. But it was Charity's stare that held her, so cold it was, and hard. Rose turned away and looked at Amy. She stood near them, shifting her weight awkwardly from leg to leg. Nicholas was behind her, staring intently at the old ladies. His hand was clenched firmly on his mother's belt.

"Do you know Karen?" Charity asked Amy.

Rose listened without looking.

"No," Amy said. "But Anson was nice to Nicholas."

"He was nice to everybody," Charity said.

"I guess you… all of you… were special friends," Amy said. "I mean, I saw you there a lot. Accidentally, I mean. I wasn't spying."

"I should hope not," Charity said.

"I'm sorry about Anson," Amy said. "I mean, you must be hurting real bad. Missing him, I mean."

"Do I look like I'm hurting?" Charity asked. "No, you give your sympathy to those really close to him. That's not likely to be us."

Rose felt the heat of her stare.

"I did talk a little to Louisa," Amy said. "She was crying a lot."

Rose glanced up. Nicholas was still looking hard at the old ladies. His face was pale.

"We better go," Amy said, tugging at Nicholas and pulling his fingers off her belt. He winced and looked away from Charity.

Rose met his eyes. She thought they were filled with words that needed to be said but couldn't find a way to his tongue and his mouth. They seemed to be locked in his head, looking out at her for help.

"Nicholas," Rose said, reaching out to him. Three old heads and Amy turned to look at her.

Nicholas locked his hand firmly back on Amy's belt and shook his head.

"He's scared of all this," Amy said, shrugging, leaning toward Rose. "I'm sorry." She took hold of Nicholas. "We have to go."

Charity signaled to Grace and June. They left too.

Rose watched them go.

❆   ❆   ❆

That night Margaret called.

"I'm sorry, Mother. I meant to spend more time with you, but Karen is so alone. Nobody to help. Louisa just sits and mopes and cries. And Greg won't talk. Goes off by himself. God knows where. Karen has no idea where his wife and boys are or why they didn't come. Anyway, I've been helping her with the arrangements. Picking the coffin. You wouldn't believe the different colors and textures of satin they've got, and she couldn't decide how to dress him, casual or dressy or even farm clothes. Only I don't think she was really serious about that … Oh, Mother, I'm sorry. Here I am rattling on and I know he was special to you. I guess it's easier to keep talking than to face your awful pain and not know how to take some of it from you. I really don't know how to help you… tell me what I can do."

"Sweetie, there's nothing. Just be you." Rose closed her eyes and held the phone tight. Right now, this second, it was enough to know Margaret's love. It filled her.

May Snow

"You should go see Anson," Margaret said. "He looks good."

"Does he wink and grin when you look down at him?" Rose whispered. She squeezed her eyes and tried not to see him.

"He looks like Anson."

"They always stretch the skin so tight over the mouth," Rose said. "Do his teeth look like they're going to push through his lips?"

"He looks like he's sleeping."

"Sleeping a prayer with folded hands," Rose said. "Why do they put them like that? He slept on his side. With his legs curled up like a little child."

"Was it like this when Dad died?"

"Worse." Rose sighed. She was once again standing by his coffin and looking at her rigid, lifeless husband, afraid to touch him, wondering where he really was. "I didn't know then that a person can bear anything, but the clock ticks and you keep on living."

There was a long silence.

"How long did it take for the hurt to stop for Dad?" Margaret asked. Her voice was soft. "When did the ache stop?"

"Never." Rose said, clenching her fingers so hard they hurt. "Margaret, I need to tell you something."

"What?"

"You mustn't laugh."

"There's not too much funny happening these days."

"Margaret." Rose drew in her breath. "I think Anson was killed."

"What?"

"I think somebody intentionally hurt him."

"That's crazy. Who would do such a thing?" Margaret

said. "Louisa? I hear Anson was kicking her out. But murder him? I don't think so. Not enough guts. Or maybe Karen? To get his money. He had plenty, but not enough to risk jail for. Mother, you'd better be getting your head together."

"I think one of the old ladies killed him," Rose said, her jaw stiff and words clear. "It was Charity or Grace. Or June."

"Why do you think that?"

"I think they were so full of hurt that they had to get rid of it. It went beyond words, and one of them was so poisoned that she let the pain and hate and anger escape, and when she exploded, Anson was there and it killed him."

"Which one of them could do that?" Margaret asked.

"I don't know, but I mean to find out."

"You really believe one of your friends killed a man they had spent happy times with? Mother, they probably shared some pretty intimate moments with him. You can't really think Charity or Grace could kill anybody."

"I do think that."

Rose heard Margaret's sigh. "Maybe you're right. There are times I'm sure I could do great injury to Forrest. Maim him. Twist him in places that would make him beg to be dead. Just pound him and pound him and pound him. Who knows, maybe Charity did kill him. Maybe she did it before. Maybe she killed Maxwell. I remember when he died. Killed in his car. Bam, against a tree. Drunk driving it was. And he had lots of insurance. He'd been trying not to drink. Maybe Charity gave him a bottle and sent him on an errand on bumpy roads or dared him to get back in five minutes or planted an inflatable girl doll on a tree branch."

May Snow

"Maybe she did," Rose said. "Maybe there was one woman too many."

"Or could it be Grace killed George. I don't know though. That's harder to picture. She's so ditzy. But from what she says, George was as ditzy as she was. She said if she'd told him to jump down the cellar steps head first, he would have. And she claims he was having some kind of a heart problem, so she probably wasn't getting sex. Everybody knows sex is everything to Grace. I know you won't believe it, but she told Forrest once that he'd really enjoy her 'cause she'd never had babies. This from a chunky, fluffy-headed, inside and out, granny-age, arthritic kook. She probably drove old George to choose a heart attack over her tongue. That's murder, isn't it?" Margaret paused. "And who knows about June? She could have murdered a dozen people and chose Canadaway for her hideout."

Rose's hand throbbed. Her fingers felt glued to the receiver. "I think one of them killed him."

"This is foolish, you know," Margaret said softly. "It was a stupid, stupid accident. Nobody killed Anson. Nobody could. *Nobody* could have killed that dear, gentle man."

"But I think somebody did. Maybe," Rose whispered, "maybe somebody could have."

❄   ❄   ❄

Soft strains of Anson's favorite hymns whispered from the speakers in the funeral home. They rolled over his friends and family members, wandered through their sad thoughts and old memories. Mourners passed by the casket, touched him with their eyes one last time, then sat in rows of folding chairs waiting for Pastor Russell's words of assurance that Anson had made the trip to Heaven, that his body was empty of spirit and ready to be put away in the ground.

Sitting apart from Charity, Grace, and June, Rose watched the procession. Someone had placed her simple bouquet of carnations next to their bigger, fuller, multi-flowered basket. Nettie Hinkle paused by the flowers, bent over the cards, turned, and glanced at Rose. Nettie's eyebrows lifted. Rose shivered and dropped her eyes.

"You okay?" Margaret asked, leaning close.

"Thank you, Sweetie, I'm fine." Rose bit her lip and rubbed the base of her throat. She lifted her eyes and caught Charity looking at her. The old woman sucked in her cheeks, patted her hair, and slowly turned her eyes from Rose. Beside Charity, Grace grinned, waved, shrugged, and looked away as Charity tugged at her. Rose's gaze slid to June sitting so still by Grace. She seemed sad, her face, pale and empty. She looked steadily at Rose.

"I have tissues," Margaret said, her hand grazing Rose's arm.

Rose shook her head. "I won't cry." She looked toward the coffin. Anson's new house. Where his bones would live alone. Her breath caught in her throat. He was gone from her. Suddenly she was overwhelmed with the bigness, the finalness, of his leaving. And, just as suddenly, the loss of Thomas rushed through her, and the dark cloud of his death enshrouded her. Inside her heart he was dying again. The pain was sharp. It covered her everywhere. Then her mother was there. And her father. And her uncles and aunts and friends and neighbors and little Benjy Applegate, rolled under a tractor. Everyone

May Snow

she ever knew who had died, died again, right there while she sat in her chair and watched Pastor Russell, Bible in hand, walk to the lectern and start to say good things about Anson, pray for him and for all of them.

She looked at the backs of Anson's old farmer friends sitting in front of her. Thomas's friends too. She wondered what they thought as they looked toward the coffin where Anson, no older than they, lay with his eyes closed and sightless, his heart empty of life. She heard the hymns, softly wafting among Pastor Russell's holy words, which were strong and filled with promise. She looked to the ceiling and wondered if Anson was watching.

Rose rode with Margaret to the cemetery. The old ladies weren't there. Nor were they at Anson's house afterward.

When Rose walked into Anson's house, she saw Dwight and Louisa in a massive, overstuffed chair. Arms tight around each other, they huddled and cried. Karen and Greg were arguing in a corner. Rose heard Nettie telling Katie Hammel that Greg wouldn't stay the night, that he'd be out of here long before it was decent, that Karen would remodel, that Louisa would make Dwight marry her now that she didn't have Anson standing between them, and what a shame it was that Anson had outlived his farm. Maybe they should have buried him in the fields or in his old cow pasture or maybe cremated him, thrown his ashes into Grimmers Pond, or out over his empty acres. Wasn't it weird to think of him buried in a little hole so close to so many dead people? Katie nodded in agreement.

Rose sat alone thinking of Anson, arms around Bernice, walking through clouds. Fading away. Leaving her alone again.

June

Oh, Thomas, she thought. *I'm so sorry I'm thinking of him. I love you, dear heart. Please wait for me. I want to walk on clouds with you. Promise you'll wait.*

20
July

Twilight, sweet smelling and elusive, briefly sparkled magic over the village. Rocking on her porch, Rose gave way to childlike fancies and dreamed herself dancing on rainbows with winged, fairy feet across the arched hues, bathing in the splendor of shiny, gold coins captured in a pot at the end of a colorful slope.

Eyes closed, she sensed Nicholas slide through the dropping darkness and ease his body down onto the steps. Pushing her chair back and forth in her slow and steady rhythm, she waited silently while he melded himself to her time and cadence.

"Rose?" he said finally.

"Nicholas," she answered, smiling.

He squirmed on the porch boards. "Did you have brothers or sisters when you were a kid?"

"Not then. Not now."

"Weren't you lonely?"

May Snow

"I was very busy," Rose said. She tapped her fingers against the smooth wooden rocker arms. "I guess it would have been nice to have a sister, someone pulling weeds alongside me, riding ponies, or carrying water out to my father — Maybe braiding each other's hair or cutting catalogue dolls together or sharing the frosting spoon." She moved forward and back. "But I never had time to be lonely."

She rocked and thought, taking herself back to the little girl who worked in the fields and the kitchen, helper to both parents, only child. She remembered that child. She became that girl again and felt her pain. "Oh, Nicholas, that's not true. I loved the farm, but I *was* lonely. So many hours alone, and no one to take some of Dad's harsh words so I could feel less of them. Nobody else making mistakes. Hours by myself, hands busy, head free to roam. Yes, dear boy, I was lonely. Is that what you are, Nicholas? Are you lonely?"

"Who did you talk to?" he asked.

"Sometimes friends. Or the preacher's wife. Sometimes my mother or father. Sometimes, nobody. Mostly, nobody."

"What did you do with all your thoughts when you didn't tell anybody?"

"I hugged them close unless they were bad. Then I pushed the ugly thoughts out and made up a wall, built it around me, and wouldn't let the bad thoughts back in." She rubbed the base of her throat and didn't tell him that too many times the wall had great cracks.

"What if you had a secret that hurt inside you?"

"Is that what you have, Nicholas?" She stopped rocking and leaned forward.

"Maybe." He paused. "In my stomach."

July

"You know, Nicholas, old people are pretty good at keeping secrets."

"I'm sorry I said you ate dogs," Nicholas said.

"That's okay." She reached and ruffled his hair. "I figured you'd think about it and realize if I didn't eat my cats, I probably didn't eat dogs either."

"Dogs are different from cats."

She heard his foot knocking the steps.

"Nicholas, do you want to tell me something?"

He dropped his head and shook it a little. "No," he whispered.

She waited.

"I won't tell anybody," she said. "I'm good at that."

He looked at her then got up in one quick motion and stood by her rocker. He reached and touched the chair, making circles on its arm with one finger.

"You should give your cats names," he said.

She covered his hand with hers. "Nicholas, I'll help you if I can."

She felt his arms come around her. His hug was frail and fleeting. He pulled away and ran off the porch, across the lawn.

She sat and watched him go.

❄   ❄   ❄

Another hot day. Rose rocked on her porch waiting for Milton Sinnicoe, Anson's attorney. He'd called and asked to see her. He wouldn't tell her why, and when she offered to go to his office, he said Anson had instructed him to see Rose at her own home. He wanted her comfortable.

Rose lifted an ice-filled glass of lemonade to her cheek,

255

May Snow

pressing its coolness to her skin. She sighed and hoped Anson hadn't left her in charge of anything. She'd felt the weight of leftover duties when Thomas had died. She didn't want to cope with Anson's. Particularly if they involved his children or Louisa. Her current path was clear and full, concentration centered and honed. If she was going to learn exactly what happened the night Anson died, she needed her energy focused on that issue. She wanted no side roads.

She sighed again. *Of course there were side roads. Tributaries in the gushing river of life.* She smiled ruefully. *There were Margaret and Nicholas, and she needed her friends. She couldn't just forget Dweebie Dwight. Forgive me, Lord, I know he's a person and doesn't need nasty adjectives stuck to his name. And she couldn't ditch weeping Louisa. Although it seemed Anson had done just that. But he would expect more from her. Men! One mold. Oh God, she wished one of hers still lived.*

She looked up and saw Milton walking up the front path. Handsome, not old yet, cool and sharp-creased, in full attorney attire. *If I were younger,* she thought, *my heart would twang.*

"Hello, Rose," he said, taking her hand gently in his own, and she wondered when he had stopped thinking of her as Mrs. Celador.

"Miltie," she said. "Your dimples are as deep as the days your mother trotted you, plump and sassy and dressed in a diaper, down the road in her old, wooden Jackson wagon with all those jiggling bottles of spices and extracts and healing lotions packed in around you. I used to think one was sure to break and cut you. But none ever did. I guess nothing ever wanted to hurt you." She squeezed his hand

and pulled hers away. "You've always had a touch of the sun gleaming off you."

He tilted his head, and she saw he was puzzled, maybe troubled.

"That's a fine thing, Milton," she said. "A warm, comforting trait." He was a good boy. Man. A good boy grown to a good man.

He smiled and slipped into the chair next to her. Anson's rocker. She swallowed and looked away.

"How's your mother?" Rose asked, watching the boys across the street.

"You should visit her. She doesn't see real well these days, but the memories in her head are still full and clear, bright with the remembering of all those farms she visited selling those Jackson products." Rose listened to the chair creak as he leaned back. "They're good stories; take me right back to what was when I was little… and even before. You're in her tales. You and Thomas. She can make me see you young."

"I was once. Young. A long time ago."

"When the big boys ran the teacher's underpants up the flag pole," Milton said.

Rose laughed. "Your mother told you."

"She did." Milton covered her hand with his own. "She was there too." Milton paused. "And Anson."

Rose sighed, rocked a little faster. "That's why you're here. To talk about Anson."

"He left you some money." He patted her hand. "Quite a little bit."

She drew in her breath. She'd not thought of money. Not once.

May Snow

"Did he want me to look after Louisa?" she whispered. One of the boys jumped and caught a high ball. The others whooped.

"No. He didn't say so. In fact, he left Louisa some money. And the house," Milton said. "I think he thought she should learn to look after herself, so he left her a boost to get her started."

"Then that's all he wanted?" she asked. "To give me some money?" It was as if he had left no part of himself. "When did he do this? Put me in his will? What about the others?"

"His children get some. And the church."

"Nobody else?"

"His fishing buddies. Not money. His gear and some other personal things."

"No other woman?"

She heard his rocker stop, felt his hand tighten. "He came to me, Rose, only a few weeks ago. You were the only one added in the will."

"He left me money," Rose said. *They had never talked about money. What a cold thing to leave her. There was no spring of flesh, no light of thought, no spark of feeling in pieces of green paper passed from hand to hand.*

"Did you want more?"

She heard his rocker roll back and forth over the floor.

"Yes," she said. "I want more. A piece of him to tuck in my pocket, to put in my heart, to keep him as real as Thomas."

"Do you have something concrete and special that helps you hold onto Thomas?"

"No, he is stitched in my heart. Anson, I'm afraid, will slip through my soul, and time will fill in the hole he made there, and I'll forget how he felt in my life."

July

Milton's rocker stopped. She smelled him as he leaned close to her.

"Then take this and be happy." He turned her hand over and slipped a soft, velvet box on her palm. "He loved you very much."

Her fingers shook as she opened it.

Lying on white satin was a small, gold rose. It caught the sun and smiled back at it. A tiny, bright diamond sparkled at its center.

"Oh my," she whispered, touching the fragile petals with one finger. "Oh, my Anson." She closed her eyes to keep in the tears.

"He loved you," Milton repeated, his head close to hers. "He was afraid if he died before you were married, you might not know it well enough to keep it clear. This was to be your wedding gift. He asked me to keep it until that day. Just in case this happened."

"In case he died?"

"Yes."

"And he did. My Anson died."

"Yes, dear lady, but he wanted you to know his love."

"You're his messenger."

"The necklace is his love."

"My poor, dear Anson."

❄   ❄   ❄

Late in the day, Rose, head down, walked through the back-yards to Anson's house. Louisa's house now. Before she knocked, she ran her fingers over the mailbox, tracing letters of his name.

May Snow

It was awhile before Louisa opened the door. Her face was flushed and damp. She rubbed her forehead with a tissue and stared at Rose through squinting eyes.

Rose did not feel welcome.

"Have I come at a bad time?" she asked, touching the top of Louisa's arm. "You look tired."

"I thought you might be Dwight," Louisa said, looking past Rose. "Or Mother. I should have known. They wouldn't have knocked." She wiped her cheeks and frowned. "And they're mad." She made no move to let Rose in.

"I'll come back later," Rose said, not sure what to do. In a world full of people, Louisa stood out different. Or maybe it was that she was sucked in, invisible and empty, and needed too much filling, and Rose was tired.

"No, stay." Louisa flung up her arms and dropped them heavy against her thighs. "I need some help."

She still just stood, so Rose took her around the waist, turned her, marched them both into the house, and closed the door behind them.

They stood in the kitchen, wordless.

Finally Rose, not wanting to hurt or impose but feeling the pain of a house full of Anson and none of it touchable, grew impatient with this woman who stayed a child and wouldn't stretch her mind to reach her years and spoke. She strained to keep her words civil and smooth. "You tell me what you want and I'll try to help you."

Louisa threw out her arms and stamped her foot. "He has so many clothes."

Rose sighed. It had to be one of the two men in Louisa's life. "Anson or Dwight?" she asked.

260

July

"Grandpa."

"And why is that a problem?"

"Because Mother left them all for me to sort and pack."
God, she didn't want to do this. "I'll help you."

"I'm working on the stuff in the tall chest in his room."

"Hand-hewn cherry," Rose said. "It was his mother's."

"I can't believe it holds so much." Louisa rolled her eyes.
"And he has *three* chests of drawers, and all of them are
crammed tight with clothes and junk. There are even some of
Grandma's old things."

Rose rubbed the base of her throat. "Let's go up and do it,"
she said.

"I don't think I should have to touch his underwear."

Rose bit her tongue. "I'll pack his underwear."

"Good," Louisa said. "Come on." She headed for the stairway.

"Well, I'm certainly glad I lifted your spirits," Rose mumbled, hobbling after her, her legs dreading the stairs, her heart
dreading Anson's bedroom.

Anson's bed was piled with shirts and socks and pants
and belts and ties and handkerchiefs. Wincing, Rose pushed
her fingers against her lips, keeping a soft moan from
spilling out, swelling, and filling the room with an anguished howl.

"Don't you be tripping over that stool," Louisa said, pointing. "It's the one that had blood all over it. Still does. Nettie
did her best, but those stains were bad, soaked right in. I've
got lots of boxes. Dwight brought them up before he went
home mad. Damn him. He should be here packing. He's happy
I got so much of Grandpa's money. Thinks I'll share the

bounty." She threw ties in a box. "Well, if he thinks he's getting any, he should be here working."

Rose picked up a shirt and held it against her body, smoothing the wrinkles before she started to fold it. It was soft and smelled of Anson.

"We had a big fight. He wants me to sell the house and move." Louisa shoved belts in with the ties. "Well, I won't. It's mine now." She threw in handkerchiefs then suddenly stopped and sat down hard on the bed. "Maybe I should. He wants his own business far away from here." She dropped her chin on her chest and started to cry, head bobbing up and down, hands clamped between her knees. "And Mother wants my money. Thinks it should be hers. Uncle Greg too. He wants it. Maybe I should give it to them. But I can't. Why can't they understand? Why do they fight me? I have to have this money. Can't you see, Rose? It means I can have Dwight. I have to have Dwight. Only he's mad at me." She looked up at Rose. Louisa's face was blotched and full; her eyes and nose, wet and running. "I don't want Dwight mad at me. Or Mother either. Or God. Especially not God. I'm not evil, Rose. I'm sorry for all the bad things I've ever done. But look at me. I'm getting so old, and I've never been pretty. No man will ever love me. Just Dwight. I have to please him. Oh Rose, should I sell the house? I don't want to. It has so many corners where I can hide. But I have to keep Dwight. Grandpa never understood that part." She sniffed deep and shuddered, stilled her body. "But I think I could do anything to keep Dwight." She got up, took another box, and started filling it with Anson's pants.

Rose pushed her hair back. Her mouth felt dry. "I think I should go," she said.

"I thought you came to help me?"

"I will. Later. I can't just now. It's too soon."

"I guess I could close the door," Louisa said, looking around. "Just forget the mess. Or I could call Nettie. She would probably help me."

Rose nodded. *Let her,* she thought. *It doesn't matter anymore.*

Rose paused at the doorway. She felt heavy. Leaning against the wood to steady herself, she turned to Louisa. "I gave Anson a little, yellow, ceramic cat. It was my grandmother's. Have you seen it?"

"You mean in here?"

"Yes," Rose said. The air seemed so thick. She struggled for breath. "It's very special to me."

"I haven't seen it. Maybe he broke it."

"He would have told me."

"Or maybe somebody took it. A kid maybe. They were all over the place after the funeral. Maybe it's just been moved. I'll ask Nettie if she's seen it."

Rose swallowed.

"I'll look," Louisa said. "I'm sure it's someplace."

"Thank you. I'd be grateful."

Leaning heavily on the rail, Rose went down the stairs. Louisa was behind her, stepping light.

"Another thing, Rose," Louisa said when they reached the bottom.

"I don't like cats and you do… do you want Gossip and Rumor?"

May Snow

❄   ❄   ❄

Rose was too tired to adjust her back to better fit the park bench bars. She concentrated on the travels of a butterfly, flitting so light through the air, setting down on a branch or blade of grass for a brief but poised moment, then soaring again as it, playfully twisted, chasing hidden targets. She watched so hard she saw nothing else, felt nothing else. She was almost inside the butterfly and, at the same time, all around it. She narrowed her eyes and kept everything else out.

Awareness trickled in, like an eye seeing inside her head and knowing the spaces she'd emptied, the thick line of directed consciousness. It was an eye sharp enough to pierce protecting walls and send a steady, growing stream of clamoring reality around and through the taut thread of her single-minded direction, her connection to the butterfly. And when it broke, a river gushed in. The hot sun and sweat rolling beneath her dress. The bench, hard and pressing painful patterns into her back, and sticking to her thighs. The rush of cars. Buzzing bugs. Water falling from the fountain top to the penny pool below. Her legs, too short, aching as they strained to keep her feet flat on the sidewalk. Her heart, aching in its need for Anson.

She sighed and made ready to get up, head for home. She had purchased bananas and milk, stopped for a rest in the park, and was now rested enough to walk home. A short way, but it was so hot. She wished she had driven her car. She felt so heavy these days. And tired.

She spread her hands on either side of her and pushed against the wooden seat, making her body lift itself. The ache of resisting bones and joints shot into every corner of her body. And as she stood, she became aware of Grace standing near her, watching.

"Why, Rose." Grace poked her arm. "It's really you."

Rose lifted her head and faced Grace square. Suddenly overwhelmed by Grace's unexpected, vivid presence and unprepared, Rose sank back onto the bench.

"The mystery woman who disappeared into the bowels of her house to mourn has appeared." Grace grinned and dropped her bulky body next to Rose.

Rose, weary and hot, stuck to the bench, and unable to slide, feeling the sharp stabs of hostility, bent away from her friend.

"I haven't disappeared," Rose said.

"You haven't been to Bible class or choir." Grace stuck her legs out straight and wiggled her toes. "I do like sandals."

Rose watched Grace admire her feet.

"Haven't seen you riding your bicycle, though I grant you, it's been pretty hot," Grace said, twisting her ankle side to side.

Rose caught sight of the butterfly dipping and touching a maverick buttercup at the base of a thick chestnut tree, then lifting, swooping out of view.

Grace jiggled Rose's arm and frowned. "Are you listening to me?" Dropping Rose's arm, she pointed at the fountain. "I made wishes with Anson at that pool and dropped pennies in the water to make them come true. But they didn't come true." She looked at Rose. "Not the best of them anyway."

"My milk is going to sour," Rose said.

"So buy more," Grace said, tapping her fingers on her thighs. "I haven't seen you at the library, either. They could use some help with the summer story hour." She batted a fly on her arm. "Charity gets bored with it."

May Snow

Rose squirmed, pulling the underside of her legs away from the bench where her dress had risen up and her skin stuck to the wood.

"Louisa says Karen's trying to get some of the money Anson left her. She even wants the house. She won't get it, though." Grace laughed. "Everybody knows Louisa is spending every cent she's got on Dweebie Dwight. Silly woman. When the money runs out, he'll be fast behind it."

Rose winced. There was a slight intake of breath and quick release, a little bubble of joyful contentment and smugness at the end of Grace's laugh. Her joy in Louisa's desperate need repulsed Rose.

"Do you suffer at all because Anson died?" Rose asked. She felt Grace's arm tighten where it touched hers.

"I've got hard candies in my pocket," Grace said. "Want one?"

"No," Rose answered. "I want to know where your pain is. How can you be prancing around like your life hasn't changed? Don't you hurt? *Where is your pain?*"

"There's pain all over," Grace said, squinting. "You just have to squish it."

"You sure do a good job of squishing," Rose said. "Your pain must be half way to China."

"Oh, I think you're pretty good yourself. Didn't you feel just a tiny bit of pain when Thomas strayed?"

There was the sound of air being taken in quickly, and Rose realized it was her own breath filling her lungs.

"You must have," Grace continued. "But I didn't see it. Nobody saw your pain. You squished it."

"Thomas never cheated," Rose whispered.

"Sometimes you're so dumb, Rose."

July

Rose closed her eyes and breathed deep, pushing against the memory, the fear that stirred in her gut. *How could Grace know what couldn't be true?*

Beside her, Grace stirred and stood. "Better get your milk home."

Rose swallowed and willed her face stolid.

"Oh. We're going fishing off the dock tomorrow. Early, before June works. You should come." Grace walked away laughing.

❄   ❄   ❄

Thomas and Anson and Charity and Grace were sharp and young in Rose's dream. They were swimming in Lake Erie, jumping the waves and splashing each other. Their mouths moved, and she could tell they were laughing, but she couldn't hear them from the beach where she lay covered with sand. Only her head was free and able to move. She called out to June as she ran past on long, luscious legs on her way to join the swimmers. But June didn't answer, didn't even glance at her as she ripped off her clothes and jumped, naked, into the water. Rose shouted to Thomas not to touch June. Evil dripped from her breast tips and would poison him, but he floated closer and stretched his arm to reach and grab. She could see Grace's jaw open and extend, and her gleeful howls rolled silently through the air, causing the clouds to split and dip and crash upon each other.

The sun hit her face, and she awoke thinking she was still on the beach. Straining, she fought the sheet that was wrapped tight around her. Sobbing, she called out to Thomas. "Don't touch her. Don't touch her."

Even as she realized the dream wasn't real, she lay in her bed, crying, wanting to save her dear husband and bring him back to her. And as her heart stilled and the vision faded, she wondered if the ladies had reached Anson and tainted him too.

Silent then, and worn, she unraveled herself from the sheet, slid out of bed, went down the stairs on legs still trembling, and let the cats out the front door onto the porch. It crossed her mind that her imagination was soaring too high and perhaps it was time to let it rest, lest she travel up there to join them, the victim of a stroke or a heart attack. Although to be cushioned on a cloud with Thomas and Anson was certainly a pleasure to contemplate. She shook her head hard to drive out the dream.

She opened the door and stepped through it to breathe in fresh, unsullied morning air. Rose thought she ought to just go down to the pier with her fishing pole and join her old friends, welcome or not. Pretend Grace's offer was real. The mending had to start someplace. But she wasn't sure she could look at their faces and not see murder.

Her bare foot landed on a round, rolling object. She stumbled and grabbed at a chair, holding tight while it rocked until she could balance herself and her feet found firm ground.

Safe, she looked down to see what had tripped her.

There were marbles strewn all over the floor.

She wondered who could have spilled them on her porch. Then she grinned and pushed one with her toe. It clacked against another and that one smashed into a third. The sun caught the rolling glass and bounced bright off the clear, crystal colors. Shooting sparkling streams of light, it teased the cats to jump and chase the shimmering spheres. They raced in circles among the marbles, pouncing and playing. Rose laughed while she watched.

I should pick them up, she thought, *before the mailman comes and falls on his fanny and sues the pants off me.* Then she laughed even harder. *But I don't have any pants on,* she thought, rubbing her bottom, bare beneath her nightdress.

I could give them to Grace to put in her vases to hold her flowers in place. Or to Charity. For her real flowers. Grace's silk posies would never do for Charity. Oh, sweet friends, how I miss you. Even with all your funny little oddities.

She sighed and bent to gather the marbles. They probably belonged to Nicholas, were left without malice, forgotten for new play. Although he usually wasn't so careless, and she'd never seen him play with marbles.

※　※　※

"How come you never named your cats?" Nicholas asked, cradling one of the nearly grown Christmas kittens.

"I never really thought about it," Rose said. "I guess I figured 'pretty kitty' took care of it."

"It doesn't. They need their own names. Everybody does. Even cats."

"I suppose you're right." Rose rocked gently, sharing her porch with Nicholas.

"What are they anyways?"

"Why, they're *cats*, Nicholas." Rose looked up from her knitting. She rubbed her eyes and hoped for a few more rows before the sun was gone.

"Yeah, but are they boy cats or girl cats?"

"Two girls. One boy."

"Okay, then they're Abbey, Betsy, and Connor."

"I like those names," Rose said, smiling. "But they're a little unusual for cats."

"They're my cousins' names."

"Do you have lots of cousins?" Rose asked, surprised he had mentioned his family, hoping to hear more, not wanting to push him too far and silence him.

"Two more. Kathryn and Jacob." He sat, back bent, feet still, stroking the cat.

The light was slipping away quickly, leaving in its wake strands of orange and pink. Even as they watched, those were swallowed by the quiet, inky night.

"What do you see when you look out into the dark?" Rose asked.

"Sometimes I make up stories." The cat jumped out of Nicholas's lap. "Sometimes I watch them hunt."

"The cats?"

"Yeah."

"You really like them, don't you?"

"They're my friends." Nicholas tapped his foot against the porch steps. "I miss the kids back home a lot." He squirmed on the wooden floorboards. "Jacob and Connor and me were buddies. We used to play tricks on the girls."

"Where's home?" Rose rocked steady. Through the night's dark cloth she could see the shape of Nicholas. He looked so small.

"Sometimes I see people doing things in the night when they don't know I'm watching."

"That's spying, Nicholas," Rose said softly. "Maybe that's not quite fair."

"I don't see on purpose. I'm just there."

They sat awhile without talking.

"Lots of times I hear Louisa and Dwight. He wants her to sell Anson's house. She doesn't want to. Then he yells and goes away and she calls for him to come back. He won't, though. She cries a lot. Women do that. They cry too much."

"It's not always a bad thing to cry."

"You don't."

"Oh, sometimes I do, dear child. Sometimes there's a need too big to stop the tears."

"Like Anson dying?"

"Yes, like that." She heard him slide along the wood, felt him brush against her legs. She held the rocker steady. He leaned into her. His body was hard and warm, so small.

"I was watching when Anson came home with Louisa," he said. "He told her she had to go back to her mother's the next day. She didn't want to, but he said she had to pack her clothes. He told her she had to go home and grow up."

"That was the night Anson died," Rose whispered.

His hair brushed her knees when he nodded. "I got scared after the lights went out." She felt him tremble. "I ran home."

"Did you see anything, Nicholas?"

Rose held her breath.

"There were bats flying all over the place. It was kind of light out. Not too much, though. There was a big moon, but the clouds kept hiding it. It kind of looked like Halloween. Spooky. I saw ghosts. And witches. Like monsters."

May Snow

Rose sighed and dropped her hands on her knitting. "What did you *really* see, Nicholas?"

"I told you. I saw ghosts. And the witches. Great big shadows stretching out like tall tree trunks with fat, waving branches. Only they moved too much. Like they were old and creaky and spooky. Out to get kids and torture them."

"Old witches?"

"Probably old. Canadaway's got a lot of old people."

"Don't you like old people?"

"Not much. You're okay, though. And Anson, he was good too. Till the witches got him."

Rose smiled sadly. It wasn't an imaginary witch that killed Anson. She leaned back and looked at the stars. Maybe Thomas and Anson were stars now. And that one hovering close was Bernice. *Save a space for me,* she thought. She wished Nicholas were in her lap. She'd like to hug him. She was tired. She put his words away and lost herself to the sky.

❄   ❄   ❄

It rained during the night, washing dust off leaf and limb, cooling the heat, and blowing a light scent of fish and seaweed through Rose's window.

She awoke smiling, thinking she should make biscuits for Thomas before he went out to milk. Then she remembered. Thomas crashed dead against her brain. She squeezed her eyes shut for a moment then hugged the sheet around her and allowed herself to pretend, to fold herself into a memory that was old enough, good enough, to give more comfort than pain.

July

Robins were singing. She went to the window to hear them better. Their song was rich in her head, and she felt herself soar, land on a branch beside them, fling her head back, and open her mouth wide, bright music pouring from her throat.

Sweeping the yards with her eyes, she caught the back door opening at Anson's house. She saw Dwight creep out, look both ways, then glance back. He lifted his finger to his lips to shush Louisa, as she stepped out after him. She was dressed in filmy nylon. She giggled and reached for Dwight.

Ah, sweet love. They were back together again, Rose thought. She moved from the window. No point in embarrassing poor Dwight should he happen to look up and see her.

She peeked through the curtains and watched him scurry down the driveway, Louisa prancing behind him. He stopped and motioned her back to the house, but she flung herself on him, clutched him tight, and covered his face with kisses. He pushed her away and stamped his foot. She laughed and ran back to the house. Before she ducked through the door, Louisa turned and posed provocatively. Dwight shook his head and covered his face with his hands.

It was early. No one would see. *And no one would care,* thought Rose. It made no difference to anyone that Dwight had spent an unmarried night with Louisa. Not anymore. Some might even rejoice and count the girl lucky. But any who did see would surely take note of the near naked limbs of the middle-aged Louisa, and there would be clucking and cackling and clatter throughout the village. The hilarious word would spread. Louisa and Dwight would know. Cruel tongues would wag in their direction, and Dwight would cower. Louisa would cry. Rose went to her dresser for clothes. Thank God, it was so early in the morning.

✳   ✳   ✳

Rose and Nicholas sat on her porch in the evening dark.

"If I find something in the garbage can, can I have it?" he asked.

"Those are things for the needy," Rose said.

"Needy for what?"

Rose smiled and rolled yarn into a growing ball. It was easier to knit that way, no knots for her gnarled fingers to untangle.

"What did you find?" she asked.

"A cat."

"A *cat*. Oh, Nicholas, not one of my kittens?" Rose put her yarn in the basket by her rocker, and started to get up. "Come give me the sweet baby. Poor pussy. How did he ever get in the garbage can?"

"Not a real cat," Nicholas said. "See, it's an ornament." Twisting on the steps, he turned so he could show her. He held the figurine out to her.

Bending toward him, she took it, cupped it in her hands, and eased back in her chair. As her fingers smoothed over the familiar curves and slopes, she gasped and touched her heart. "Oh, Nicholas, this is *my* cat."

"You said it was for poor people."

"Where did you get it?" She stroked the porcelain animal. It felt crusty in spots, dirty. Her heart was beating fast.

"I told you. In the garbage can."

July

"How could it get there? I gave it to someone special. Like my grandmother gave it to me a long time ago. It's all I have left of her. It was a gift. To me. Then him. How could it end up in a garbage can?"

"Do you love it?"

"Oh yes."

"Then why didn't you take care of it?"

"I thought I did." Rose rocked slowly. She closed her eyes and saw the cat in Anson's bedroom.

"You have lots of cats," Nicholas said.

Rose swallowed and clutched her treasure.

"Rose?" Nicholas whispered.

"Yes, Nicholas."

"I think I might be needy."

She bent forward and put the cat in his hands.

21
Mid-July

Rose sat at her kitchen table, her face buried in her hands, fingers tight against her forehead. A jumble of memories and feelings and wants, fuzzy-edged and painfully dull, tumbled and crashed and exploded inside her head. Pushing her palms hard, she gritted her teeth and kept in the wail that pulsed wild, straining for release. Her body shuddered in its struggle to defend its control.

At the center of the table was a little carved dog.

A soft moan escaped. She trembled and pushed harder.

The phone rang.

She took her hands from her face, leaned her forehead into the cradle of one palm, closed her eyes, and listened to the ring.

By the time it was silent, she had emptied thought from her head, and weary and spent, she rose, took the carved wooden love gift gently in her hands, and walked to the china cabinet, keeper of her treasures, in her living room. She placed the dog on the center shelf in front, the most special of spots.

May Snow

Then she took a folding lawn chair from the back entry-way, lugged it down the steps, and headed for the beach at the end of Washington Avenue.

It wasn't until she had crossed the road that ran along Lake Erie's shore and had inched her way down the steep, cement stairs that led to the sand, clasping the iron pipe handrail for support, that she wondered who had called her on the phone. She worried that it might have been Margaret.

Stopping at the bottom of the steps, feet sinking in the soft, grainy soil — washed and worn and battered and broken for thousands of years by fierce, pulsing water then thrown to the edge of the lake — she lifted her face to the lake's breeze and let the thought go.

The beach was almost empty. Manley Warner was lying on a blanket next to Leeza Hinkle, Nettie's great-grand-daughter. Leeza was on her back, her body glistening where the sun touched oil. Manley lay on his stomach, face turned toward her. Rose thought his eyes were probably open and enjoying all that sparkle.

Further down, Maylene Peterson was digging a sand ditch with her sweet girl, Ashley.

And there was June standing at the water's edge, where the waves let loose little white humps that scurried toward shore on liquid legs that stretched and spread. Rose dropped her eyes and watched the water splash against June's feet, then circle and run back into the lake. June bent, picked up a pebble, flung it into the water. She picked up another stone and walked along the beach.

Rose sighed. She was too weary to trudge back up the steps and home. She unfolded her chair, sat, closed her eyes, and waited for the breeze to touch her face. The hot sun and the lapping, lulling water soothed her thoughts.

When finally there was nothing, and at the same time, a great sense of fullness, Thomas came and spread himself within her, touching every spot, every slope, and every corner that she was. She could hear him in the singing of the water, feel him in the silky touch of moving air, the soft whisper of sun against her skin. He was all around and in her.

She kept him as long as she could. But it was too hard, and she could feel him start to shrink, to leave her.

Her cheeks were cooled by tears.

She wasn't sad. Only longing.

When she opened her eyes, calmer now, she saw June swimming in the water. From this distance, she could have been a young woman. Rose ached to run through the sand, leap into the water, and slip through the waves with her. Swim with bones young and limber, bones of long ago that moved as the mind commanded.

Even while her body yearned in silence, Rose watched June, her former friend, pull herself from the heavy, drawing water and run with strong and able legs to the beach. As June's feet met the sand, Rose, sitting still with hands clasped tight, closed her eyes and imagined the wet, soggy soil squeezing through her own toes, spreading over them cool and grainy. She sighed and lifted her face to the sun. She couldn't take her shoes off. Not today. Her feet were swollen from the heat and the walk. The shoes would not go back on. The sun and breeze kissed her cheeks. That was enough. She leaned her head against the chair's webbing and smiled.

May Snow

The sun was hot. The lake roared. She dozed.

A hand was on her shoulder, pressing gently. Rose opened her eyes.

"Shh. Don't be frightened. It's only me."

"June?" Rose breathed in deep. Her head was heavy. She wanted to close her eyes again.

"You shouldn't be out in the sun too long." June dropped her hand against her thigh. She sat on her knees on a beach towel spread by Rose's chair.

"What about you?" Rose said. "You're showing more skin than I am."

June smiled. "I'm well oiled."

"Have I been sleeping long?."

"Awhile."

"I wanted to walk in the water," Rose commented.

"I'll walk with you." June stood and held out her hand.

"I can't take off my shoes."

"Then leave them on."

Rose gazed wistfully at the waves rolling and breaking. She cocked her head and nodded. "I will."

They walked along the edge of the water until Rose's legs were too weak to carry her further, and June ran back and got the folding chair. She set it up at the water's edge so Rose could rest.

"Thank you," Rose said.

June sank in the wet, packed sand beside her. Water lapped against them then flowed back. She hugged her knees and shivered.

"Are you cold?" Rose asked.

June shook her head, looked across the lake.

"I guess you're mad at me," Rose said softly. The sun shot shimmering sparks upon the water, darting, dancing.

"Not mad," June said. She bent her head to her knees.

"You think I took Anson away from you."

June picked up a stone, held it up to the sky, threw it down. "I miss him."

"I know," Rose said.

"I want to go to his house. Go inside without knocking. See him happy to see me and ready to listen to whatever words I give him. I want to touch his hair, run my fingers over the bunches on his fingers, touch his lumpy veins." She picked up another stone, rubbed it over her knee. "Mostly I want him to hold me. Just hold me."

Rose reached and touched June's hair.

June shook her hand away. "I wanted him always to be my friend," she said.

"He would have stayed your friend."

"He told me once I should get a cat. He said I was young enough that it would die before I did."

"He gave us cats for Christmas," Rose said.

"He knew how lonely I was."

"He would have stayed your friend," Rose said again.

"No," June said. "You took it away. You took it away from all of us."

"He would have been a friend to all of us."

June slammed the stone into the water. "Stop saying that! We wanted more than *friends*."

"Did you love him?" Rose whispered.

June swung her head and glared at her. "Did you?"

"I loved him." Rose bit her lip. The sun stung her eyes. "I

think I loved him. I did." She struggled to be true. "I almost loved him. I would have if he hadn't died ... I would have loved him as much as I could." She strained to keep the tears in. "I must have loved him. I miss him so."

"We could have done that too. Loved him as much as we could."

"He was our chance to feel again," Rose said.

"He was *your* chance, Rose. Not ours. You stepped quick and hard on our hopes. Pledges don't seem to mean much to you."

"I didn't mean to break the rules."

"Yes you did," June said. "You wanted him to be just yours."

"I missed Thomas so much. And Anson, Anson helped me. He separated me from Thomas. I wasn't a pair anymore, the second half of Thomas. I was a separate woman. I needed that so much." She couldn't stop the tears.

"We all needed something from him," June said. "That's why we had the rules. So we could share and we could all get a part of him. The part we needed. You took that away and he let you. He cheated too. Why shouldn't we be angry? Why shouldn't we want to shake you and hurt you and see you cry? What else have we got?"

Rose shuddered. "Did you want to hurt Anson too?"

"Sure I did," June said. "When you get hurt, you try to hurt back. Otherwise that pain pushes you way down to the black center of the earth, and you feel like nothing there. You have to fight back."

"Did you hurt Anson?" Rose asked.

June's body slumped against her knees. Rose couldn't tell if it was from pain or from sadness.

Mid-July

They sat quietly for awhile. When June got up, Rose thought she moved old.

"Let's go back," June said. She helped Rose up and carried her chair across the sand and up the steps. They didn't talk.

❄   ❄   ❄

"Gracie tells me Anson's granddaughter has bought a whole lot of stuff for her sleep-in boyfriend, so he could start himself a business right in Anson's house."

"When did she tell you that?" Rose asked, sliding her fingers around the jars of lotion and nail polish on Myrtle's bedside table and pushing through sample perfume packets, pencils, stamps, and rubber bands. She avoided the used tissues, pinching up little, heart-shaped, cinnamon candies. She enjoyed the time she spent volunteering at the nursing home. "You really ought to get rid of some of this stuff."

"I need it," Myrtle said. She sat in her wheelchair on the other side of the bed combing the long, blond curls of an angel-faced doll dressed in pale blue velvet. Its costume was banded with white fur on the hem, sleeves, and neck. The doll wore ice skates. "She was here today. With Charity. Old sober sides. At least Grace knows how to laugh."

"Charity can be funny too," Rose said. She held the candies in her hand. "Can I throw these out? They're pretty sticky."

"Charity's a skinny stick, cold fish," Myrtle said, dropping the comb and stroking the doll's hair. "You keep that candy where I can reach it."

"I'll bring you some in cellophane."

"See these fingers." Myrtle lifted her hands, stretched her

fingers, and groaned. "They don't work good enough to unwind any old cellophane."

Rose smiled. She'd seen those fingers tear wrappers from cookies with speed and dexterity. "They work fine." She wrapped the candies in a tissue and dropped them in a glass ashtray that was filled with paper clips and a grubby eraser shaped like a mouse. "Were they both here?"

"Who? Charity and Grace? Of course. What else? They're always together." Myrtle stuffed her fingers under her thighs. "Where were you?"

Rose came around the bed and took the doll from Myrtle's lap. "Around," she said, patting the sick old lady's head. This was the part she really liked, chatting with the old ladies. And Myrtle, with her long, flowing, white hair and ample bottom, was Rose's favorite. Let Charity write the letters and read the newspapers in her crisp, informative manner and let Grace lead the dances and song fests and swing among the games and birthday socials. Rose preferred talk and touch. She loved her ladies who were strong in endurance and able to grasp and enjoy the little moments of deliberate disobedience when they feigned misunderstanding, loss of intelligence, failed hearing or when they pulled forth latent bull-headed stubbornness, trickery, foolishness, and mischievous glee at the expense of the staff. Myrtle — sometimes child, sometimes seer, sometimes sweet saint, always charming chameleon — could do it all.

Rose placed the doll on a shelf lined with fancy, frilled, porcelain beauties and softer stuffed or plastic pretend people. "Whose turn is it now?" she asked.

"Give me a fat baby doll," Myrtle said. "I feel like cuddling."

There were several to choose from. Rose picked a soft,

spongy newborn, pink-skinned and smelling like powder. Before she put it in Myrtle's arms, she held it to her own chest a moment.

"I named her Grace," Myrtle said. "They smell alike. I've got a Charity doll too. That one." She pointed to a tall, slim lady doll, elegant and lovely in simple-cut silk. "She's proper."

"Is there a Rose doll?"

"Yep, the one in the strawberry print. Holding the kitten. The one with the pink cheeks and dimples."

"I don't have dimples."

"You do inside."

"How do you know?"

Myrtle shrugged. "You like to joke. And gossip."

"Only if it's true," Rose said.

"Nothing's true." Myrtle cradled her doll, dropped a kiss on its head. "There are too many sides. Here, take this." She lifted the doll to Rose. "It doesn't feel like a real baby. Sometimes it does, though."

Rose took the doll. It felt like dead rubber and cloth and bristly fake hair. As she lay it on the bed, one eye stuck open and staring, glassy blue, looking at the ceiling.

"You're having troubles, aren't you?" Myrtle asked. "With Charity and Grace."

"And June," Rose said.

"Don't know her."

"She's new in town. Sort of."

"She taking your place with Charity and Grace?"

"Not exactly." Rose went to the window and watched the sun dropping. "I've got to be going. I don't like driving in the dark."

May Snow

"You drove?"

"My legs get tired."

"Long day, huh?"

"Kind of," Rose said. She put her finger on the glass and traced a tree.

"You see the stuff in Anson's yard?"

"It's Louisa's yard."

"His granddaughter. The inheritor."

Rose nodded and turned. Myrtle deserved to know everything she could tell her. It was her town too. Had been for years.

"Louisa has a boyfriend. Dwight Wilson and she wants to keep him. Really wants to keep him. Anyway, Anson gave her the house and a lot of money. Her thinking's all messed up. She thinks you can buy a person by giving him what he wants, like matching the price tag you think you see hanging on him. She wants to buy Dwight. Keep him where she wants him to be. So she bought him a business. Gonna make him a king in his little kingdom. Bought him a tractor with all kinds of gadgets — plow, cutting blades, cultivator. Got him a sign, 'Dwight's Lawn Care.' And she thinks she bought herself a man. I told you. She's got a messed up head."

※ ※ ※

On her way home from the preschooler soccer game, Rose stopped at the convenience store for English muffins and peanut butter. All those little legs chasing the elusive black-and-white ball had stirred her own child-like appetites, and she meant to give herself a dinner that fed that kiddy craving.

As she stepped into the store, Rose immediately spotted

Mid-July

Louisa. A candy bar in either hand, shoulders hunched, Anson's granddaughter peered intently at the magnificent array of sweet candy bar choices laid out on the shelves before her. Frowning, she put a bar back, took another, put them both back, wrung her hands. Her hair was greasy, and her skirt hung baggy over her sandals. Moving closer, Rose could see that Louisa's toenails needed cutting. Rose considered backing up and tiptoeing into the next aisle.

This is for you, Anson, she thought and forced her legs to take her to Louisa. The faces of laughing children running in a pack after the ball, kicking it in any direction, tumbling, sliding, sometimes falling, and being lifted by parent coaches who cuddled the pain away faded and so did the energy she'd soaked in from watching them.

"My favorites are chocolate-covered peanuts," Rose said.

Louisa's head slowly rotated, a quarter turn and back. She didn't blink; she didn't flinch; she didn't speak.

If I'd never left the path of friendship and stepped onto the wide road of passion, I could walk out of here right now, Rose telepathed to Anson. *But no, I gave you my heart and you gave me guilt. And here stands Louisa. Obviously in need of some kind of a jump-start. This is one of the rare times I wish I had not known you.* Rose sighed. *No, erase that. I don't really mean that. Not quite, anyway.*

"Maybe a peppermint patty," Rose said.

Louisa grabbed a peppermint patty and shoved it into Rose's hand.

"I know you're hurting," Rose said and put the candy back on the shelf, "but I don't know why."

"Would you care?"

Rose nodded. She lifted her hand to touch Louisa in her pain, to soothe her and Louisa quickly lifted her own arm to ward her off. Rose stopped midway.

"Dwight wants to marry me."

"But that's good," Rose said. "That's what you want."

"It's not enough. He teases and teases. He wants us to move."

"Out of Anson's house?

Out of Grandpa's *town*. I bought him a tractor and a lawn-shredder and a wagon. And a pile of rakes and hoes and a posthole digger and bags and bags and *bags* of dirt. He's got everything. *Everything.* He wanted his own business. Well, I bought him a business, and he still wants to go."

"Maybe he has to," Rose said and wished for a place to sit down. More guilt. *Were legs more important than lives?* she wondered

"Maybe *I* can't." Louisa swung around to face Rose. "Maybe God wants me to stay here and take care of Grandpa's house, you know? That's why Grandpa gave me money. To take care of his house. But I need the money to keep Dwight. I got the house and I got the money, and it's all part of the package. If I don't keep the house, I don't get the money. And then I'll have nothing to keep Dwight with. Poof. He'll be gone. I don't know how else to keep him. I buy and I buy and I buy. And he still wants more from me."

"I don't think he's looking for money," Rose said.

"Well, it's all I've got. And I worked hard to get it."

Rose pulled her chin to her throat, wrinkled her brow, and pressed her lips together.

"Well, I did. You think it was easy living with Grandpa? Well, it wasn't. He made me feel dumb and clumsy and *young.*"

Mid-July

Louisa flung up her arms. "I did all I could, and I got the money. And the house to boot. I earned them and I'm not about to give them up. I paid the price. They're mine."

❄   ❄   ❄

Rose stood admiring her reflection in the long, coat-tree mirror. There were no wrinkles in the face she saw, and her soft, white curls had deepened to gold-touched brown. When she lifted her arms and swayed to the song in her heart, there was no sag, no skin hanging, and when she lifted her hips in a provocative roll, her belly, gently rounded, did not jiggle.

She tilted her head, turned it to follow the flow of her arms, and caught the sparkle of the diamond at the center of the golden rose necklace circling her neck, catching the light while she danced.

Loud pounding at the front door jarred her vision, transforming the graceful image in the mirror to an indisputable old lady, gawky and incongruous but twinkling in the eye.

Hey, she thought, *the outside shell may be cracked, but the inside yolk is still pretty juicy.*

She opened the door, a whisper of a young Rose still swinging in dance, kissing the eyes of her brain.

Nicholas stood on the porch. His face was white. He shook.

Rose bent to him, cupped his face. "Something is wrong, child. Tell me quickly." His mouth trembled and his eyes were wet.

"I can help you, Nicholas."

"My mom's crying bad. I can't stop her."

"Is she hurt?"

May Snow

His head jerked back and forth. "I don't think so. Nobody hit her. She can't quit, Rose. I don't know what to do."

Rose kissed him quick on the forehead and took his hand. "We'll fix it, Sweetie." It crossed her mind to send him into her house to wait, but she dared not leave him alone.

They crossed the yards together. She heard the wails before they got to the door. Nicholas, in his haste, had left it open.

He tugged her arm and looked up at her. She saw his face and stopped.

"You can stay outside, Nicholas," Rose said, keeping her eyes on his. "I can take care of your mom alone."

"No," he whispered.

"I'll come back out as soon as I can. I won't forget you."

"No."

"Please wait here, sweet boy."

"I'm afraid to be alone."

She thought of the nights he whisked through the dark or sat silent disappearing into it. "Okay. Stay close. You can hang onto my skirt if you want to." She squeezed his hand. She wanted him near her, but she might need her hands free.

They stepped into the house, Rose before Nicholas.

The sun filled the living room, brightening the toys strewn about.

Amy sat on the floor by the far wall, knees drawn up, arms hugging them tight. Her head bent low, her forehead rested on her raised knees and her hanging hair covered her face. Her cries were ragged, turning to moans, pulled deep from her innards, wrenching and harsh.

Rose hurried to her and stooped down though her ankles screamed their distress.

"Are you hurt?" she asked softly, running her hands all over Amy's body. There was no blood and no flinch from sudden pain.

She felt Amy shudder. Amy lifted her face. It was swollen and wet, blotched red. She lifted a fist to her mouth, pressed it tight, started to rock.

Rose folded the young woman into her arms and rocked with her.

Slowly the cries grew more shallow and eased to gasping sobs. Amy buried her face in the comfort of Rose.

Rose heard her lurching whisper.

"I'm so sorry. I'm so sorry. Poor, poor Nicholas. Whatever will become of my baby?"

Nicholas held tight to Rose's skirt.

Rose held Amy for a long time. Amy did not explain her sorrow, and Rose did not ask.

❄   ❄   ❄

Rose got up early and packed her bicycle to go fishing. If she were lucky, the old ladies would be there. If they weren't, well, she'd just enjoy the thrust of the line and the wait for the tug, and if the walleye cooperated, she would bring home supper.

As she turned out of her driveway, she looked toward Nicholas's house. Nothing was happening. The drapes were closed. The morning paper lay on the steps. Before Rose had left their house last night, Amy had promised Nicholas a picnic. She said he could take someone with him, a friend. Rose hoped it would happen, but she'd never seen Nicholas with a playmate, and he'd said nothing when his mother pledged a

291

day of shared fun. He just stared, silent. Rose suspected his head was too filled with feelings to find words to fit.

It was pleasant to be on her bike, pumping slow and savoring the crisp, sweet juices of morning. Her mind was fresh. Her veins cried no pain. Her joints moved smoothly. Sometimes the gods were good.

It took little time to get to the pier.

Joy surged sharp when she saw that the old ladies were there. And June.

Bodies poised on the concrete dock and set against a clear, blue sky, the women stood like moving statues, clear-cut and plain. Charity and June, tall and sharp-edged, fished side by side. Charity's silhouette stood regal and haughty, not to be touched. June's appeared harsher, almost as if she was made out of cheaper material. Standing apart from them, Grace, who was shorter and rounder, seemed to have cracks in her seams as if she had moved before her boundaries had hardened. They were intent on their business and offered no welcome.

Rose parked her bike and fixed her gear, took her readied pole, and stood with them. They kept their silence.

The water was clear. It sparkled and peaked in little moving mountains, percolating up and down. She cast her bait into it.

They let her stay.

It was comfortable for a little while. She absorbed their presence. Accepted. A part of.

She couldn't see their faces. They confronted the lake with concentration as if mesmerized, dazed by its steady throbbing flow. They didn't turn their heads to look at her.

June lowered herself to a sitting position. Her legs hung over the dock. Charity unfolded two lawn chairs, passed one to Grace, and sat in the other. A third chair — Rose surmised it was for June — lay flat bedside Charity. It wasn't offered to her, and no one asked how her legs were holding up.

The sense of oneness gone, Rose sat on the bolted-down dock bench.

They were four ladies sitting close to each other and fishing.

Glancing at the others, checking to see if they would finally meet her eyes, seeing that they would not, Rose grasped her pole tight and spoke to the water.

"I have this awful feeling that something bad happened to Anson. I walk through the day and sleep at night with that fear." She paused. There was no sound except the lap of lake against the piling, the call of gulls, the distant roar of traffic. No friend offered a response.

So Rose continued. "Something bad. That made him die. It scares me." She swallowed, waited a moment, and went on. "Like he didn't die naturally. Maybe he had help. Maybe he died accidentally. Not with intentional help. It goes without saying that he certainly didn't bump his own leg on purpose." She knew she was rambling. "He knew the vein could burst. And he was careful. Maybe someone kind of pushed him. Or hit him. Or something. Accidentally. You know, not on purpose. And she's afraid to say it."

Silence.

She spoke again, her eyes straight out on the water and her heart, solid and beating fast.

"What do you think?" she asked. "Maybe someone went there to talk that night. And got mad and maybe hurt him. But didn't mean to. And now she doesn't know what to say. What do you think? Do you think that could have happened?"

May Snow

Charity cast her line with seeming determination. "What do you think, Rose?"

The others didn't move their poles.

"It could have happened that way," Rose responded. "An accident, though. Not intentional."

Charity reeled her line in. Grace and June did the same.

"I think he could have accidentally smashed his leg against the bed," Charity said. She picked up her equipment. Grace and June did likewise. "This isn't pleasant conversation, Rose. It had better stop."

The old ladies walked away.

❄ ❄ ❄

That night in her sleep, Rose chased Thomas through skies shot with lightening. She called him to stop, shouted his name, but her voice fell on heavy, gray clouds that sucked her words into their thick, grainy mass and slowed them to muffled whispers. Then Anson was there and he promised to help. When Thomas saw them, he roared thunder-like bellows. Then Anson pushed her away. He left her and ran to help Thomas. Worms dangled from their fingertips and they reached into a barrel, dipping their wormed fingers in and yanking out their catch — huge, squirming fish with eyes round and glassy, reflecting the light of the storm. Laughing, they hurled the glistening fish at Rose.

She was back in her bed, and a fish hit the roof. One after another pounded the shingles.

She opened her eyes. The phone was ringing, shrill and insistent.

Mid-July

It stopped.

She lay frozen, wide-awake, waiting.

It didn't ring again.

❄   ❄   ❄

Early the next morning while it was still dark, Rose went out to drink coffee on the porch and watch the sun come up. There she found Margaret sitting in a rocker, arms wound tight around her body, rocking slowly, humming softly.

"Doesn't it look peaceful?" Margaret asked sadly without turning. "It's so lovely it makes my heart stop."

Rose watched the orange glow spread and the tree limbs start to show and the telephone lines and the birds perched still and the housetops, crisp-lined and clean.

She passed her coffee to Margaret, who untangled her arms, took a sip, gave it back, and hugged herself again.

"Did you call me last night?" Rose asked, afraid she had been frightened by her own child's need.

"No."

"Have you been here long?"

Margaret shook her head. "I wish it could stay half-dark forever."

Leaning against the back of Margaret's chair, settling its motion, Rose stroked her daughter's hair. Margaret reached and covered her mother's hand with her own.

"I love you, darling daughter," Rose whispered.

"Come sit with me and watch the night disappear."

"Are you cold?" Rose asked, sliding into the chair next to Margaret. "I'll get you an afghan."

May Snow

"It goes so fast — the dark, safe night. That's my blanket lately. Soft and hazy, it creeps around and warms me. The only pictures I see are those I make. It's the bright sunlight that shows distinctly, stark and ugly. I can't pretend away what I see clear."

Rose clasped her hands and rocked. Her heart was sliding down.

"I have looked for help everywhere," Margaret said. "There's a black void in me, an inside ache that I can't touch."

Rose bit her lip.

"I've been to church. I've been for counseling. I've called the help line. I sit for hours wondering what I did wrong. What can I do to fix it? Who is he with now? Why does he want to be with her instead of me? Nothing helps. Nothing. What can I do? Help me, please help me, Mother."

Rose took her daughter's hand and squeezed it tight. She couldn't tell her that the only help was inside herself, that piece of God that waits. She would only know that when she was ready and able to see. And she wasn't there yet.

"I'm walking with you, dear Margaret," Rose said, aching to take her daughter's pain. But even if she could, she should not rob her child of growth, that glorious summit of a hard-climbed mountain.

They rocked together and daylight came.

22
Late July

There were two envelopes in the mailbox.

Rose opened the top one first. It was thick and white with curlicue letters splashed across the front. She knew the moment she felt its weight that it was an invitation to a wedding.

Before she ran her finger under the flap, she lifted the envelope to her nose. It smelled faintly of lilacs. She hoped the inside paper was tinged with light purple, fragrant and fragile. But it wasn't. The whole of the envelope, inside and out, was snowy white, virginal white, and so was the card inside the second envelope. White with gold lettering. Plain other than a border of embossed white roses.

A touch of lavender would color it a bit more appropriately, Rose thought. Then she smiled. *What's the difference? Louisa had caught Dwight. And how many virgins were left in the world, anyway? Let her send white. Let her wear white, throw a veil over her head, keep him from her bed on the eve of her marriage. It was a wedding, a joining, a time to rejoice. She'd go and she'd dance and she'd tip a cup to her lips. For a moment the world would shine bright.*

The second envelope was also white. But there was no stamp or return address. The flap was sealed tight.

Rose frowned as she turned it over. She shoved her finger into a tiny hole at the top of the envelope and ripped.

There was a single sheet of paper inside.

> *If you're looking for a murderer, look in the mirror. You broke the rules. You caused him to change direction and walk toward you alone. It wasn't fair. You were going to get everything. You should have played the game right, and Anson would still be alive.* You *killed him.*

❄   ❄   ❄

After choir practice, the ladies walked over to the park to watch the high school glee club perform. Ambling three abreast, arms locked together, hips bumping as they struggled to stay on the sidewalk, Rose walked between Helen Bond and Nettie Hinkle. Ahead of them, hips swaying, fingers snapping in time to the lilting harmonies swinging through the air, Grace strolled beside Charity. Occasionally, Charity grabbed her sister and tugged her to dignity.

"Good crowd," Nettie said. "See any seats?"

"There's a bench on the other side." Charity pointed without looking back.

"That's not enough room for all of us," Helen said.

"Some of us have legs good enough to stand on," Charity said.

Grace turned with eyebrows lifted, lips stretched downward and glanced quick at Rose. She shrugged and looked forward again.

"I can sit on the grass," Helen said.

"Too damp," Nettie said.

"I'll bunch up my sweater and sit on it."

"Like you could get back up," Grace said.

Rose wished they would stop. They should have brought lawn chairs. Or got there earlier. The last few minutes of choir practice had not made them better warblers.

"All we have to do is get there," Charity said. She motioned them forward, picking up speed. "Canadaway boys are polite. They'll get us seats."

She was right. Manley Warner and Sammy Gugino marched over with folding chairs as soon as the ladies drew near the empty park bench. They opened the chairs, set them on sturdy level spots, stepped up to Helen and Nettie, took them by the arm, and led them smartly to comfort, and then they ran and flopped on the grass by their friends. Their mothers smiled approval.

Rose sat down carefully on the bench next to Grace. Grace turned and grinned then looked away. Charity was on her other side partially hidden from Rose by Grace's bulk.

Grace stuck her foot out and moved her ankle back and forth.

"Put it down," Rose said. "I've seen it before."

Grace winked at her and crossed her legs at the ankles.

Sweet sounds touched their ears, voices young and confi-

May Snow

dent. Rose leaned back and closed her eyes. The smell of grass was clean and heavy, baby-skin sweet inside her nose.

Grace wiggled next to her and strummed her fingers on the wooden seat. "Charity hid my skate key in the window box," she whispered to Rose. "But I found it." She tapped her foot on the sidewalk. "Don't tell her I know where it is."

Rose frowned. Charity had always hidden the skate key. Years ago. When they were children. Why would Grace want a skate key now?

Nettie passed out root beer barrel candy.

Helen's head swayed to the rhythm.

Shadows dropped. The streetlights glowed soft amber, brightening as the night darkened. The music flowed steady, ebbing, rising, circling. A cloud of notes, spreading and dropping, gently covered the ladies with dreams and tranquility.

It was over too fast. Bodies stirred, gathered belongings, nodded to the ladies as they passed, and then the park was empty, quiet.

Charity lit a cigarette. Smoke swirled under Rose's nose, acrid and unpleasant. She wrinkled her face.

"Dark night," Nettie said. "Probably should get on home."

"Peaceful," Helen said, hugging herself. "I could burrow right in. Just let the black curl around, keep me warm and hidden."

"It's spooky," Nettie said. "I don't like it. Not unless I know where everything is. I don't want no dark, pointy stuff poking out at me."

"Murdering creatures in Canadaway. Hiding behind trees." Grace giggled. "I don't think so."

"There could be people living here who make other people

die. Why not?" Rose spoke low, wishing she hadn't, willing her words back, hoping them unheard.

"No doubt," Charity said. The tip of her cigarette blazed. "What do you think, Helen? A coven of killers in Canadaway? It's almost poetic."

"Not poetic and not possible," Nettie said, "and it's time for me to go. Before God snuffs out the streetlights from all this ugly talk."

"No," Helen said. "We're a good town." She got up, folded her chair, and leaned it against an oak tree. "A good, safe town. Come on, Nettie, I'll walk you home."

The chairs would be okay, Rose thought. *The boys would get them the next morning. Nettie and Helen would be safe. No monsters would jump from bushes and attack them. Canadaway was a safe town. But Anson was dead.*

Helen took Nettie's arm and walked her away into the night.

"Trusting, isn't she?" Charity said.

Grace swung her legs.

"Do you like the dark, Rose?" Charity asked.

"Sometimes it's comfortable," Rose said.

"They should let old people join the glee club," Grace said.

"Nicholas next door plays in the dark," Rose said. She smoothed her dress over her knees. "The dark gives him power."

"Over what?" Grace asked

"His loneliness," Rose said.

"How strange," Charity said, "that a child would play alone in the night."

"Maybe it's easier to pretend you have friends in the dark," Rose said. "He saw witches the night Anson died."

May Snow

The bench moaned as Charity moved against it. "Quite an imagination," she said.

"He said he saw them," Rose said. "They were real to him."

"It's dark in the yards by his house," Charity said. "So many trees and bushes. I suppose it's easy to imagine what you can't see."

Rose smelled Charity's cigarette smoke, sharp and piercing, as Charity drew deep and blew it out slow.

"The night Anson died there was a big moon," Grace said.

Rose felt her throat grow tight.

Charity stood. "It's time to go home." She dropped her cigarette, rubbed it into the grass with her shoe. Rose saw her face in the streetlight.

"We all remember that night, Rose." Charity turned and walked away.

❄   ❄   ❄

Rose was sweeping cobwebs from the ceiling corners in the living room when the phone rang. Startled, she dragged the broom straws down the wall. Straggly, gray, web strands streaked the wallpaper. She sighed and wiped her face with her apron. She picked up the phone, hoping it was Margaret.

"Took you long enough to get to the phone," Charity said.

Rose gripped the receiver. "I was cleaning cobwebs."

"Messy job."

"Yes." Rose waited for words she knew would not come.

"Sarah Hunter asked me to call. Bingo's cancelled. They're varnishing the church hall floor."

"Next week then?"

"Yes," Charity said.

"Okay." Rose bit her lip. "Charity?"

"Sarah wanted me to tell you."

"Charity?" Rose didn't want her to hang up.

"What?"

"If you wanted, I could drive next week. Pick up June and maybe we could go for ice cream after."

"It's too hard for you to drive in the dark."

"I could manage one time."

"Probably would kill us all."

"Or we could go for dinner before bingo."

"We could."

"I'll pick you up."

"One thing, Rose."

"What?" Rose rubbed the gold rose at her neck.

"It's best if you let this Anson thing go. Don't be making any more remarks that some monster came and killed him..."

"Not a monster," Rose said softly.

"Or a neighbor, then. Or a stranger passing through. Or a *friend*. Don't be delving any deeper. It was an accident. Let it be."

"I want to," Rose said. "I want it to be over."

"Then let it be over."

"I can't be sure," Rose said. She didn't *know*, but she felt something was wrong and it wouldn't leave her.

"You think it was one of us," Charity stated flatly.

"Was it?" The words were a struggle.

"I thought we were working on being friends again."

"Was it one of you?" Rose asked again.

"If it was one of us," Charity said, "do you think we'd tell you.? Righteous you. You won't even pluck a grape from an open market. You'd send us straight to jail."

"It's stealing," Rose said.

"It is stealing," Charity agreed. "But a *grape*? Get real."

"It's still stealing. And how do you know who touched it last or where their hands had been? How could you eat it knowing it was dirty?"

"I'll see you next week, Rose."

"Wait."

"What?"

"You didn't answer me: was it one of you?" Rose asked, wanting badly for her friend to say, "No, no, definitely, no."

A new voice came on. Grace. On another phone. Probably in her bedroom.

"You know, Rose, if somebody really did kill Anson, you'd better let it alone. I saw Louisa in the market. She thinks you're a nosey, old biddy. People will think you're weird if you keep telling everybody you see that you think Anson was murdered."

"You've been listening." Rose could feel Grace shrug and grin. "I haven't been telling people anything. Why are you so mean and angry? How can I help what I feel?"

"You're right," Charity said. "Grace is angry. You broke a pact. You think we're killers, so why shouldn't she be mad. How can we help how *we* feel?"

"I hate this," Rose said.

"Why don't *you* be a friend?" Charity asked. Her voice was gentle.

"Hey, maybe you killed him, Rose," Grace said. "You live the closest. Maybe you thought he decided to ditch you."

Late July

❄   ❄   ❄

Later that evening, as Rose spooned chicken soup into her mouth, the liquid hot and heavy with carrot and celery and sweet chicken pieces, a pain shot from her jaw through her tooth to her cheek bone, leaving a throb within the walls of her enamel.

She waited long, painful moments for the ache to subside. When it didn't, she climbed on a chair, reached far back in the cupboard, and pulled out the whiskey bottle Thomas thought he had hidden. She uncapped and tilted it, her fingers over the top catching the liquid, then she rubbed it over her gum. She left the bottle on the counter in case the numbness wore off.

When Nicholas came and sat with her on the porch in the dark, she mumbled her pain through teeth clenched together to protect the aching tooth from the movement of jaw and the rush of air.

Nicholas patted her knee and murmured his sympathy. Then he sat, cross-legged and silent, close to her rocker.

❄   ❄   ❄

Her forehead resting heavily against her palm, Rose sat at her kitchen table. She clutched her jaw with her other hand, hoping to contain the pain in one spot and keep it from filling her whole mouth, spreading with the saliva that she tried to suck in and swallow, a well that kept spilling over.

She'd been up all night. She knew there had been moments of sleep, little catnaps ending when her face slid from her hand and pain jerked her awake.

May Snow

The throbbing stayed with her. She marveled that a spot so small could take over the whole of her body, rendering it totally concentrated on that steady pulse.

She rubbed more whiskey around the swollen tooth. Ignoring the sense of her brain, she was convinced the tooth had grown and was still growing and maybe would burst. If the pain would end in the explosion, she hoped it was so. She knew it was not.

She felt every one of her seventy-three years. Inside and out. There was no youthful soul struggling to push unwilling old bones into jumping and dance today. Her soul, too, was old on this day. If she lifted any part of her body, she knew the skin on that piece would sag to the floor.

There was a knock at her door. She sighed and carefully turned her head to the sound.

Another rap, sharper. She pushed herself up. Slowly, keeping her body stiff, she stepped to the door, all thought fixed on a jar-free walk.

Gingerly she opened the door.

"Oh, you poor soul. You look awful."

It was Amy. Nicholas was with her. Rose tried to smile. It hurt.

"Have you called the dentist?" Amy asked, stepping in.

"Not yet." Rose's lips barely moved.

"I'll do it for you. Do you have a number?"

Rose pointed to the living room. She wagged her fingers when Amy hesitated. "The book's on the table. Under the phone." Not meaning to, not wanting to, she pushed her tongue against the tooth. And it *hurt*.

"You sit down. I'll go call. Nicholas, you stay with her."

Amy went to the other room, came back. "Oh, I brought you some oil of cloves. Rub it on your gums. It'll help. My gramma taught me." She shoved the small bottle into Rose's hands and headed back to the living room.

Rose slumped in her chair.

"It hurts bad, doesn't it?" Nicholas said.

Rose, face stern and unmoving, winked at him.

"I told Mom."

Rose dropped her forehead onto her palm, squeezed it, rubbed it.

"She feels bad for you," Nicholas said, patting her shoulder. "Sometimes she gets toothaches."

Rose twisted, reached, grasped his arm. Pain surged deep. She moaned softly.

"It's all right," Nicholas said. "You don't have to talk to me. I'll just talk to you."

"You're a good boy," Rose whispered. His touch was comfort.

Amy came back. "I got him. Dr. Minnow. He says come now. I'll drive you."

"I need a bath."

"He's going to look at your mouth, not your body."

"Just let me brush my teeth."

"You don't have enough pain? You want more?" Amy stooped behind her, rubbed Rose's arms gently. "Come along, Rose. You need some help. Dr. Minnow won't care if your tooth doesn't sparkle."

"Thank you," Rose said, letting Amy steady her as she stood.

"Hey, I was coming over anyway."

Rose stood a moment, hunched, arms wrapped tight around her body, holding herself together.

May Snow

"I wanted to tell you," Amy said low into Rose's ear. She hesitated. "I wanted to tell you that if you want to check on Nicholas once in awhile, it's okay. But not too much. And keep him away from your mean, old, lady friends."

Swallowing, pushing the pain where it belonged, Rose smiled.

※　※　※

Rose dug deep in the chest that sat in the bedroom she'd slept in with Anson. Reaching deep, she pulled out an off-white afghan patterned with cable and seed and popcorn stitches. She sat back on her heels and bent her head into the soft yarn. It smelled faintly of lilies of the valley, of backyards in spring.

Rose closed her eyes and times of old seeped in and filled her — Charity laughing, her arms filled with the first wedding afghan Rose had made, white and lacy and thick-fringed, stitches not always in the exact, right spot; Grace dancing with her squares of many colors slung over her shoulders, yarn dipping and dragging behind her flouncing feet; Margaret, dear Margaret, crying, knowing the love in every stitch — many special friends, much special family. All were with Rose as she held this afghan, knit for Margaret's child, for the time when she would find someone to love and to marry and to sleep with under the gift of Rose's wedding blanket. And now she was going to give that afghan to Louisa, Anson's grandchild — a gift to Anson. She would make another for Emily. And that would be stitched with love too.

Rose got up. She folded the blanket. She wrapped it in white tissue.

Late July

It was ready. It was time to walk across the backyards and take the gift to Louisa. Rose held the package in her arms, tight against her chest, for a long time.

There was a set of knives in her cupboard, a bonus for buying her dryer at Mad Mattie's Appliances. It was still in sealed, unbroken plastic. She could wrap that and give it to Louisa, keep the wedding afghan for the grandchild she loved. That's how it should be. That's how it had always been. Given with love.

Anson would want her to love Louisa.

She breathed deep and swallowed her sadness. She carried the afghan out of her house and across the yards to the house where Anson had lived.

Dwight was in the driveway loading his tractor onto a trailer hitched to a brand new pickup.

"Nice truck," Rose said.

Dwight grinned. "Early wedding present from Louisa."

"Nice gift."

"Yeah." Dwight patted a fender. "It's got everything. Power windows, air conditioning, four-wheel drive. You name it, it's got it."

"What did you get Louisa?" Rose asked.

"Huh?"

"For a wedding gift."

"Oh. Nothing." Dwight repositioned his baseball cap. "She doesn't want anything." He cocked his head, winked. "She got me."

"I see." Rose shifted her package. She bent over its bulk, peered at Dwight. "But you got her. Wasn't that enough?"

Dwight looked down at his shoes. When he looked back up

May Snow

into Rose's eyes, his smile was gone. "It should be, shouldn't it?" he said.

"You're young, Dwight," Rose said. "Make sure you choose a path that will make you happy."

"Not so young anymore," Dwight said, "and this path looks as good as any other right now." He swung his arm to the truck. "Hey, not so bad, you know."

"It'll lose its shine and get rusty."

"I'll get a new one."

"It's easy to get another truck."

"But not another wife."

"Not so easy," Rose said.

Dwight shrugged. "Maybe not. I don't know, but this is what I'm taking right now."

Louisa was in the kitchen poring over cookbooks.

"Interesting reading," Rose said, putting her package on top of volumes of cookery, thick covers shellacked with plump chickens, steamy loaves of bread, tall dark cakes with whipped cream and cherries, marvelous, sumptuous, enticing calories. The table was full of their pages. "There must be a bookstore manager somewhere lifting a toast to you."

"Some are from the library," Louisa said, circling a recipe with red pen.

"Are you looking for something special?"

"Meat loaf," Louisa said. "Dwight loves meat loaf."

"Sounds good. Not too complex."

"Every recipe needs something I don't have. Grandpa wasn't big on spices."

"Ground beef, bread crumbs, onion, and milk," Rose said, "and eggs. That should do it."

"Too easy. I want mine special."

"A little ketchup on top."

"I need to go shopping," Louisa said, sighing. "This house-keeping stuff is a lot of work."

"I brought you a present."

Louisa smiled. "It's a big one."

"You can open it if you want to."

"It's my first present." She clasped her hands and smiled at Rose. "Except for the stuff Mother brings over ... I should wait for Dwight."

"You could."

"I don't want to."

"Open it."

"Okay, I will." Louisa laughed, grabbed the package, and tore the tissue. Mounds of soft yarn fell in her lap. She buried her arms in the afghan and lifted it to her face. It covered her shoulders and chest. Her eyes were wet. "Oh Rose, it's so lovely. And you made it, didn't you? For me."

Rose swallowed. "I made it. It's for you."

"It looks like a wedding."

Rose nodded.

"Grandma used to knit. She and Grandpa would sit next to each other for hours. She knit and he read the paper. Or just sat watching her. They didn't talk much, just sat happy." Louisa smoothed her hand over the raised knitted pattern. "I still have a sweater she made me when I was little. I miss her."

"Your grandmother was a good woman."

"She should be here. Grandpa too. But if they were, this wouldn't be happening. I wouldn't be living here. This wouldn't be my house. Grandpa would have sent me back home, and Dwight would have been out of my life. Isn't it sad that Grandpa had to die so I could be happy?"

Rose shuddered.

"Do you think they're watching from Heaven?"

"I don't know," Rose whispered.

"Do you want some cookies?" Louisa asked. "I make really good peanut butter ones. I use crunchy peanut butter. If there isn't any crunchy in the cupboard, I chop up regular peanuts. Dwight likes little pieces of nuts in his cookies.

"I don't think I'd better eat one," Rose said. "I just had a tooth filled and I'm kind of scared to eat anything hard."

"Your loss," Louisa said, shrugging. "They're the only thing I know how to make that turns out good. Except brownies and mashed potatoes. I make super-fluffy mashed potatoes."

Rose thought of Anson making roads in his potatoes, crossing lines, eating them, one section at a time.

"Your grandfather was a potato man," Rose said.

"I know. Mom made a big batch for supper the night he took me home and said I had to stay there."

"He brought you back here, though," Rose said, rubbing her fingers over the glossy cookbooks.

"To pack. He was making me go back home the next day."

"But you didn't have to go home after all."

"No, he died." Louisa frowned. "But I wasn't glad he died. I didn't want him to."

"Didn't you hear anything that night?"

"How could I? I was sleeping."

"But if he banged his leg, or fell, there must have been some noise."

"My door was closed."

Late July

Absently Rose piled the books, one on top of another: a chicken stack, a salad stack, a pastry stack. Walls in old houses were not so thick they erased thumps and cries for help.

"What if someone else was in the house, wouldn't you have heard that?"

"My door was closed."

"So someone could have been here and you wouldn't have known it?"

"You better stop it, Rose." Louisa pushed the afghan off her shoulders and leaned across the table. "Nobody was here. Nobody killed Grandpa. You're just starting up trouble for nothing."

❄   ❄   ❄

All the next day clouds hung low and dark over Canadaway. Although the damp swelled her ankles and caused her joints to ache, Rose moved restlessly through her house, Anson heavy on her mind. He lay there in her head spread out in blood, still and silent and alone. Her love. But she could not touch the place in her mind where he'd traveled without her, where he'd walked to his death. Or was pushed. Her face was not there. She had not heard his final cry or seen his soul lift up to God. Yet, by his body, quiet in death, there was a void in the picture in her head. Gaping large was an empty, evil place, a hole that covered a hidden face.

She looked out the window at the overcast sky. *Please God, let me be wrong.*

Since she'd seen Louisa, grave suspicions rumbled through her thoughts, unbidden, without warning. Maybe it wasn't the old ladies, her friends. Or June. But, oh, it could not have been the flesh of his own that had emptied his body of blood. Not for a house. Not for the price of a husband.

She placed her hand over the glass where the carved dog sat in her china cabinet. Had this grandchild been given so much love that there was not enough left for another grandchild to feel?

Suddenly the room was dark and the sky shed rain with pounding vengeance. Rose rushed to the windows, pulled the curtains in from the sucking air, and slammed them shut.

Thunder rolled and lightning flashed. Rose stood in the middle of her kitchen away from windows that could shatter and throw glass at her. She feared the sink that could shoot a streaking bolt of lightning through its faucet. Her mother had taught her to be afraid of storms. She had shooed little Rose onto the davenport in the middle of the night, shoes on and laced, so if the house was struck by lightning and lit by fire, she could run without pain over stones and sticks to a safe place.

The phone rang. Her hand jerked to her mouth and she looked to the living room. An evil conductor, an instrument of possible death in a storm. Her mother had not let her touch the phone while thunder rolled and lightning spit.

The phone rang again.

Almost simultaneously a thick, jagged streak of blazing light brightened the sky and fired the room with a radiant glow.

It could be Margaret in need.

Rose crossed the rooms, drew in her breath, and lifted the receiver.

She heard breathing.

"Margaret?"

Late July

"You need to stop. Anson is dead. Let him rest easy in his grave."

The voice was muffled. She didn't recognize it.

"Who are you?" Rose whispered. Her knuckles were white as she held tight to the phone.

"Don't cause more pain."

"Please, who are you?"

"Let it go."

"I can't."

The pause was long.

"Then be prepared for what you cause."

"Just tell me," Rose begged, "so it can be over."

The line was still.

Rain beat against the windows. Rose put the phone down.

❄   ❄   ❄

Rose could have called the police right away, but instead, she sat through the night in a soft-cushioned chair waiting for the phone to ring again. Sometimes her eyes would close for long moments and the pictures in her head would fade. Then her head would fall, and she'd catch herself sharp, jerk herself back to the thunder rumbling outside, growing fainter, further from the dimming flashes until there was only the steady pelt of rain on her house.

She waited for morning. The phone sat silent. Over and over she listened to the threatening words that rolled in her head. She couldn't place the voice. She hoped for another call. She needed to hear the sound of her caller again, the cadence, the lilt. It had to be someone she knew. She was only a little afraid. She already stood on both sides of being. A push would send her to Thomas. And Anson. But away from Margaret. Even in the shadow of joy, that could be too painful to bear.

Leaning deep into the plush cushions, resting without the comfort of sleep, Rose sat through the night and found no answers.

With first light, she briefly gave in to slumber. It was enough to give her some strength.

She rose and splashed her face with water, slicked back her hair, put on fresh underclothing, scrubbed her teeth. Bending to the mirror, she patted life into her cheeks.

Then Rose went out into the washed morning. She folded her hands around a perfect, pink rose, dipped her face, and drew in its scent. She kept her eyes away from Anson's house.

She got in her car and drove to the police station — a little white building, brick-faced and plain, sandwiched between the library and the post office.

Willis Redman was there talking with Officer Joseph Abramowicz. They stopped when they saw her and greeted her with nods and smiles.

Rose put her hand on Willis's arm. "I don't care if you stay," she said, "but it's Joseph I'm here to see."

Willis looked at Joseph. The young officer lifted his eyebrows and shrugged.

"I don't know tact or lead-in words for this," Rose said. She bit her lip, released it slowly. "What if I knew someone had hurt someone else? Badly. Maybe even killed him. And it was a friend. It wasn't done maliciously. It couldn't have been. It had to be an accident. What if I knew that? What if I was almost positive in my heart?"

"You're saying," Joseph Abramowicz said, "you know of a murder?"

"Not exactly a murder."

"A kind of murder."

"Maybe not."

"What then, Rose?"

Rose looked at Willis. He frowned and shook his head when she caught his eye. She lifted her chin and turned away.

"An accident," she said. "But somebody died."

"Who died, Rose?" Joseph asked.

"It was Anson."

"Oh Rose," Willis said.

"You think someone killed him?" Joseph said.

"I do. I don't want to, but I do."

"Anson's vein ruptured," Willis said. "He bled to death. There was nothing to show another person caused his vein to break."

"But what if it happened?"

"Why do you think it did?" Joseph asked.

"Somebody called me last night and threatened me."

"Who called you?"

"I don't know."

"What did this person say?"

Rose breathed deep. "To stop saying Anson was murdered."

"Is there someone you've been accusing?"

"Maybe."

"Why would someone kill Anson?" Joseph asked quietly.

Rose dropped her eyes. Her thumb picked at the nail on the pointer finger of her other hand. She couldn't tell this young man that four old ladies were lonely and decided to share one old man. And she couldn't give Willis reason to think her foolish.

"I don't know," she whispered.

"Let it go, Rose," Joseph said.

Those famous words, Rose thought. *Let it go. But I can't.*

"What if it were true?" Rose asked. "What would happen if someone did it and got convicted?"

"Prison."

"What if they were old?"

"Prison."

"What would happen to them in prison?"

"It depends."

Rose could find no more words.

"If there's more," Joseph said, "come back and tell me."

❄   ❄   ❄

"Does your tooth still hurt?" asked Nicholas.

"No."

"Wanna cookie? I got some." Nicholas reached in his pocket and pulled out a plastic sandwich bag filled with broken cookie pieces.

Rose smiled. "I don't think so."

"Louisa gave them to me. They're peanut butter."

"How about instead we go to Hunter's and get ice cream?"

They were sitting on Rose's porch. It was the last day of July, and it was hot. Amy was filling in for a lunch waitress then doing her own dinner shift and had asked Rose to keep an eye on Nicholas now and then. She was concerned because she'd be gone so long. But things were tight and she needed the money.

"Just make sure he doesn't get in a car with anybody you don't know. Actually, just keep him close and out of all cars."

With a touch of amusement, Rose agreed it probably wasn't a good idea to allow him into cars driven by unknown persons. She'd been a mother. She hadn't forgotten the risks.

Amy had opened her mouth, closed it quickly, and pressed her lips together. She only touched the top of Nicholas's head and hurried off to work.

"I don't want to go to Hunter's."

"You don't want ice cream?"

"I don't want to go to Hunter's."

"You want to drive all the way to Northridge?"

"Okay."

"Hunter's is closer."

"I don't like to go there."

"Why not?"

"A witch works there."

"What?"

"I don't wanna talk anymore." Nicholas started down the steps.

"How about a drive to Northridge, a swim at the Y, and then ice cream?"

"Cool."

23
August

On the first Saturday in August, Louisa Talber, robed in flowing white with a crown of flowers on her head, married Dwight Wilson, tuxedoed and awkward.

They said their vows beneath a bower in Anson's backyard. Friends, family, and other invited guests sat on white plastic chairs lined in rows behind the couple and watched. From that distance and that angle, Louisa looked young.

Immediately after the ceremony, a reception was held in the same place. There was a band, a sumptuous buffet, abundant and diverse drink. A mime, face painted, flitted among the revelers, strewing laughter, gaiety, and imaginary balloons.

Small, round tables with plates of tiny cookies, dishes of mints and peanuts, bowls of pink and purple and yellow flowers, were scattered over the yard.

"Karen did well on such short notice," Helen Bond said,

choosing a small, round, chocolate cookie laced with walnuts. She plunked it, whole, into her mouth.

"She's a good organizer," Rose said, rubbing the spot at the base of her throat, thinking she should feel joy for Louisa, wanting to keep her body and mind empty and pain-free for awhile. She shared a table with Helen. Nicholas was sitting with them. Amy had asked Rose if Nicholas could go with her to the wedding. She had to work and couldn't take him. She'd seemed uneasy. "It's a crowd. Watch over him good."

Rose stroked Nicholas's arm. He looked at her and smiled.

"They say all brides are beautiful," Helen said, looking at Louisa hauling Dwight over to the band. "So I guess this is as close to beautiful as Louisa will ever get."

Rose glanced at Louisa. The bride stood close to the clarinet player. Her lips moved fast and her face was flushed. Dwight tugged at her, and she slapped him away.

"That glow on her cheeks is anger," Helen commented. "Not quite as attractive as the bridal blush of innocence."

"Are you all right?" Rose asked. Helen was a kind, sweet soul, a peacemaker.

"I like Dwight."

Rose nodded. Helen was also smart. Rose watched Louisa and Dwight walk away from the band and suddenly the music was loud and the beat was hard. She looked at Helen and they laughed.

"Hey, Nicholas," Helen said, "want to dance?"

"Nope. Don't know how."

"Then I've got a better idea. How about you and me go find my friend Jenny Porter and her grandson, Adam? He's just about your age and doesn't know a soul from around here.

Seems like you and him could scare up some fun that's a whole lot better than hanging around two old ladies."

Staring up at Helen, his face blank, Nicholas cracked a peanut and put it in his mouth.

Rose bit her lip. *Watch over him carefully.*

Helen bent close to the boy, smoothed back his hair. "Wouldn't it be nice to have someone to play with?"

Nicholas chewed the peanut. He turned his head and looked at Rose.

"Do you want to go?" Rose asked

He nodded.

"Then go and have yourself a good time."

He smiled as Helen took his hand and led him away. She patted Rose's shoulder as they passed her chair.

There are many ways to watch over a child, Rose thought. *And this boy needs a new way.*

Rose squirmed. The sun was too hot on her face. She dropped her head to stop its glare from burning her eyes. Her hands lay idle in her lap, limp. The veins were swollen and blue. She wondered how far the blood would spurt if she punctured that puffed up streak of skin. She shuddered. There was no warmth of sun inside her.

She felt a gentle squeeze on her shoulder, the scent of vanilla wafted sweet, and Charity slipped by her and slid into the chair Helen had emptied.

"Hello, Rose."

Rose wanted to cry. She wanted to crawl onto Charity's lap, put her head on her friend's shoulder, and cry.

"You look very nice," Rose said. She pressed her hands together. "You always look nice."

May Snow

"Come sit with us, Rose. It's a wedding and we're always together at weddings."

Rose felt her heart drumming fast. She bit the inside of her cheek hard. They always sang together, danced together, laughed, ate, gossiped, frolicked, cried all in a bunch at weddings.

"I've missed you," Rose whispered.

"Today you're our Rose and you belong with us. Like it used to be."

❄   ❄   ❄

On the day after the wedding, the sun beat hot on Rose's house. It seeped through roof and windows and covered every surface, filling every space with heat.

Rose awoke, skin already wet from the sun pushing through her windows. She lay awake, eyes closed, mind fighting body into movement. Although her body was reluctant, her mind won, and she eased herself, slowly with resistance, out of the bed and into the bathroom.

Rose was too tired to go to church. She sat at her kitchen table, sliced apple and iced tea in front her, and debated with her soul. Sunday was God's day. He might sit, stand, and walk with her every day of her life, but on Sunday it was her job to acknowledge her debt and concentrate on His goodness and power. There had been few Sundays she had not immersed herself in church worship and sung His praises, whispered thanks and pleas to Him, listened to the sermon on His message. But this day she couldn't go to church. Her body just wouldn't hear the begging of her heart. It was too tired. Too heavy. Too hot. Too drained.

Although she wasn't exactly sad, tears hung at the edge of her eyes. Mingled with the heavy heat that sat within her body was a floating shimmer of airy light, a breaking up of pain balled tight. She dared not dwell on the hope that paths were merging and hers was meeting again with Charity's and Grace's.

She took her Bible to the living room, turned the fan to blow across her body, and sank into a thick-cushioned chair. Closing her eyes, she felt a prayer, and when its calm strength had stilled her, she opened the Holy Book and read.

She fell asleep in the chair and didn't wake until the phone rang beside her.

"Rose?"

"Yes," she whispered. Her body trembled. It was Charity. She dared to hope.

"You weren't in church today."

"No. I'm very tired."

"You're all right?"

Rose nodded, then aware, spoke into the phone. "Yes."

"I thought I'd check."

"Thank you."

"Well, then. I'll see you around… I'm glad you're well."

"I'll see you around."

The next day was no better. The heat droned on. Rose changed her sheets, washed them, and hung them out to dry. When she was done, she eased into a rocker on the front porch and watched the boys across the street batting and running and hopping and throwing as if there was no sun beating the earth, sucking the sap from all humans below.

Lunchtime came. Her bones wouldn't lift out of the chair. She should open a can of soup. Too hot. She could make a sandwich, tuna or peanut butter. Too much effort. Fruit would be good. Cool. A sweet, juicy melon. She only had apples. Her stomach rumbling gently, she rocked and thought about food.

Closing her eyes, she imagined a giant mountain of melons — great, round, rough-skinned cantaloupes. She made the top one roll, and as it dropped, banging the fat fruit it passed, they, too, fell rolling and bouncing, crashing into each other, breaking open, splitting, bursting forth sweet orange flesh. Her mouth juiced and she licked her lips. Breakfast had been meager. She was hungry.

So she pushed her body out of the rocker, got her purse, counted the painful steps to her car, and drove downtown to Hunter's. Easier than cooking, more choice, and Hunter's had overhead fans.

It was early enough that the lunch rush hadn't started. A couple of kids were flipping through magazines in the comic section, and a man Rose didn't know was sitting at the counter sipping lemonade while he read a newspaper. *Probably waiting for the bus*, she thought. Head cocked, one arm stretched in front of her, fingers wiggling, Willow Warner sat two seats down from the stranger. She dipped her other hand into a bag of potato chips and popped a chip, whole, into her mouth then took a swig of soda.

"Cool, huh?" Willow queried, waving her fingers as Rose passed her.

"Cool," Rose agreed, smiling. Willow's fingernails sparkled bright, a "cool" lime green.

June was at the end of the counter swiping crumbs, polishing the countertop. Rose slid onto the stool there and, eyes downcast, took a menu from the rack. She flicked her eyes upward. June was looking at her. Face empty, not showing the turmoil behind it, Rose stared back and waited.

June reached, patted Rose on the hand, and it was all right.

"Hot day," June said. "Want some lemonade?"

"Cherry cola," Rose said, looking at the menu. Hamburgers, hot dogs, tuna, grilled cheese. She pushed the list away. "Do you have any melon?"

"I've got even better. Chicken salad in a fancy-cut half melon."

"Ooh, my stomach rumbles at the thought."

"For a friend, I'll toss on an extra scoop of chicken," June said, moving away to make Rose's lunch.

For a friend, Rose thought. *For a friend.*

The counter was filling with hungry people. June scurried to satisfy their needs, keep them happy, and fill their mouths.

"Sorry," she said, sliding Rose's melon, shining wet and heaped with chicken, in front of her. "Busy. Can't talk. Maybe later."

Rose nodded. She bit her lip. It looked so good, so *big*. She dipped her fork, spearing a plump piece of white chicken. Bits of walnut clung to the flesh. It was delicious.

"There's Charity," June said, hurrying by. "By the door."

Rose watched Charity pause at the door, look around, catch her eye. The hesitation was brief. Charity lifted her hand in greeting. Rose waved back. She let out her breath as Charity walked toward her.

"Grace is next door getting her hair washed," Charity said, sitting down next to Rose.

Rose lifted her eyebrows. "I thought she didn't like Debbys-Do."

"She's tired," Charity said, eyeing Rose's salad. "And it's only a wash. That looks good."

"It is."

"I think I'll get one."

"Want some of mine? There's a lot."

"You eat it," Charity said, trying to get June's attention. "You can stand the calories ... well, will you look at that. Here comes the bride."

"She looks mad," Rose said, observing Louisa march into the shop and head straight for June.

"Shh," Charity said. "Listen."

"I need some ant traps," Louisa shouted toward June.

"Don't have any," June said, not slowing her pace as she filled cups, cut bread, wiped the counter. "Try the grocery."

"You gotta have some. Where's Sarah? I need some help here."

"She's home sick. I'm alone. We don't have any ant traps. And I don't have time to argue."

"I've got ants all over my kitchen. Somebody's got to help me. Dwight's off God knows where cutting somebody's lawn. He should be taking care of this. I *hate* ants. In fact, I shouldn't even be here. I should be off someplace nice. On a beach or a resort or gazing at some famous landmark. On a *honeymoon.* But no. He cuts grass, and I fight *ants.*"

"This is the season to keep lawns tidy," Charity said loud enough to get Louisa's attention. "And that's what Dwight does for a living these days. Per your choice."

"Damn." Louisa threw up her arms and stalked out.

"Looks like things aren't too rosy at home," Charity said. She picked up Rose's spoon and scooped some salad.

"I don't think she'll ever have a happy marriage," Rose said. "Not unless she learns to look outside her own little circle of self."

"She's awfully old to start that."

"She probably never learned what happy is. Or that she deserves it. Karen doesn't always see those things that aren't how she wants them."

"I used to hope for a happy marriage," Charity said, lighting a cigarette. "And sometimes I had one. Bits and pieces anyway. Not like yours, though. You had it good."

"Thomas was good to me," Rose said. "Most times anyway. But I remember times I felt stifled. All pushed in and not able to spill out what was real to me. But Thomas usually was right. I would have liked to have been consulted more, though."

"Nothing's perfect." Charity frowned at the stranger waving her smoke away with his newspaper.

"No, nothing is." Rose would have liked to push the smoke away too, but she figured this wasn't the opportune time to imply fault.

"You probably would have had it again with Anson. Perfection. The ideal couple. Twice in a lifetime she finds the perfect mate."

Rose drew in her breath, let it out slowly. "That would have bothered you, wouldn't it?"

Charity shrugged.

"It wasn't meant to go so far, you know. It just did."

"Don't talk about it. Just let it drop. It's over."

"You keep saying that like it's easy. Like just forget doubts and fears. Snap, they're gone. I can't do that. They roll in my head. They push hard at my brain, and I can't lose them. I try to shut down and ignore them away, but they're too strong. They sneak through the barriers and tease me with questions, and I feel like I just have to *know*."

"It's back to the old accusation," Charity said, grinding her cigarette into an ashtray. She lit another. "Do you really think we're killers, Rose?" She blew smoke at the ceiling.

Rose put her hands in her lap and looked down at her plate.

"Does some murder gene kick in on our sixtieth or seventy-fifth or eightieth birthday? Just laying dormant there waiting for old age to set in, for ligaments to stiffen, and veins to wilt. Then that evil gene pushes our brittle, old bones to karate chop a neck or crouch in a tree to do an arthritic killing, a bone-crushing leap onto an unsuspecting victim, or that gene makes us pull a trigger and hurl a bullet into an enemy."

Rose trembled.

"Is that what you think?" Charity asked.

"Maybe it wasn't you. It just doesn't feel right. He was so careful. He watched where that leg went."

"When he thought about it," Charity said.

"He didn't want to bump it."

"I'm sure he didn't bang it on a stool or the side of the bed on purpose."

"Maybe it was a burglar," Rose said.

"Nothing was taken."

"My cat's missing." Rose wrung her hands. She wanted what she had started to stop, but her mouth kept talking.

Charity threw up her arms. Ashes flew. "Now, it's a cat burglar. Maybe it was Dwight sneaking in to see Louisa. Maybe it was Louisa herself hoping to inherit money to buy Dwight."

Rose smiled ruefully. "Looks like she might want to return her purchase."

Charity leaned into Rose, connected her eyes to Rose's, and took the hands in Rose's lap into her own.

"Do you think we are killers, Rose? Any of us? Grace or June or me? Do you think we could choose to make someone die?"

Rose heard the ugly words spoken gently. She saw pleading love in her friend's eyes. Her heart filled. She had known them so long.

"Charity, I love you."

Charity squeezed Rose's hand tenderly. "Let it go."

Rose bit her lip. She nodded. "I'll try ... no, more than that. I'll *believe* you."

"When?" Charity's eyes were cloudy.

"I think when the hurt's gone, when Anson has faded to dim memory, when I can talk to Thomas without seeing Anson's shadow. Then it won't matter. Then it can go."

"That's not soon enough, dear friend."

Rose reached and touched Charity's wet cheek. In all the years Rose had known Charity, there had never been lies. Until her own lies with Anson. The lies were hers, not Charity's.

"I *do* believe you, Charity."

May Snow

"I got more cookies."

"You *have* more cookies," Rose corrected.

Nicholas wrinkled his nose. "How come you say that?"

"Well, it's correct." The evening was cool. The smell of the lake was fresh and in the distance, waves splashed soft.

"I don't like to be correct with you," Nicholas said.

"Why not?"

"It makes you old."

Rose laughed and kept on knitting.

"Can I give the cats some cookie?" Nicholas asked.

"They like mice better."

"Cookies are sweeter."

"Okay," Rose said. "Give them some cookie. But just a teeny, little bit."

"Can cats get cavities?"

"Don't see why not."

"You got one."

"I did."

"I thought old people had false teeth."

"Some do."

"My grandma can push with her tongue and lift her teeth right out of her mouth."

"That's a talent, I guess." Rose rested her needles in her lap. "Where's your grandma live?"

Nicholas stuffed a cookie in his mouth, chewed for awhile. "Louisa and Dwight fight a lot. Dwight wants to dump the lawn care stuff and move."

"Don't you think it'd be a good idea to make some friends and quit the spying?"

Nicholas threw cookie pieces at the cats. "Dwight says the lawn junk aggravates his allergies. He's always itching and his eyes get teary." Nicholas stomped his feet on the steps and the cats ran. "Probably people think he's crying. Mom says don't make friends. We're moving out of here soon."

Rose's heart dropped. "Where are you going?"

"I dunno." He scooped up a cat, buried his face in fur. "Louisa says he should be satisfied with all the toys she bought him and she's got no money left." He sat the cat down and tickled her.

"Let Betsy go play," Rose said. "Where are you moving to?"

"I told you, I dunno." Nicholas let the cat go. "Louisa gives me cookies when she's mad at Dwight. They're good. Peanut butter."

"You shouldn't spy on them, Nicholas."

"It's interesting."

"But not too nice."

"I don't like them very much anyway."

"That doesn't make it better."

Nicholas shrugged. He slid back and forth over the steps.

"Who *do* you like, Nicholas?"

"I like you and Mom."

"And?"

"Nobody else around here."

"Don't you want friends?"

"I don't think so. Big people like to hurt you, and kids, they just like other kids who stick around and can play a lot."

"Well, I'm glad I'm your friend, and I'm glad you're my friend. I need friends."

"Those old ladies aren't your friends," Nicholas said.

"What old ladies?"

The days were still long, and the sky was just beginning to layer orange over the lake.

Nicholas looked at Rose and winced.

"What old ladies?" she asked again, though she knew.

"The ones who went to Anson's house that night when he died."

"Oh Nicholas." She did not want to hear this.

"They did. But don't tell. They're big. I saw their shadows go all the way to the sky." He looked away. "They could hurt you too."

"Nicholas, the moon plays tricks."

"The round one put stones in your mailbox once. I took them out."

"Maybe you mixed up the nights," Rose said.

"I don't think so. I seen them before, sneak in and see him. You too. I seen you sneak in there."

"Saw, Nicholas, you *saw*."

"There you go again." Nicholas jumped off the porch and chased the cats.

❅　❅　❅

"Forrest wants to come back," said Margaret. "He's sorry and confused, and he loves me."

Rose clutched the phone. It had rung ominous clamor into the morning.

"What are you going to do?" Rose asked.

August

"Oh, Mother, I'm so happy. Everyone is entitled to a mistake. Forrest made his, and now it's over."

Rose shook her head. A hard rock soared and punched her solid in the gut. "You're taking him back." Not a question.

"Of course, I am."

Rose could think of nothing to say. This day, which had started clear-pathed, weightless, and joyous in its promise to move her closer to the comfort of old and familiar friendship, was breaking down. She could see her daughter whipping through space from despair to ecstasy, dropping pieces of strength, independence, and growth as she flew. Flying too fast, spinning out of control and reason.

"I can forgive him," Margaret said. "He's sorry. He made a mistake and he's sorry."

"You won't forget what he did."

"I forgive him."

"But you won't forget," Rose said. "There'll be a baby he's responsible for."

"I can live with that."

Oh Margaret. "It will hurt."

"Yes, I know," Margaret said softly. "But he'll be home."

"It will hit you at strange times, haunt you. For the rest of your years," Rose said, sadness welling within. *How can I know that?* she wondered. *Where is my pain coming from?*

"Mom, he chose *me.* He loves *me.*"

"Do you love him?" Rose asked. "Don't answer fast. Think."

"Of course, I do," Margaret said immediately. "Would I have hung in there alone, not telling anyone but you, if I didn't?"

May Snow

"*Why* do you love him?"

"I knew from the day I met him that he was right for me. He's strong and kind and loyal, and he takes care of me."

"But he didn't take care of you. He left you."

"I need him."

Such anguish. Rose squeezed her eyes shut, held in tears. *Where was her strong, beautiful daughter? Was she drowning in a sea of weak genes gushed from her own body into her infant's? But she had sent power too. Oh Margaret, be wise.*

"I know," Rose said. "I know you think you need him. But need isn't love."

"Mom, I'm happy. Don't ruin it."

I did this too, Rose thought. *closed my eyes many times. I needed Thomas. I loved him. I still love him. I turned my head and didn't see. I shrouded my brain and suffocated what my eyes couldn't veil. Maybe not infidelity. But looks and words that hurt. Not infidelity. No. I'm sure, I don't just think. And I was okay. Why am I so sad for my Margaret?*

"Think this through, dear daughter."

"I did."

"And be sure."

"I'm sure."

"So he's coming home."

"Yes… Mother, don't hate me."

24
Late August

Darkness had covered the heat and pushed it away. Cool breezes wafted through the deep gray and circled around Rose as she rocked on her porch. The gentle wind lifted stray, curly strands from her forehead, whispering sweet kisses against her cheek.

She was waiting for Nicholas.

It was late when she felt him slip through the night, settle on her steps.

"I was starting to miss you," she said. She had grown used to his company, the comfort of shared presence.

"Nicholas?" she said when he didn't answer.

She watched his shape turn, stand up slowly, and come to her. She felt his hand upon her knee.

She reached and touched his face. His eyes leaked tears. She felt their wet.

She pulled him into her lap. His growing bones bent and twisted and shaped a cave against her body that fit exactly.

"Can you tell me?" she asked.

"I have to give the china cat back."

Rose rubbed his back. Her hand was steady and sure.

"Mom doesn't like you anymore," Nicholas said.

"Why is that?" Her hand moved up and down.

"I don't know." He pressed his head against her breast. "I can't come over anymore."

"I'll talk to her."

"Won't do any good. She'll be madder."

"Will she hit you, Nicholas?" She held her breath. She had wanted to ask for a very long time.

"Naw, she doesn't hit much. Only a little. And not very hard ... and then she cries."

"Does anybody hit you?"

"Her old boyfriend used to. Till we moved away." He squirmed against her. "But don't tell. Not ever."

"I won't tell anything I shouldn't. We're friends, remember?"

"Not anymore."

"Forever, Nicholas. Whether we talk again or not. You're on my line for always."

"What does that mean?"

"That you touched my heart and it sucked you in and you're part of my life for always."

"Like you and the old witch ladies?"

"Yes, like that." Charity and Grace and June. She sighed and hugged him tight.

He squirmed against her. "Did you know Dwight was in the hospital? His face got all red and he couldn't breath and they had to give him oxygen."

"No, I didn't know." Rose relaxed her hold and he slid into a looser position. "Must be his allergies."

"I wish I could keep the cat. Mom washed him so he's all shiny again."

"I'll keep him for you."

"When I'm a man, I'll come get him back."

❄   ❄   ❄

Rose couldn't sleep. The weight of Nicholas in her lap, in her heart, stayed with her. Restless, sure-footed, she prowled the house, walking through streaks of moonlight fallen from the windows onto her walls and carpet. Knowing every corner and mystery of her house, she slipped safely through patches of black where the glow didn't reach. She meandered out to the porch and thought of Amy earlier that night hurrying across the yard to where she and Nicholas sat together. Nicholas had fallen asleep in her arms. She'd held him and rocked, softly crooning lullabies into his hair. When Amy got home from work and couldn't find Nicholas, she must have guessed that he was with Rose. She had come across the yard, fast, and had taken her son from Rose.

"He can't come here anymore," Amy had said, "and I hold you responsible to respect that order and not let him in your yard or on your porch."

"Why, Amy?"

"Don't make trouble for him. He's just a little boy. He doesn't need anymore hurt."

"Why, Amy?" Rose asked again.

Amy carried Nicholas, heavy and awkward, across the

yards. She didn't wake him, although it would have been easier. Rose wondered why, when she seemed to love him so, Amy took her son's friend away from him.

And now the house across the way was silent and dark. Rose stood on her porch and pondered the reasons that pain rained so heavy from those that we love.

A shadow fell across her yard. It moved, long and black, across the grass from the sidewalk, coming to her porch.

Startled, she stepped back, crouched behind her rocker. She heard the crunch of stone on her driveway, the measured step of a weighted body. Carefully, she crept away from the chair, sidled over quiet, dry floorboards. Peering over the railing, she saw Grace plodding steadily down her driveway, past the porch, past the garbage cans, stopping at the edge of her garage.

Puzzled, Rose slipped down her porch steps and followed Grace's path. Rose kept her feet on grass. She didn't want to frighten the old woman.

She watched Grace stoop and pick at the impatiens bordering the garage. She gasped and covered her mouth as she realized her friend was tearing the flowers out by their roots. She stood and looked as Grace dropped on the ground and sat in the grass. Arms wrapped around her body, her old friend cried.

Swiftly, Rose went to her, bent, and touched her. "Grace?" she whispered close to her ear.

"Go away." The old lady swayed back and forth. "Go away."

"What is it, dear friend?"

"Leave me alone." Grace dropped her face forward, swinging her arms over her head as if to protect herself. Her sobs were intense and wrenching.

Late August

"Oh Grace." Rose stood unsteady beside her.

Grace drew in a deep breath. Her body shuddered. "Where is Charity? Please. I need her."

Rose hurried into her house and called Charity. Charity came, and without explanation, took Grace away.

❄   ❄   ❄

The night before had been long and Rose hadn't slept much. When the frenzied mix of troubled friends with guarded secrets finally hammered her brain to exhaustion and she dropped deep into a well of slumber, ugly dreams jerked her awake. She roamed her rooms, her head awhirl with questions and pain. She felt jailed in an unknown dungeon.

Daylight slew the dragon. Nothing was so big it couldn't be fixed. The key was finding the problem.

Big key, she thought, *when nobody's talking. But it's time that they did, Amy and Charity and Louisa and Grace and Nicholas. Time that they opened their mouths and spoke clear.*

She sighed and made a strong pot of coffee. What she wanted, what she thought was right and made sense, was not always the way the river flowed. Well, maybe she could build a few dikes.

She took her coffee to the front porch. She planned to sit, drink, pull her thoughts together, and figure out a way to make sense out of all this.

She was through the front door before she realized she had company. There was Charity, rocking steady and sipping coffee from the top of a thermos,the rest of which rested on the floor at her feet.

May Snow

"Have you been here long?" Rose asked. The sky was still streaked pink. But only a little.

"Your rockers need painting." Charity coughed and reached in her pocket, took out her cigarettes. "I know I should stop, but what difference does it make at my age?" She dragged deep. "They make life a little easier. And I'm bound to die soon anyway."

"I don't think so," Rose said sitting. "You're too tough."

"I've missed you, Rosie."

"And I, you." Rose set her own chair to rocking. The rhythm calmed her. "I'm sorry, you know. I should have told you that Anson and I were going beyond the rules. But it was a special time for him and me, a secret time that grew to a lie between you and me and Grace. It wounded our friendship. For that, I'm sorry."

"Sometimes it's hard to be honest," Charity said.

"Yes."

"But it's also hard to kill old feelings. And ours are mighty old. I love you, Rose Celador."

"We'll be okay."

"In time." Charity's voice trembled.

"No more lies," Rose said.

"Sometimes that's hard," Charity repeated, blowing smoke.

Rose watched a robin, summer fat, peck at treasure in her lawn.

"Grace is sick," Charity said. "She's taken to wandering. I think she's mixing her days and nights. Try not to be angry when she does strange things. She's angry with you, Rose. She blames you for lost love. She dreamed of dancing through the years with Anson. Still does sometimes. It makes me cry. But there's nothing I can do. Just keep her safe."

"It's only me she's angry at?"

"Just you. And only sometimes. It keeps her busy when the demons strike."

"Her sickness? That's the demon?"

Charity hesitated. "Yes."

"What is it?" Rose asked, her voice low.

"A killing cancer," Charity said. "And old age. The ravishes of a mind worn out. She'll be all right. I'll make sure."

Rose rubbed her throat. "She's the baby of us."

"June is now."

"But Grace always was. And in my heart, still is."

"Yes. Well, hey, we're having a bonfire down on the beach tonight. Marshmallows and wieners. Right around sunset. Bring a dessert. Your brownies would be good. Or whatever if it's too hot to bake. That's what I stopped to tell you."

"I'm glad you did."

"Me too."

Afterward, Rose pulled her rocker to a sunny spot and napped.

When she awoke, she saw Amy carrying boxes to her car. There was a trailer hooked behind it and Manley Warner struggled to fit a chair into it. Nicholas stood at the front door of his house looking her way. His face was without expression. He clutched a brown paper bag. He looked so small.

"Oh my." Rose stood up fast, wobbled briefly, caught her balance, and hurried down the steps and across the yard.

"Amy," she called. "What are you doing?"

May Snow

Amy stopped by the car. Rose could see her face was tired and troubled, set hard.

Rose's heart beat fast. This was too sudden. It always seemed as if life's pain came too fast, and when she grabbed and squeezed it, got a grip, got a little control, even more trouble spilled over her. She stopped and pressed her hand to her heart.

"Why are you going?" Rose whispered as Amy stepped close, lifting her arms as if to hold Rose, but then dropped them.

"I should have told you when we came," Amy said, "but I didn't know you, didn't know I could trust you."

"What?" Rose asked softly. "What should you have told me?" She sensed Nicholas steal across the yard, and stand near her.

"We're hiding, Rose. From Nicholas's father. From my father. From my old boyfriend. All those stupid men who hit me and hit me and hit me and then hit Nicholas. I've had enough. So we came here. To hide. They won't hit us if they can't find us."

"You should have told me."

"I almost did. The day you came and held me and didn't ask and didn't make me tell. I almost did. But it felt so good to lie in your arms and to finally just be quiet."

"You should have told me. I could have helped."

"Yes, I should have told you, and then maybe, you would have been more careful."

"What do you mean?"

"At Louisa's wedding. You let Nicholas go and play with a strange child who knew my boyfriend's aunt's youngest daughter — who told her mother, who told her sister, who told her son, who was one of those awful men who hit me

— and he found out where I work and they told him where I live. I told you to be careful and to watch Nicholas. And you didn't do that."

"It's because of me you're going." The world grew dark and pressed against her soul. Rose felt Nicholas's arm slide around her waist. She swallowed and willed her head to stop spinning.

"You could stay and fight and end this running," Rose said.

"I'm sorry, Rose. It's not that easy."

"Nicholas needs friends."

"I know. And Nicholas needs to be safe."

They stood and faced each other, and Rose knew there would be no relenting.

"Nicholas can sit with you on your porch until I'm done packing and ready to go," Amy said.

Rose nodded. She slipped her arm over Nicholas's shoulders and walked back to her house with him. He held her steady as she planted each step with care.

They sat together on the steps, bodies touching until Amy called him to come.

He gave her the brown paper bag. "It's cookies Louisa made. You keep them."

"No, Nicholas, they're for you."

"It's a present." He shoved the bag into her hands.

"Let me get the cat." She wanted him to have the little, yellow, ceramic cat. "I'll make your mother understand that it's okay for you to have it."

"No." Nicholas shook his head. "You keep it. When I'm grown up, I'll come and get it."

"I'll remember that. And keep it safe for you."

"I love you, Rose."

May Snow

"I love you too, dear child."

❄   ❄   ❄

Rose put the cocoa can on the kitchen table then the flour and sugar canisters. She took her heavy mixing bowl, a wedding gift faded pink, from the cupboard and carried it slowly to the table. She rummaged through her odds and ends drawer, found the wooden spoon that had stirred a thousand brownie batters, and laid it next to the bowl.

Then she pulled out a chair, sat, folded her hands in her lap, and stared at the wares she would use to whisk together a mouth-watering confection. And tears ran down her face.

"I need you, Thomas," she whispered. "My strength is gone."

The phone rang. She shuddered. She closed her eyes and waited for the ringing to stop.

It would not stop and she could not ignore it. She lifted her weary body and went to the living room, bent over the phone, balancing against the table that held it.

"Mother, it's Margaret."

Rose envisioned her daughter's face, drawn with sadness. She felt it from her voice. Trembling, Rose dropped into the soft-cushioned chair by the phone.

"You're right," Margaret said. "There are pictures in my head."

Her hurt is greater than mine, Rose thought. *God, give me some of it. Let me take her pain. It will help me to help her. Please.*

"What are you doing to erase the pictures?" Rose asked.

"I'm still planting flowers around the library and city hall, watering them anyway, too late to plant much more. Though

350

we'll probably put in bulbs later, the other good ladies and me, civic-minded people that we are. And I'm feeding the homeless. At the church shelter."

"Is that what you want to do?"

"Forrest says it will help him politically and keep me busy."

"Is that what you want?"

"I want to paint pictures. Paint my sadness away."

"Then paint pictures," Rose said. Thomas was with her, and she was angry with him. He would think his daughter frivolous and he would be wrong.

"I have no talent."

"Who cares?"

"I want to paint pictures of men loving wives. I want my head to be filled with images of men loving their wives. Like Dad loved you. And I want to paint them. In bold, bright, splashy colors."

"If you do that, paint the women bigger."

"Forrest never was like Dad."

"Your father wasn't perfect."

"He always loved you."

"I made it easy for him to love me."

"I'm trying to do that with Forrest."

Damn you, Thomas, Rose thought.

"Margaret, dear Margaret," Rose said firmly into the phone, "be you. Paint those pictures."

❄   ❄   ❄

Rose didn't make brownies for the beach picnic. Instead she took the cookies Louisa had made.

May Snow

As she walked to the lake, Rose looked to the sky. The sun streaked orange behind the breaking clouds, hemming them with a blinding light that hinted at the brilliance of God's Heaven. Someday she'd climb those clouds, sink into the light, fill up with love, and let troubles be gone. Someday.

She dragged her chair down the steps to the sand. Charity and June were scouring the beach for driftwood. Rose expected to find Grace prone on a blanket soaking up the last warmth of the day, but Grace was not lolling on smooth sand and soft fleece. Instead she stood balanced on one leg in the water, her body bent forward, free leg straight back and pointed, arms spread, head up. *Like a skater*, Rose thought, *skimming the ice, soaring alone.* She watched the old lady straighten, stretch her arms to the sky, and go around and around, twirling in the water. In the corner of her eye, Rose saw that Charity had stopped gathering wood and was poised to pounce and grab her sister from hurt if need be.

Grace slipped and went down. Charity moved forward. But Grace was up again and laughing, slapping the water and kicking. Charity stopped, hand to her mouth, then turned, stepped back, bent, and picked up wood.

Wrapped in blankets, they sat on chairs around the fire. Leftover marshmallows were packed away with the ketchup and mustard and stray bits of cellophane and napkins. Louisa's cookies, still in the paper bag, passed from hand to hand.

Leaning back in her chair, stomach full, bare toes curled in the still-warm sand, Rose let her thoughts drift with the rhythmic splash of the rolling water. The sound was soothing, healing to her sore soul. June hummed softly beside her.

Late August

"Remember way back, when Stanley and Max snuck us to the beach?" Grace said. "We'd lie and snuggle and kiss under the stars."

"Mamma never knew," Charity said.

It was a good night for remembering, Rose thought. The breezes were gentle and pushed out worry, left only pleasant old moments to ponder and share. "Thomas took me out to Grimmers Pond on nights just like this," she said and smiled. "He tried to get me to take my clothes off."

"I bet you didn't," Charity said.

"Bet Dweebie Dwight got Louisa's clothes off fast," Grace said, and June laughed. "Bet she waited for years for someone to see her naked."

"They're fighting real bad," Charity said. "Louisa and Dwight."

"That's good for us," June said, grabbing the sack off Rose's lap. "We get his cookies."

"She gave them to Nicholas," Rose said.

"Probably 'cause Dwight wouldn't eat them," Grace said.

"Maybe that's what put him in the hospital," June said. "Louisa's baking."

"She told me it was strawberries," Charity said. "I saw her at the grocery. She didn't seem too concerned."

"Maybe he's mean to her too," Grace said. "We always say ugly things about her, but maybe he's the instigator and she just needs to fight back."

"I don't think so," Rose said. She closed her eyes and concentrated on the peaceful lap of water hitting sand.

"Remember the time Stanley broke all my cups and saucers?" Grace said. "I told you."

May Snow

Rose heard Charity's chair shift in the dark.

"Why would you think of that now?" Charity asked.

"Bone china, they were. All different patterns and colors. You bought me some, Charity. And Rose brought me back a cup covered with little, blue forget me nots when she went to the Thousand Islands with Thomas. Remember, Rose?"

"I remember."

"He broke them all. Because I'd spent some money on I don't remember what and didn't ask him if I could."

"This is supposed to be a night for good memories," Charity said.

"I took a knife and cut him. It was lying there on the counter, and I picked it up without thinking and slashed him right across the cheek."

June squirmed and her leg brushed against Rose. She pulled it back quickly.

"I cried so bad," Grace said.

"Did he hit you?" June asked.

"No, I think he was in shock. I called Charity, and she came and cleaned him up, and she bandaged his face. He never mentioned it again. Remember, Charity?"

"It was a long time ago," Charity said, "and best forgotten."

Rose smelled the smoke of Charity's cigarette. *Let it go.* She quivered as a shiver stalked her body.

Later walking home, Rose pulled a cookie out of the bag and bit into it. It was her first taste, and with horror she realized the nut chunks in the cookies were cashews. Not peanuts. Cashews. Dwight was allergic to cashews. *Deadly allergic.*

Late August

❄   ❄   ❄

Rose stood in her backyard staring through the dark at Anson's house. *Anson's* house. The air was cool, but it didn't soothe the churning heat that beat within and puffed her face, made her body heavy. She dropped the chair she'd dragged home from the beach. She held tight to the bag of peanut butter cookies laced with cashews.

Lights were on in Anson's kitchen. Louisa's shadow passed by the window. Clenching her teeth, Rose shook her fist at the wispy, black silhouette.

"You made him sick on purpose," she whispered harshly through teeth pressed tight. "You knew cashews could kill him, and you knew cashews tasted the same as peanuts to him."

What else did you do? swam unspoken through her mind.

Ignoring the ache that gnawed in her thighs from fatigue and walking and the pains that shot through her ankles, fed by her anger, she took strength from the frenzy that crashed in her soul. With deliberate step, she marched to the house that still should be Anson's.

Rose banged on the door and walked in.

Louisa sat at the kitchen table pushing a marshmallow across a lake of cocoa in a cow- shaped mug. Her chin rested on the palm of one hand. She barely glanced at Rose before drowning the marshmallow with the back of her spoon.

"Is Dwight better?" Rose asked.

Louisa lifted the spoon and licked it. "I miss him."

"I'll bet."

Raising her head, Louisa frowned. "What's that mean?"

"Louisa, you gave him cashews. *Cashews.* You know he

can't eat them. They could kill him. So you made him cookies with great big cashew nuts. What were you thinking!"

"I wasn't thinking," Louisa said, swiping her hand under her nose and wiping it on her skirt.

"You were thinking, all right. You were thinking you were tired of a husband who spent all your money and wanted to move you out of the house you stole from Anson."

Louisa slammed the spoon against the table. "Grandpa left me this house!"

"You killed him for this house!" There. It was said. Words in a whoosh barreling out of her mouth. And all the stones in her body settled to her feet. She swayed and reached for a chair to stay balanced.

Louisa looked and didn't offer to help.

Rose groped the chair and, hand over hand, pulled herself into it.

"I don't want you to stay," Louisa said. "I want you out of my house."

"You did it, didn't you? You killed him."

"No, and I didn't hurt Dwight on purpose. You're a vicious, old woman. Grandpa never should have loved you."

"There's no way he would have bled to death without calling for help."

"He was sleeping." Tears slid down Louisa's face. "There wasn't any noise."

"You're lying." Rose couldn't stop. Her face felt sunken white, and she was so cold. "You let him die, so you could have Dwight, and now you don't even want him."

"I didn't hear Grandpa call for help."

"You did. He stumbled and hurt himself, and you didn't

help him." Her hands were fists, squeezed tight and shaking in her lap. "You're a bad, evil woman."

"It wasn't me!"

"You should be punished."

"No!"

"Put in jail."

"Don't you hear?" Louisa banged the table. Her eyes were wet. Her skin, pulled tight. "It wasn't me!"

A shudder moved swiftly through Rose's stomach and chest, shot through her arms and legs. Shivering, she wrapped her arms around her torso and sank back against the chair. "Who then?" she whispered.

"You know who it was."

"Tell me."

"Your friends, that's who. Your old, lady friends."

Oh God, I don't want to hear this.

"I don't think they knew I was here." Louisa blew her nose on a paper napkin, rubbing her eyes hard. "I was supposed to have gone back home."

"Both of them?" Rose could barely ask. "Charity *and* Grace?"

"Just Grace first, then Charity. And June."

"What do you mean? Grace first?"

"She came alone. They were downstairs talking. Then Grace started crying, and Grandpa tried to be nice, but she was yelling and carrying on, and he finally told her to go."

"You listened."

"It was hard not to. Anyway, she wouldn't go, so Grandpa said, 'okay, stay, but I'm going up to bed.' And he did. And she stayed down there for awhile. Finally it was quiet down there, and I thought she'd gone."

"But she didn't." Rose clenched her hands together, rubbing her thumbs over each other.

"No. She came upstairs. I shut my door. She went into Grandpa's room and they talked some, then she cried. But I didn't hear any thumps or screams, so I didn't know anything was wrong. It got quiet, so I thought she stayed ... in his bed."

Rose winced.

"Then the next thing I knew, I heard more people coming up the stairs, and I was scared, so I pushed a chair under the doorknob."

"How do you know it was Charity and June?"

"I could tell their voices. They were talking low, but it was them. I was afraid to move. I didn't want them to know I was there."

"What did they say?"

"I don't know. Grace was crying and they kept running water in the bathroom."

"And you just stayed in your bedroom?"

"What could I do?"

"Then what happened?"

"They left."

"Then what?"

"Nothing. I went to sleep."

"You went and saw him, didn't you?"

Louisa took her spoon and stirred her cocoa with fast, hard strokes.

"You did. Why didn't you help him?"

"He was all bloody," Louisa said, her voice choking, dropping. "He wasn't breathing."

"Why didn't you call Dr. Kenny? Or the police?"

"He was dead. They couldn't make him live again."

"How could you be so sure?"

"I *knew*."

"You should have called them." Rose's shoulders slumped. Louisa had thought only of herself. She hadn't called for help. She had never lost sight of her own wants. His own grandchild.

"It wouldn't have changed his being gone," Louisa said.

"And you never told?"

Louisa shook her head.

"You wanted his money."

Louisa stared into the cow-shaped mug.

"You knew you wouldn't get it so fast if the police thought there was a crime."

Louisa looked at Rose. "I wanted Dwight."

Rose's head dropped, her chin lay on her chest. She thought she could never lift it again. She didn't want to. But there was no way to suspend time and pain, except to travel deep into the dark, and Rose had more to do.

Hands against the table, she pushed herself up. She was weary, used up and wrung out. She felt old. Inside and out.

She shuffled to the door. Turning, Rose looked at Louisa. "What a sad, selfish woman you are. How can you ever be happy?"

May Snow

✳   ✳   ✳

This time it was Rose who waited in the early morning hours while the sky turned blue and hid the stars. Absently pushing one foot against Charity's porch floor, moving the glider upon which she sat slowly, smoothly, back and forth, she watched two fat crows perched on a telephone line. They seemed to be staring back at her, and she wondered what they were thinking.

In a moment, swift and glorious, one of them cawed, spread his wings, lifted, and soared. The second crow answered his call and followed. Rose set her feet down, bent forward, eyes on the birds, yearning to be with them. She opened her mind, let it loose, and flew beside them until the flick of a wind chime, pushed by the breeze, flashed in the corner of her eye and brought her rushing back to the dimension she knew and could touch. She leaned back against the glider, pressed it to movement again, closed her eyes, and concentrated on the wind chime's gentle tinkle.

She nearly slept.

She felt Charity ease herself onto the glider beside her, heard her cup against its saucer, smelled her soap.

"I'm awake," said Rose.

"I thought you might be." Charity rose and moved to a white wicker rocker, turned it a little toward Rose, and sat. "I can see you better." She set her coffee on a low table nearby and folded her hands in her lap. She did not rock.

"It's a beautiful day," Rose said. There was wetness on her cheeks.

"It is." Charity sat quiet.

"I'm very tired," Rose said, feeling as if she were fading, not understanding how tears could come for no reason, unbidden, unwanted.

"Tell me why you're here," Charity said gently.

"I talked with Louisa." She didn't know from where the calm within, the emptiness, had come.

"I see."

"I thought it was Louisa that had hurt Anson." It was not calm. It was sadness.

Briefly Charity lowered her head, and then she sighed and raised her face to Rose.

"You know what she told me," Rose said.

"All this time she said nothing," Charity said. "We thought she would be still forever. It served her purpose."

"She's weak."

"We should have given that factor more strength."

"You lied to me."

"Yes." Charity ran her tongue over her lips. "It was better for you."

"We never lied before this."

"No, we didn't." Charity spoke low.

"But we agreed we wouldn't lie anymore. Such a little time ago. On my porch."

"From that time forward," Charity said.

"It has to be forever, from bloomers and bobby socks to gray hair and canes."

Charity wiped her eyes. "I know."

"It was Grace." Rose swallowed, rested her fingers on the gold chain at her neck. "It was Grace."

"Yes. and she has suffered so from it."

"It's me that she hates."

"It's you she is able to hate. She lays the blame on you, so she can bear what she did."

"Why did she do it?"

"I don't know. Anger, maybe. Pride. She offered him every-thing that night. Everything a woman can give. And he turned her down."

"But to kill him?"

"She didn't mean to."

"She meant to *harm* him." Rose pushed her fingers hard against the gold rose in the hollow of her throat.

"I think only to hurt him," Charity said. "The cat was there. That little, yellow, ceramic cat of yours. She poked at him with it, with its sharp pointed tail. And in her frenzy she saw the vein that everyone made so much of and she sank the cat's tail into the bulge … ahh." Charity dropped her head in her hands. Her body heaved and shook. "She didn't mean to kill him. She doesn't think. Her head doesn't think. She went for his vulnerable spot. She wanted him shamed as much as she was. She went too far and couldn't stop."

"You helped her," Rose whispered. Her lips trembled.

"She called. I couldn't say no."

"And June?"

"I needed help. I knew I could trust her."

"You didn't call a doctor?"

"We didn't know it was so bad until we got there. He was dead." Charity gulped air. "Grace sat beside him while he bled to death. There was no reason to call a doctor. It was done, and it had to be hidden."

"Didn't he fight?"

"Grace said he did. Just a little. At first. But anger has strength, and her anger lasted longer than his struggle... he was old, dear Rose."

"You protected her."

"I always have."

"Didn't you think Louisa would tell?"

"We didn't know she was there, and after, when we did, she didn't say anything. We thought she never would. I told you. It served her purpose. She got what she wanted. Money and Dwight."

"So you thought you were safe."

"Never safe, Rose." Charity straightened, wiped her hands across her face. "There's still God."

They sat without speaking. A car door slammed down the road. Someone was whistling close by. A woman yelled out for her son to come in and put some proper clothes on.

"Why didn't you tell me?" Rose asked.

"You would have gone straight to the police."

"I don't know."

"Oh, Rose," Charity said, tapping a cigarette out of the pack. "You always do the right thing." Charity lit the cigarette, dragged deep, coughed out smoke.

Rose thought of Nicholas crouching in the dark watching shadows, seeing things he shouldn't.

"I don't know what to do," Rose whispered.

"I can't help you."

"Isn't it funny," Rose said. "I'd like to ask Anson, what's the next step here? What do I do?"

"Look to yourself, Rose. Look to your heart."

"I really needed Anson," Rose said.

May Snow

"We all needed him. The difference between you and us was that we could be satisfied with just a piece of him. We didn't want him to fill our whole lives. All we wanted was a little help to remember the fullness of being a woman."

"I needed more."

"You thought you did."

"Thomas left a hole so big."

"You filled it a long time ago. You just never looked true at yourself. You might talk to Thomas, but the answers he gives you come straight from your own head."

"I can't hear anymore. I'm just so tired."

"Will you tell Grace that you know?" Charity asked.

"Should I?"

"Let me. I'll know how to say it."

Rose nodded. "To protect her."

"She needs that."

Rose nodded again. "The mud on the house and the marbles and the phone calls, it was her, wasn't it?"

"I told you before."

"Poor Grace."

"She'll want to know what you're going to do."

Rose looked at her friend. There was nothing inside her, no answers. "I don't know."

❉   ❉   ❉

Rose went home and lay on her couch. It was warm in her house and quiet.

Slowly she emptied her weary head, and as she let Margaret and Louisa and Grace and Nicholas and Charity and Anson shrink and fade and slip from thought, the sounds of her house seeped into their holes and lulled her. The old clock on the china cabinet ticked. Floorboards groaned, stretching and compressing. A fly tapped inside a lampshade, one side to the other. The refrigerator whirred. A sudden rustle in the walls, and little feet scurried. And, from a distance, came the crack of bat against ball.

She smelled vanilla candles, roses outside the window, lemon polish, hot cat breath, grass, and cologne on the cushions of her couch.

Eyes closed, she sighed and pulled an afghan from the couch to fill her arms. Before she drifted off to sleep, she opened her mind to Thomas and hoped he would flood her dreams with love and power.

When she awoke, the sun was high. It streaked bright through the prisms hanging in the window. She saw rainbows glimmering on her ceiling.

Without her summons, Charity and Grace pierced her heart and pain gushed through. They had betrayed her.

She was hot. The afghan stuck to her. She pushed it off and it fell on the floor in a soft, colorful heap.

She had always known they had made Anson die. Nicholas had known. She hadn't wanted to listen. She hadn't wanted to believe. But down deep where secrets lie, she had known.

She swung her feet over the cushions into the supple, warm pile that was her blanket.

She lifted her hands over her face and wept.

Ugly thoughts came to cover the pain, make it bearable. Selfish old ladies. Mean-spirited. They couldn't stand for her to be happy.

She should call Joseph Abramowicz. See, Mr. Policeman,

you didn't do your job. You didn't hear the words that could have pushed you to do justice.

She swayed back and forth. *I want them in prison. God forgive me, I want them to hurt.*

❉   ❉   ❉

The days passed and Rose felt as if a great sickness had fallen upon her. A gray haze that dulled sight and sound and smell covered her. She could not taste, and the texture of her world was flat.

Sometimes she peeked out, but the panic was too large. Quickly she ducked within the cloak of non-being.

Floating in and out of her space were June and Grace and Charity. They were at church. At the grocery. Peering off Charity's porch when she walked by. At the bakery. On the dock. Ever polite. Never touching her. She couldn't see their faces clearly.

She waited for someone to help her.

No one did.

One day sitting on the beach with no one near, she lifted her head and heard the crash of waves — the echo as the mighty water hit land hard, hurled back, and rushed into the next breaking crest.

The water was blue and so was the sky. The sun was so bright it hurt her eyes. The sand was hot under her feet, and the grains poured heavy over her toes when she dug in her hands, scooped, and dropped the sifted earth down on herself. Sand blew in the breezes and sprinkled her arms and her legs. The lake smelled fishy, like it needed a bath. And she laughed.

25
September

The night was cool. Huddled in an old, thick sweater, Rose sat on her porch and rocked. It was time to decide, and she was ready. She had healed enough to know she must go to her soul, to the Spirit that dwelled within, for the counsel she could get nowhere else.

Anson was gone. Forever. It was Thomas who would meet her and walk her through the clouds.

Biting her lip, she took the gold chain from her neck and laid it carefully in her lap. She drew a deep breath. She was wrong. Anson *was* there, a small, sad spot in her heart. She hoped he would melt to bittersweet memory, a sweet pang rarely felt.

She leaned back, lifted her face to the clean, night air. There really was no choice. They had all killed Anson. Together they had walked him to a place where he could not stay if they were to hold tight to a friendship that was old and good and necessary. He would not be shared equally, could not be, and so the weakest link had broken, and dear Grace, weak and impulsive, had picked up a little ceramic cat and attacked him. And he had died. They had all helped put that cat in her hand.

Rose rubbed the empty spot at the base of her neck.

They were her friends and she loved them. There was no choice.

❄   ❄   ❄

"Margaret, what on earth are you doing?" Rose put her paring knife down and rubbed her fingers. She was peeling potatoes, and the cold, moist vegetables made her fingers ache.

"I'm just looking to see if I can find stuff from when I was a kid," Margaret said. She was sitting on her knees peering into Rose's bottom cupboards. "See?" She pulled out a rusty grater and held it up. "You used to make me shred cheese on this old thing. I hated it. I thought it would shred the tips of my fingers right into the cheese."

"Toss it out," Rose said, flexing her fingers, wincing. "I don't use it anymore. Or maybe you could paint it a pretty color and glue silk flowers on it."

"I don't think so." Margaret put the grater back in the cupboard and leaned back on her heels. "Don't you have a butter churn somewhere?"

"I think I might." Rose picked up a potato. "Someplace."

"If you'll just wait a minute, I'll pare those for you." Margaret stuck her head in the cupboard and called out from inside, "Remember how you made me churn and churn and churn, whip that cream into butter until I thought my arm would break."

"The only time you churned was when Dad wanted buttermilk. By the time you were old enough to crank the paddles, we were using store-bought butter."

"Maybe." Margaret took the knife from Rose and bent and kissed her mother's fingers. "My turn. How many do you need?"

"Lots."

"How come you offered to make potato salad? All that chopping — celery, onions, potatoes — with your fingers so bad. Not too smart, Mother."

"The church's food committee counts on my salad at the harvest picnic every year. It's my signature dish."

"Get a new pen."

"Your father liked my salad." Rose pulled a bowl of hard-boiled eggs toward her, took one and rolled it to crack the shell.

"He did, indeed. With buttermilk. Cranked by yours truly." Margaret piled peeled potatoes in a pot to be washed and cooked. "Mom?"

Rose looked up from the egg she was peeling.

"I'm leaving Forrest."

Rose put the egg down.

"Are you sure?" Rose asked.

"That I want to leave him?"

Rose nodded.

"I'm not sure." Margaret rubbed a finger around the rim of the pot. "But I'm not sure I want to stay either."

"Where will you go?"

"Not very far. Just another part of town, a cheaper part. Into a little apartment. I've already rented it. And I've got a job. Selling hosiery."

"Forrest should take care of you."

"I don't want to need him."

May Snow

"You're stronger than I was," Rose said. "I could never have walked away from your father. I would have fallen like a weed without water."

"You really believe that, don't you?" Margaret said.

"What?"

"That Dad was the strong one."

"He was."

Margaret folded her hands in her lap and leaned across the table toward Rose. "Do you remember when I was little, maybe eight or ten? Dad would make me walk behind the tractor while he cultivated the tomatoes so I could brush off the dirt if he covered a plant?"

Rose nodded. Oh yes, she remembered. Her child, so small, walking up and down those hot rows.

"Sometimes," Margaret said, "he would drive down a whole row and not cover one plant"

"Yes," Rose said, wincing.

"You told him I was too little for so much work and he said you were wrong."

"I remember," Rose said.

"Then one morning as you were filling the water jugs we took to the fields, you turned and told Dad that it wasn't fair that he got all those hours of help from me and you got no help with your chores."

Rose smiled.

"So he said, 'what chores?' And you said you had a whole long list and he could have me help him in the morning, but you were going to have me in the afternoon."

"I taped the list on the refrigerator," Rose said, "and when you came in for lunch, I showed him the list and said when you had finished the list, he could have you back. If there was any time left."

"He didn't read the list," Margaret said.

"I didn't think he would," Rose said, smiling.

"I read it," Margaret said. "After he left and went back to the tomato fields."

"And you laughed," Rose said. "Then you came and hugged me."

"The first chore was: Sit by the window and read a story to your dolly."

"Then go to the far meadow," Rose said, "and pick me some buttercups."

"Play two hours." Margaret's voice trembled. "That was the best."

"Knead bread with your mother who loves you so much."

"Sing songs with your mother." Margaret took Rose's hands in her own.

"Set the table," Rose said, a catch in her throat.

"When Dad came home, he said he'd seen me running through the pasture, hands full of flowers."

"He didn't think it was work," Rose said.

"And you looked at him," Margaret said, patting her mother's hand, "and you dared him with your eyes sparking fire, your back set straight, and your lips stretched thin — you dared him to deny you my help with your list of chores."

"He let me have you every afternoon."

"You *took* me every afternoon."

"I loved your father so much."

"I'm going away from Forrest, Mother. And I'm going to

think hard about him. See if I need him. See if I love him. See if I want him. Like you wanted Dad."

"I hope some day you find what I had."

"I hope so too."

❄ ❄ ❄

Rose set the cake — angel food frosted with whipped cream, four pink candles sunk in its fluff, and a cascade of pink and white and lavender-tinted carnations flowing from the center hole — on a front porch table. Pots of plum-colored mums and baskets of pink and white and mauve mums were scattered over the wooden floor. Balloons, pink and white and filled to near bursting, were strung all over the porch.

Smiling, Rose tapped a fat, pink, rubber bubble hung from the ceiling and sent it swinging with a thump into another. Watching the balloons play as they bumped and twirled, she lowered herself into a freshly painted rocker. She'd spent some of the money Anson left her to hire Manley Warner to paint her front porch rockers — dusty rose, magenta, and the darkened, softened blue and green of colonial times.

She sat, comfortable and free inside, and waited for Charity, Grace, and June. She had asked them to come. They said they would.

And they did.

Her pleasure soared when she saw them pull up to the curb. She pressed her fingers to her lips and knew the swell of old love, given and returned, in her heart. They were coming out of the car smiling.

"The balloons are dancing," Grace said. Her face shone

happy. Pulling away from Charity's hold, Rose heard her plead, "Let me." And Grace did a quick, graceful shuffle, laughing, "See, I still can."

"I see," Charity said softly, taking her sister's arm again. "And it was beautiful."

"Prima donna stuff," June said, grinning.

"At least," Rose said from the top of the steps.

They came and they hugged her.

"Did you ever find your porcelain cat?" Grace whispered as she rested in Rose's arms. "I put it in the garbage can. Afterward. So no one could find it. Not you or the police. Especially not you."

Rose nodded, her arms gentle around the treasured body — less round than it had been but not yet frail. "Nicholas found it. I'm glad you want me to have it again."

"I'm not mad anymore."

"Me either," Rose said.

"A cake," Grace said, turning. "And candles. Whose birthday? It's nobody's birthday, is it? Is it yours, June?"

June shook her head. "No, but it looks good."

"It's a rebirth cake," Rose said, "with a candle for each of us to light and wish on."

Charity squeezed Rose's arm.

June looked at Rose and smiled. "A candle for me."

Rose nodded, smiled back. "Make a good wish."

"Well, let's light, wish, and eat," Grace said.

And they did.

26
October

Early in October on a cool day that smelled of drying leaves and sweet, ripe grapes, Rose pedaled down to Grimmers Pond. She parked her bike and strolled along the water's edge, singing hymns and pop tunes and Christmas carols at the top of her lungs.

Just for herself.

Because it felt good.